1

As quickly as Richard's life had been transformed by the miracle of Natasha, it was over. Gone. In an instant. And everything after, everything that was to follow, was like some bad dream, a dream from which it seemed he would never wake. . .

Her text message had said simply: 'Meet me at Joe's. Half an hour.' He'd shut the apartment door behind him and put his keys in his pocket. He'd stepped out into the street and, stopping at a newsstand, had grabbed a *New York Post*. Then he'd walked the next block to Joe's Place. He'd checked his watch. It was 1.10 p.m.

She should have been there. But she wasn't. 'Hey, Richard, how you doing?' Richard returned Joe's greeting as he entered the busy café. He smiled and nodded, scanning the small tables for Natasha. No sign. She should have been here by now. She must have got caught up. All that wedding planning. He sat at the only spare table by the window. Sandra, one of Joe's long-term staff, looked over. 'Coffee, Richard?'

'Sure, thanks, Sandra. Usual.' Yeah, that was bound to be it, so much to do, so little time. It wasn't as if theirs was going to be a grand affair. Small, discreet, classy. But still, these things took some doing, and Natasha had thrown herself wholeheartedly at the task. As she did with everything. As she had with him, with their new life, with their glorious, miraculous future. . .

* * *

They'd met through a mutual friend. Jane, Ted's partner, had brought Natasha with her and they were introduced. It had gone from there. They'd seen each other a few times, but Richard had not seemed that interested. Then, gradually, he'd started calling her and they'd enjoyed each other's company. It was just a kind of friendship, at first, a few meals, but neither seemed to want to take the next step. Then, one night, they'd met at The Huston bar after they'd both completed a stressful week's work. The evening had worn on. Eventually he'd asked her whether she would like to come and see his place; it was close by.

They had told each other their life stories. How he'd been brought up in the Bronx. Richard had not really known his parents. He'd been orphaned at the age of five; a fire had broken out on the fourth floor of the building in the early hours of a Sunday morning, and engulfed the entire block. His parents, the subsequent Fire Department report concluded, had been overcome by fumes.

Richard told Natasha how he'd been sleeping in the other small bedroom, adjacent to the front door. He'd woken and after knocking desperately on his parents' locked door he'd gone to the apartment door and opened it. A neighbour had grabbed the child and taken him down the stairwell emergency exit as he screamed for his parents. But the neighbour simply continued on until she was out of the building, at which point she released the child into the arms of a Fire Department officer. Richard remembered vividly the fireman's piercing blue eyes and rugged face, as he asked, 'Where are your mum and dad?'

'It was strange,' he told Natasha that first night in his Manhattan apartment, 'I don't remember another thing, only the funeral and that rainy day in September. I was dressed in a little black suit and tie.' He had seen a programme about the tragedy that befell the Kennedy family in 1963, and saw that small boy, John Jr, wiping his eyes and saluting his father's coffin. 'I didn't salute,' he told Natasha, 'just looked and felt empty.'

That night he had discovered that Natasha was a good listener. It was an admirable quality, he'd thought. He still thought so,

THE MEDUSA CONSPIRACY

THE MEDUSA CONSPIRACY

Andrew Lowe

Book Guild Publishing
Sussex, England

First published in Great Britain in 2012 by
The Book Guild Ltd
19 New Road
Brighton, BN1 1UF

Typeset in Baskerville by Ellipsis Digital Limited, Glasgow

Printed in Great Britain by
CPI Group (UK) Ltd, Croydon, CR0 4YY

A catalogue record for this book is available from The British Library.

ISBN 978 1 84624 754 5

'Life is either a daring adventure or nothing. Security does not exist in nature ... avoiding danger is no safer in the long run than exposure.'

Helen Keller

'... the female of the species is more deadly than the male.'

Rudyard Kipling

Acknowledgements

To Carol Biss and all her team at Book Guild Publishing. A very special thanks for encouraging me at the beginning of the publishing process and for their perseverance, advice and invaluable assistance throughout.

I wish to say a big thanks to my sister and brother-in-law Barbara and Phil Manby and their daughter Louise for their help in the early drafts.

Special thanks to my friend Subhash for his support, my cousin Monica for advice and to the many friends who believed in me.

Most importantly to my son and daughter Natalie and Ian, my cousin Sonia and her family in Australia, Maria, Brian and Bernard in Canada, and all my friends both here and around the world who are always in my thoughts.

A final word to the lady on whom I loosely based the central character: thanks for the times we had together and I wish you well for the future. I hope she will return in a second book soon. Always the survivor.

sitting here in Joe's Place, waiting for his future wife. Where was she? He looked at his watch again. Half an hour had gone by. It was unlike her.

Yes, a good listener. She'd sat patiently while he regaled the tragedy of his early life. '*Do I blame anybody?*' he'd asked in response to her question. 'Not really, the investigation established that a water heater had caught fire in the adjacent apartment. They said it was lack of maintenance. The landlord was prosecuted and I think he got two years for culpable manslaughter. But I really don't care. If I went out and shot him would it bring them back? No, and what's the point of bitterness? It only destroys you in the most pernicious way, from the inside, and that's dangerous because you can't see it eating away at you. No, I've moved on. I had to.'

And he *had* moved on, *hadn't he*? Yes, he had, but everything he had done thereafter, in the shadow of their death, he had done for them, at least in some respect. He had this obsessive drive to do well, to prove to his parents that their lives weren't wasted; to show that their death and his survival meant something. He often visited them at the cemetery and told them how his deals were going, about his promotion, his life in general. It was a kind of catharsis. . . Maybe it seemed a little odd, but it just felt right somehow, to him, at least.

Richard was getting worried. Another ten minutes had gone by and still no Natasha. When had he received her text? He checked his phone again. If she was running late why hadn't she called or texted again? She wasn't the sort to let him sweat it out. That was what he loved about her: she always knew the right thing to do, the right thing to say. He'd known she was special that night, the way she didn't judge him, didn't patronise him when he confided in her, just listened and said the right thing.

'Thank you for telling me that story. I never realised that you'd . . .'

'Been through all that?'

'Well, yes, I guess so.'

He'd handed her a fresh drink and sat down opposite. He appreciated how attentive she'd been, but now it was time to talk about her. 'So, *you* must have a story, with a name like Sevinski. Is it Russian or Polish?'

'Russian; well it's more my grandparents' story really.'

'They were immigrants?' he said, more statement than question.

'Yes,' she said. 'They had a tough time coming here, fleeing the Nazis like so many others. They were lucky and managed to get out in time. Made their way to England, and stayed there till the end of the war. Then Grandpa was offered a teaching post here in the States.'

'What did he teach?' Richard interrupted.

'He was a mathematics professor.'

'I knew you were from smart stock.'

She laughed. 'But that was after the war. Before that, in England, he was at Bletchley.'

'Ah, a code breaker,' said Richard. He'd read about this, about Bletchley and the enigma codes; all those great minds coming together to try and outfox the Nazis. And Natasha's grandfather at the heart of it. He was impressed.

'Well, sort of,' laughed Natasha. 'He worked with Turing anyway, for a while at least.'

Richard was doubly impressed. Alan Turing – the original super geek; the man who had pretty much invented computer science and helped save the world from Hitler and his evil cronies while he was at it. Lofty company in anyone's estimation. 'Impressive,' he said.

'I guess,' said Natasha. 'Most people just look at me blankly when I mention Turing and Bletchley.'

Richard smiled.

'But he wasn't really on the code-breaking team. Probability theory, that was more his area.'

Richard looked a little blank. This was beyond his knowledge ballpark. So she filled him in. She told him about how the Americans and English had been convinced that the Germans had lost the war, and how they'd been using mathematical models to try and establish how the new world order would look. About number theory and game theory and subjective probability.

Then, at Richard's insistence (he was intrigued by her knowledge), she elaborated: about the cold war and how the world's greatest mathematicians had used probability theory – basically laying bets on a whole set of variables – to locate a missing US nuclear warhead and prevented an international incident sometime in the mid-sixties. What it all boiled down to was that pretty much any problem could be resolved with a mathematical solution; even sniffing out errant nuclear missiles. It was all about probability. Except, of course, there was always the unknown, or the unknowable.

'The fly in the ointment,' she said, 'is always that unknown factor, the bit that nobody is aware of ... the spanner in the works, if you like. You can take a good guess as to what is round the corner but in truth, well, life is a lottery; there's always the unknown.'

Richard nodded. He thought of his parents, the fire, and the unfathomable randomness of it all. Yes indeed, there was always the unknown. 'In other words,' said Richard, 'shit just happens.'

'Precisely!' laughed Natasha. Richard noticed what a charming laugh she had. It lit up the room.

They had talked and talked into the small hours of the morning. She told him about her family, her father, the Harvard graduate turned chemist, and her loving mother, whom she cherished above all. He asked her about her work. She'd always had a methodical mind and her real love was journalism. 'I took a degree in it and after working for a few of the big papers I just decided to go freelance. It's, well, I really love it. Over the past two years I have had some really good stories; they don't always get attributed to you, but, well, the money is good, and sometimes you operate in a twilight world, so as an investigative reporter sometimes it's good to not be too much in the limelight. I've got something I am working on at the moment, though I can't say anything; really I never do but, well, it's going to be a great story once it's all exposed.'

Natasha leaned back and prompted him to say a bit more about himself. 'Come on, Richard, enough about my boring life, tell me how you got to where you are now.'

Richard told her how he'd been brought up by his aunt after his parents' death, about flunking high school, poor grades, hanging with the wrong set, the usual stuff. And how his aunt's partner – a volatile guy, but a formative influence nevertheless – had set him on the right course with one succinct sentence: 'If you want to make money, son, work with it.' And he'd got the boy a position at a small real estate and mortgage opera-tion run by a friend near Brooklyn. 'All I had to do was call clients, tell them how their sale was going, liaise with the vendor, nothing special.' This had gone on for about a year and he'd been so bored, but had wanted to do well, wanted to go places, just didn't know how. And then he got his first real break, going the extra mile for a client, who'd tried to throw him a back-hander but he'd done it straight. And the guy – it turned out he was head of international client accounts at Bank of America no less – had been suitably impressed and offered Richard a job. The rest, as they say, was history, and here he was, now, at Bank of America looking after big-league clients, top-drawer accounts.

And then they'd had enough of talking. They'd probed each other's minds long enough; now they wanted more.

'Looks like I am here for the night then?' she'd said, 'have you got a spare room?'

'Let me show you.' They'd walked to his room. 'How about this one?'

'Fine, which side of the bed do I go on?'

Richard had taken her in his arms and said, 'The same side

as me, Natasha.' And with that, they'd slipped under the sheets and into each other's lives . . .

From that moment he knew that she was the one, the missing piece of the jigsaw of his life. After only a few weeks of blissful romance he'd done the deed: he'd asked her to marry him. In Central Park, of all places, among the usual throng of tourists, joggers and dog walkers. And she'd said yes, she'd only gone and said yes!

They had decided to sell her place, perhaps buy a bigger house in Upstate New York, whilst retaining Richard's Manhattan apartment, which was ideally located. He had two bedrooms, plenty of space and a spare parking spot for Natasha's car. Not that they needed to economise: he had secured a new job with a specialist company dealing with wealthy clients from the Middle East and loved the view from his new office. At a conservative estimate, if all his client accounts paid off, he'd be making around three hundred thousand dollars this year. Not bad for a kid from the Bronx. Added to Natasha's own salary, they were doing just fine: your typical high-flying glamorous young New York couple. Life was cool, pretty cool. And now here they were, planning for the future, a future together, and neither of them had ever been so happy.

But where was she? Where the hell was she? He'd been sitting in Joe's Place, nursing the same cup of cold coffee for over an hour now. Something wasn't right. He pulled his cell phone from his pocket and dialled her number. It rang and rang, then went dead. He tried again. This time it rang and then a voice said, 'Hello?'

It was a man's voice. 'Who the hell is this?' Richard said aggressively.

'Sir, I'm a police officer. Are you sitting down?'

2

Richard fled Joe's Place as if his life depended on it. He had to get to the hospital. New York State. She'd been in an accident. There'd been no time for details. The NYPD officer (Officer Wilson? Williams? No, *Williamson*) had made Richard verify his identity and had only managed to convey the most scant of cold hard facts – car crash, Brooklyn, ambulance, personal effects – *fuck*! before Richard had cut him dead and was off . . . tearing down Eighth Street, scanning frantically for a yellow cab, eventually finding one. The ride was just a blur.

'Can you help me?' Richard said to the petite nurse standing at the reception desk. 'My fiancée was brought in here, around an hour ago. There was some sort of accident. Her name is Natasha . . . Natasha Sevinski . . . do you know where she is or how she is?'

The girl turned and picked up a phone on the desk directly behind her, stabbing out three numbers. He could see her head nodding, but did not hear the conversation, just the last few seconds before she replaced the receiver: 'Okay, yes. I'll send him straight there. Yes . . . yes . . . no. Okay.'

'I'm just going to call someone who will take you to a doctor.'

'Yes, but can I see her?' He was getting impatient.

'Please don't worry; I'm going to get a porter to go with you.'

He followed the porter along a long corridor to an elevator. They got in and went up two or three floors. Richard did not really notice. From the elevator, they passed two doors, and then stopped at a third. He noted the number and the name: 'Dr Leberman – 402'. The porter tapped on the door and a few seconds later a nurse opened it.

'This is Mr Lombardi,' said the porter.

The nurse asked Richard to come inside. 'Take a seat, please. Dr Leberman will be out in a few seconds.'

Where was Natasha? What was going on? Richard stared down at the carpet. Why had he not gone straight to the ward? Why was he waiting here?

'Mr Lombardi I'm Doctor Leberman. Would you step into my office, please?'

Richard followed the doctor into the small room.

'How's Natasha?' asked Richard, with urgency in his voice.

'Mr Lombardi, you need to prepare yourself for a shock. I have some bad news.'

'God, what's happened?' Richard leaned forward. His hands were sweating, his mouth was dry, he could feel a rumbling in his stomach. He felt awful.

'Mr Lombardi . . .' Doctor Leberman put his hands on the desk. 'Mr Lombardi, I have to tell you that Natasha died. She was brought in here two hours ago. There was a car accident. We did everything we could. Please, give yourself a few minutes.'

Richard sat back. Was this a dream? He wished he were in some crazy dream. He wished this would all go away. It seemed like an eternity as he sat there.

'Mr Lombardi, I am so sorry. Your fiancée crashed her car into the rear of a truck at around 12.45 p.m., just past the Brooklyn-Battery Tunnel. The truck was stationary and she hit it very hard. She has a Mercedes 500, is that right?' Richard nodded.

'Both the airbags were deployed, but the police will tell you more. I just want to tell you this; for what it's worth . . . she arrived here by ambulance at around one. She'd been pronounced dead at the scene, but I was here in the trauma room when she came in. As the senior physician, I was asked to make the official declaration. I made some routine examinations and I have to tell you that she did not die as a result of a motor vehicle accident.'

Richard looked puzzled. 'What do you mean?'

'She was already dead before the vehicle crashed. . .'

3

Richard was sitting in the waiting room of Fifth Precinct, his head in his hands. Time itself seemed to have stopped. His world was shattered. *Dead!* His precious Natasha was *dead!* He would never see her beautiful face again. Never hear that joyous laugh. Never share her wonderful life. She was gone. The fly in the ointment. The dreadful, unfathomable unknown . . .

He'd seen her at the hospital; Doctor Leberman had taken him down to the morgue that afternoon. And now this was it. What was he supposed to do? There were the formalities, of course, contacting her parents, her brother, her work, but, Jesus, that would have to wait. Doctor Leberman's words danced around his brain: '*already dead before the vehicle crashed . . .*' Already dead! It didn't make sense. Something about a possible weak heart, congenital failure. But so young? So full of life . . . No, it just didn't make sense. He needed to see Officer Williamson. Perhaps *he* could throw some more light on what had happened. And he needed to get Natasha's phone. What if people were trying to contact her?

He had arrived at the precinct around five. There were people milling around, a few waiting to be seen. He'd been in no mood to wait. Officers were coming and going from a door in the far corner. Some were obviously detectives but mainly uniformed officers. He moved closer. Two plain-clothes officers came out. He touched one on the arm. 'Excuse me . . . can you help me?'

'Sorry, sir. You need to go to reception. I can't help you.'

Cutting straight in, he told the officer what had happened, that he needed to get Natasha's effects and speak with Officer Williamson.

'Hang on, buddy.' The man turned around, keyed a code into the matt gold entry panel, then disappeared back inside. Richard could not see through the heavily tinted glass; he assumed it was some sort of one-way mirror. He did not wait long.

The detective came through the heavy door after about three minutes: 'He's still on duty, but they've put a call out for him. Listen, take a seat over there and just keep watching this door. I reckon about fifteen or twenty minutes, okay, buddy?'

'Yeah, thanks,' Richard replied. He'd been sitting there ever since: twenty minutes, half an hour, a lifetime, who knew?

'Mr Lombardi' A heavy-set New York cop was standing about a foot away from Richard.

'Yes. Officer Williamson?'

'Yeah that's me. Would you come with me, please?' He went back to the large security door and, after punching the entry code, beckoned Richard inside. The room was noisy and hot. The officer directed him to an empty desk in the far corner of the room. He motioned to Richard to sit down, and went to the other side of the desk, pulling out a bag from the bottom drawer. It was Natasha's Gucci bag; the one she had been carrying when they first met.

'I am really sorry, sir, I was the first on the scene, and had to smash the driver's window to get in as the impact had jammed the doors. She actually looked okay, but I just wanted to get her out. I was thinking that maybe her heart had stopped; this often happens in heavy impacts.'

Richard just nodded.

'I was pulling at the door when the Fire Department arrived; they were quick; they prised the door open and by that time the paramedics were there . . . but it was too late, you understand, they did try, but it was just too late.'

'Yes,' said Richard, 'I understand. Officer Williamson, there's something, something that Doctor Leberman said . . . something that doesn't make sense. . . He said, he said that. . .' Richard struggled to get the words out. Officer Williamson saved him the effort: 'That she was already dead before impact . . .'

Richard nodded again. This was an ordeal.

'And the resultant crash was due to her dying at the wheel. . .'

Richard hadn't thought of that. He guessed it made sense, if anything made sense in this crazy bloody awful mess.

'But how, why?' begged Richard. 'She was so young, so healthy . . .'

'We don't know yet, Mr Lombardi, we will have to wait for the autopsy. Again, I'm so sorry. . .'

The officer then went through the usual formalities with Richard: identification of the body, some preliminary investigation checks, the autopsy; and then asked Richard to sign for Natasha's personal effects.

Phone, bag, a bundle of work files and her driving shoes.

'Oh, and this,' said Officer Williamson, just as Richard got up to leave the office. 'We found it on the passenger seat. It looks like her personal diary. I did just have a quick look you understand, though a lot of it is in shorthand. She was a journalist I understand? Well anyhow that's the only other thing I have for you.'

As he walked out the door, Richard flicked through her diary. It was practically full, lots of contact numbers scribbled in various places corresponding with dates and names. Some pages were in shorthand, some just her normal handwriting, others just illegible scribble. He sighed and closed the diary.

A few moments later he was back out on the busy New York street.

4

What a nightmare . . . what a fucking nightmare! He wanted to cry but still could not. He just walked and walked, not even realising he was holding Natasha's bag. He could not even feel it, could not feel anything. He was numb, simply numb. *Perhaps I will wake up soon,* he thought. In the space of a few hours his life had changed completely. Natasha's words came back to him: *'A random event, something you could never know.'* He hated those words now.

Back at his apartment, he dropped his keys carelessly onto the table, and walked straight into the kitchen. He went to the lower cupboard and, pushing various bottles aside, located the whiskey at the very back. Grabbing a small tumbler, he poured himself the biggest shot he could ever remember taking, took the glass back to the dining table and sat bolt upright in the heavy wooden chair. He sat there for a moment or two and took a large swig, desperately trying to find some courage. There was no delaying any longer, he must phone Natasha's parents – Vika and Zandras – and tell them the tragic news. . .

Richard woke in the early hours of Monday morning. The whiskey he had consumed after the phone call, together with the day's events, had taken its inevitable toll. He called his friend Ted at work. He didn't recall the words, but that one call connected him to his working network and Ted would inform the Director of

Team Operations. So, by nine that morning the entire 'ops team' would be aware of what had transpired; and why the normally punctual and reliable Richard was not in the office or available.

Now, everyone would know. He remembered Zandras coming on the phone, Natasha's father. All he could hear was Vika crying in the background. Richard could hardly get the words out. What could he say? What was he supposed to say? *There is no fucking god in this fucking godforsaken world?*

He walked to the window of his apartment, and looked out onto the East River and all the lights of the city. He touched the glass panel and slid it to one side. Walking out onto the balcony, he gripped the rail and looked up at the sky. 'You took my parents from me, now her. You're just fucking nothing, nothing! You don't fucking exist, and if you do . . .' He turned to walk back in, then twisting his head around, he looked back up, and yelled, 'And if you do exist . . . *fuck you!*' He slammed the door closed, lay face down and cried until he fell asleep.

Ten days had passed since he had last seen Natasha. He had taken Vika and Zandras to see her at the hospital the day they flew in from Toronto, where they had been staying with friends when he broke the terrible news. Today was going to be the last time. Over the last week, they had been making arrangements for the funeral and Richard did not understand how the day had suddenly arrived. As he dressed alone in his apartment, he recalled Dr Leberman's words of a few days back. The doctor, as he promised he would, had called them all in for the autopsy report.

'Natasha had a heart failure basically, although she was a young healthy woman. This is very rare, but not unprecedented. Sometimes these things just happen.'

Richard thought of the conversation he'd had with Natasha that first night in his apartment. About probability. He thought of the irony of it now. Chance events could indeed be life-changing.

Dr Leberman went on to explain the technical details but the basic story was that Natasha's heart had simply given out. It had stopped instantaneously; she'd collapsed at the wheel and driven straight into the back of the Hertz truck. The paramedics attending the scene had suspected this, as there was no sign of blood and no indication that the accident had been responsible for her death. It was just a tragic quirk of fate. That unknown factor. The only other noteworthy finding was bruising around the base of the neck, which, the doctor assured them, could be explained by the whiplash from the seatbelt.

As Richard struggled with his tie, he sat on the bed and began to cry. He missed her. He loved her. He was a broken man.

It had started to rain that afternoon. Richard wanted it to be a miserable day. He did not care what other people thought. He wanted a gloomy day for such a terrible event; it was as simple as that.

As the coffin was lowered into the ground Richard threw his flowers in and blew her a kiss. After inspecting all the flowers that had been sent by friends and family, he and Natasha's parents climbed into the car and slowly drove from the cemetery.

After dropping Vika and Zandras off, he headed back to his apartment. He drove around for a while, then, after circling the apartment block a few times, he eventually pulled into the underground parking lot.

5

The train pulled into Grand Central Station. Richard looked at his watch. It was 11.35 a.m. A few people had already got up and were waiting by the door; then that final jolt and the hiss of the air brakes as the train came to a halt. Richard stepped off the last rung of the exit platform and was glad to be back in New York. The brief trip had gone well and he had picked up a new client, but his mind would wander; it came and went like a wave. It had been eight weeks and two days since Natasha's death. Over the first couple of weeks he had been over to her parents many times, and stayed overnight once or twice. He understood that it probably helped them more than it helped him, but he was trying to achieve some sort of catharsis for himself, something to allow him to come to terms with events. He didn't want to keep making connections. After the death of his parents when he was so young, he had learnt his own survival techniques. He could not say what they were, but he did know that one of the things he had done throughout his life was to disconnect. He justified it by reasoning that he had to do whatever it took. So if he had to cut people off, then so be it. He was trying to let Natasha's parents down gently. Gradually, he did not return their calls, or would say his work was piling up. He had to deal with his clients and, whilst sympathetic to his loss, his company expected results. They knew the pressure he was under and that he frequently had to travel, so they tried to accept the long silences from him.

He passed the ticket gate and walked towards the exit of the magnificent, cavernous station. He loved the building. He and Natasha had occasionally taken lunch here. He glanced at the restaurant, and decided to use the lower exit. *Why punish yourself?* He was looking forward to being back in the office; suddenly his cell phone rang.

'Hello, Vika. How are you?'

'Richard, the reason I'm calling is that I have something here I want you to see; some papers we found.'

'What papers? What are they about?'

'I'd rather not say. I'd like you to come over as soon as you can. I think it's important that you see them for yourself. It was something Natasha was working on.'

'What do you mean?'

'Richard, just come over, please, when you can, but soon. . .'

She paused. 'No, I'm bringing them over. I'll leave now and be in Manhattan within the hour. I'll call you or your secretary, so you can meet me near your office. We can grab a coffee, okay?'

'Yes, okay, that's fine but. . .' Abruptly the phone went dead.

It was nearly 2 p.m. when Richard entered the coffee shop just around the corner from his offices.

'So, Vika, what's all the mystery?'

Vika leaned down and pulled the diary from her handbag.

'I know you gave this back to me. I know how you are feeling and I guess as you could not read it . . .' She cut herself short.

'Well, I guess I wanted you to have it, Vika. Even if I could read it, I don't want to see what she wrote about, and, please, if you are going to tell me she was having an affair or she did not really want to marry me, or. . .'

'Richard! I am so shocked that you would even say a thing like this.'

Richard, realising he had upset her, changed tack.

'Vika, look I am really, really sorry, it's just me, I have got a thing about reading other people's diaries, cell phone texts, anything; you know the old saying: don't look through keyholes, you might not like what you see.'

'It's okay, Richard, I understand, you just upset me, but listen, it's nothing like that, but, please, I have to tell you what some of it is about. It's . . . well, it's something I think Natasha was working on . . . and . . . well . . . you take a look.'

She passed the diary and a stack of papers to Richard. Vika had numbered pages that corresponded with Natasha's shorthand diary entries, but written in plain English so Richard could read the notes. A few moments of silence passed. Vika sipped her coffee, as Richard read his way through the pages.

'I am sorry, Vika, but what is all this?'

'You see for yourself, Richard, she was working on something. I have translated it from shorthand for you, and for some odd words she has used Russian, but you can see it involves your firm, Albright and Newson, and people who are clients of yours.'

'Why would she be investigating clients of mine? I never would have discussed my clients with her, well not in that way, only in general terms. Our ethics have to be beyond reproach. If it got out that I was passing information of a financial nature to anybody, let alone a journalist, I would be finished in the financial world. What I want to know is where she got all this?' Richard could see that two names kept recurring; they were clients of his firm. Jesus, after everything he had been through, the last thing he needed now was a suggestion that he had colluded with her to pass information about his clients. If that came out his life really would be fucked.

'Why don't you believe me? I tell you, Richard, this is serious what she was working on, look at those other notes when it mentions. . .' Richard stood up and handed Vika the diary and her notes.

'Vika, I am sorry but I don't want to know, Natasha died of a heart attack, she just happened to be in her car. My life is fucked and you have lost a daughter, but sorry that's it, goodbye Vika.'

'Richard, please.' Vika was standing now and walking to the other side of the table. Richard took her hand.

'Vika, I told you, I'm sorry but that's it; now I have to go, goodbye.' With that he dropped her hand, turned and within ten minutes was back in his offices. He had to get on with his life; his work was all he had left now and he was not going to jeopardise that on the whims of Natasha's mother. She was distraught, he understood that, but she was finding conspiracies where none existed. He had to move on.

6

Greg was not really interested: the report was vague and obscure. He was working on a scandal involving a high-ranking official at the mayor's office, but was still awaiting some concrete evidence from somebody at the Finance Department. As usual with a lot of these things, people got cold feet, reconsidered and then just dropped the matter. Greg wanted to try some other sources but his editor was getting impatient. The person at the centre of this had already realised somebody had been making preliminary enquiries. He had contacted Greg's boss and demanded an explanation. He'd told him in no uncertain terms that if this was not dropped he would sue. It was the usual opening gambit of any politician and Gerry was used to the empty threats, but he was getting the feeling that Greg was beginning to flog a dead horse. They had spoken at length only yesterday and Gerry told Greg that if his source was not going to give him something then to wrap it up, they would go back to it at a later date if anything subsequently turned up. That was when he dropped this new lead on Greg's desk.

'It doesn't seem much to me, Gerry, I just looked it up: *The Post* covered it a couple of weeks ago, sad story but I didn't hear anything else on the wires.' Greg dropped the file back down on Gerry's desk.

'Listen, Greg, do me a favour, just go and see the woman please, she just wants to talk, says she has evidence that her daughter was working on something. Look, you knew her, she did a bit of freelance work for us a couple of years back. To be honest I thought she was in Australia, but then I read about this.' Gerry leaned back in his chair, chewing on the pencil he always carried. It was a nervous habit he'd seemingly acquired. His wife had told him about it and his secretary was always hiding them, but to no avail. Taking the pencil from his mouth, he began tapping his leather-bound desk. He continued . . . 'Look, you know the other situation: we are going to have to drop it for the time being. I'm not going to authorise anything further on that until your man puts some evidence on the table, so come on, do me a favour, have a quick look into this. Who knows, you may actually have a real story!'

Greg rolled his eyes at Gerry's sarcasm but he had to accept that his source was unlikely to give anything now. It seemed he might have been bought off, and he had given up calling him. Greg accepted that blind alleys were often an inevitable and frustrating conclusion to a promising investigation. He picked the file back up. 'Okay, Gerry, I will give it a look over but I am not spending long on this.'

'Appreciated, Greg. Look, I am out the office for a couple of days so let's say we tie up Friday.'

'Okay, Gerry, and thanks, I know you always save the good jobs for me!'

Gerry flicked his hand at Greg. 'Just fuck off and get me something.'

Greg smiled and closed the door behind him. He spent a few moments clearing his desk, then within three minutes he was out of the office and riding the elevator down to the lower concourse.

Greg's offices were on the eighty-second floor. Noble and Black specialised in political and financial scandals, often exposing high net worth individuals who lived in a world where politics and multi-million dollar contracts merged. And when the lines became blurred there was often corruption. Greg, Gerry and a small team had all come from the hard-baked school of investigative jour-

22

nalism. Most had worked for the big newspapers and some the television networks.

Gerry had wanted to start a specialist business that would not have the restrictions of the heavyweights, and would have only first-class hardened reporters, brilliant at discerning the facts, and able to dig into any small nugget of information and unearth the truth. It was a lucrative business: the stories were sold on to the big boys, who would get the credit and the improved circulations, but for Noble and Black it was big money. They took the risks and thrived on the buzz of breaking a story that others had failed at or were unwilling to take on. So it was not only well paid but intoxicating. For some, like Greg, it had become almost a narcotic; he loved it. Sometimes they fell short, but most of the time they had great stories that the broadsheets were only too willing to pay for. Though occasionally they'd leave them with the liabilities if the story ended up uncorroborated. Either way, it was a heady mix.

So this obscure story about a girl who'd crashed her car close to the Brooklyn Bridge was something that would never even get to their radar. But Gerry had taken a call from her mother, Vika, and she'd asked him just to do some digging. The girl was about to get married and then this happened. Now this Vika wanted someone to come over and speak with her in private. Apparently she had not mentioned it to anybody, not even Natasha's fiancé, some high-flying guy with a large hedge fund in Manhattan who would have no doubt had the money and probably the connections to look into anything suspicious if he'd chosen to do so. Anyway she was worried, and eventually Gerry agreed and he'd passed the file to Greg.

Greg quickly grabbed himself a coffee and made his way to the underground parking lot. Five minutes later he was on his way, heading out to Stamford, which was twenty-odd kilometres north of the Bronx. It was heavy traffic that morning and raining hard. Greg cursed himself for failing to inform the service station the last time his car was in to replace the wiper blades. But a car to him was just a functional item; he had considered getting rid of it as he hardly used it now; his apartment in downtown Manhattan was central to his work and most of his close friends. His girlfriend, Sonia, also lived close by, in the Murray Hill area of central Manhattan. They had been going together for a few weeks now. She was an advertising consultant. They had met briefly at a charity function and exchanged numbers. He was glad now he'd made contact: she was pretty, sexy and good fun. They had been planning a trip to London for some time but the usual stress of New York working schedules meant they kept moving the date. He was thinking to himself, *Yeah, we got to get this trip going,* when he realised he was close to Vika's address. About an hour had passed when he finally stopped outside her home.

7

Greg took the diary from Vika. He looked up at her questioningly before scanning down at the pages in front of him. He placed those to one side.

Vika then said: 'I see you can read shorthand, Greg.' He looked up from the diary.

'Yes, Vika, I don't use it a lot now, but let me see how I get on.' He perused the three pages Vika had marked, quietly scanning each one in turn.

Each page was a spider's web of hastily scribbled notes and annotations, connections and correlations, linking places and names with figures and underlined cross-references. Lots of complex notes about financial transactions from places like Libya, Saudi Arabia and Dubai. She had obviously been investigating something, something big by the looks of things. But what?

'Keep reading,' said Vika, 'keep reading.'

One name kept reappearing, circled in red ink: *Ahmed*. He seemed to be connected with everything else, whatever 'everything else' might be. Greg couldn't make head nor tail of it. He flicked on. More of the same. Names, places, connections, crossings out. What was it all about? Again, *'Ahmed'*, and now a new reference he hadn't noticed before, *'North Korea???'* Then: *'Money laundering, millions!! Client of Richard's company! Do I want to drag him into this??'*

Finally Greg got to the last page. Two lines in shorthand stood out; she had changed the style slightly, almost as if she really did not want anybody to be able to unravel the thread.

That bitch, who was she? Surely they don't think that they can carry on like this in New York? Fuck her, tomorrow I will document what happened just to cover my arse. Evil-looking bitch and those eyes, cold . . .

But, again, what did it all mean? She was onto something, that was for sure; she had stumbled across some strange conspiracy, but what did it all add up to? Who was Ahmed? And North Korea? Wasn't North Korea a closed book?

Greg ran his hands through his hair in frustration. What was he supposed to do with all this? Why had Vika brought this to Gerry? He looked at Vika.

'Yes, well I can see she was onto something here but, Vika, without a lot more information than this, well I don't know what to say?'

'You know what I think, Greg, I am sure Gerry has told you: I never believed my daughter had a heart attack; look at all this, it's big money involved.'

'But, Vika, I really don't—'

She cut in. 'Greg, look, you can see what that last note says.'

Greg looked back at the page. He had seen it but he was aware that Natasha had passed some work to them before, a couple of years ago, and it had been pretty low level stuff. He read Natasha's final note out loud: '*Get this over to Noble and Black, think boys will be interested, getting heavy!*'

'You see, Greg, *getting heavy*, that's what my daughter was saying and all that money! Millions, according to these notes. And not just there, but other places in the diary . . . I have found references to it.'

'Okay, Vika, but did you, or are you going to say anything to Richard, Natasha's fiancé? I mean this does tie in with his company, or it seems to.'

'He just rubbished the whole thing, said it was all fantasy and these clients he knew were all beyond reproach. He is upset, you understand. Yes, I may have lost a beautiful daughter, but he was looking forward and preparing for a whole life with her; he really loved her, you know.' Vika wiped away a tear, and then got up.

'Would you like some more coffee, Greg?'

'No thanks,' he said. 'Vika, I looked at the file before I came over; it says they suspected a heart attack.'

'That's rubbish I tell you, Greg. They did an autopsy and could find nothing. I demanded another one, but the mayor's office, which eventually agreed to see me, refused, citing the fact that the New York coroner was one of the most respected in the state, but I don't believe it. Something happened, Greg, I just sense it.' Vika looked sad but she had an anger in her; he could see that she was determined to pursue this.

'Vika, I understand but look, please, with all due respect, are you suggesting she was killed for this? Look, I know we take risks, I have exposed some quite heavy people in my time, but well . . .'

She cut him off. 'Greg, you know I am Russian?'

'Yes.'

'Well we have a saying in Russia: wherever you go, however far you travel, eventually we will get you. I am sure you know the story of Trotsky and what happened to him?' Greg pursed his lips and looked surprised.

'Yes I do, Vika, but this is nothing to do with the Russians is it?'

'No, Greg, but those North Koreans and the regime they run is fuelled by fear and the system is more Stalinist than Stalin himself. I am not educated like my daughter but I tell you, Greg, something has happened here. Please, for me, just make a few enquiries. I promise you if you say it was all nothing, well then I won't bother you any more. However, I am going to press for a second autopsy. If I could I would pay myself but, well things are not so good at the moment. Look, please just read the diary, my daughter's diary.'

'Look, I tell you what I will do, give me a few days, I will dig around and let you know.'

'You promise to give it a good shot, Greg, promise?'

'Yes, listen, Vika, I didn't really know your daughter but at the end of the day she was a fellow journalist, and we all know the difficulties of the job and, well, look, if there is anything here I will find it, you got my word on that.'

'Thank you, Greg.' Vika kissed him and squeezed his hand. 'Take care, Greg.'

Five minutes later Greg was on his way back to Manhattan Island. Ten minutes into the journey, momentarily lost in his thoughts, he decided just to head back to his apartment. Sonia was due over later and he had decided he was not going back to the office. He glanced down at Natasha's diary and decided the first thing he was going to do was read the whole thing. A modicum of interest had stirred in him. The New York winter had started to bite. He twisted his heater control round and flicked the fan round a couple of notches. Checking his speed, he pushed the throttle a bit harder. It should be a nice evening, he was thinking, looking forward to seeing Sonia again.

8

Over the next week Greg carefully studied Natasha's diary. He was making a few notes when he noticed that she had on two occasions linked the names of a guy called Ahmed with Namir, and that was the somewhat tenuous connection to her fiancé's firm, Albright and Newson. Who, as Greg had known from his discussions with Vika and some preliminary enquiries, were specialists in high net worth clients, providing investment funding, financial advice and stock investments, mainly for Middle Eastern clients. So, how was this firm tied up in some complex conspiracy involving the Middle East, North Korea, money-laundering, forgery and whatever else? Natasha had obviously been investigating some major fraud, and the more Greg thought about it, the more he became suspicious that her death was somehow connected. After all, how does a perfectly healthy young woman suddenly die of a heart attack behind the wheel of her car, with no previous medical history of a heart condition? Bruises on her neck were mentioned in the autopsy but there was no evidence of outside physical pressure, and it was concluded that her heart had just stopped. Rare in such a fit young woman but not unheard of. Her heart had been examined and it had shown all the signs of an aneurism, a sudden stopping of the heart due to . . . due to what exactly?

Meanwhile, Richard tried to get on with his life. In truth, he was severely depressed, but he hid it well. Work was the only glue holding him together now, and despite everything, things were going well for the team. The boss, Harry, was pleased with his guys. Over the last six years, he had honed a great team and together they were bringing in staggering sums of money from clients around the world: Europe, China, India, the Middle East.

Richard and his four associates, together with Harry, would meet and go over all the information, and make decisions as to where they might place their various clients' money. Then they would visit them personally, inform them of their findings and invest accordingly. Richard wished he were a bit better at analysing company accounts. He was a real salesman. He had a good enough grasp of the mechanics of the investment game and a solid overview. He possessed common sense, was very intuitive and trusted his own judgement. A client had once told him, 'Remember the quote, Richard: "take my wife, take my home, but never take my good name." You can get another home and wife, but once your reputation is gone, man, it's gone.'

Around this time, Richard's closest friend and associate, Ted, was called away to a client who wished to discuss his portfolio and was keen to invest further. The client was based in Dubai; the place had become a hothouse of investment, with money pouring in from investors across the globe. Buildings were going up all over the place; land being reclaimed, desalination plants, banks on every corner and a planned shopping complex that would become the biggest in the world. Ted called Richard just to let him know he was away for a few days and to come for dinner when he got back, with him and his wife.

'Yeah, will do. Who are you seeing in Dubai?'

'You remember Mohammed Said? Well, it's a friend of his looking for a big placement with us. I think the guy's name is Ahmed. I'll tell you all about it when I get back.' The conversation ended.

After days of trying to piece things together from Natasha's diary entries, Greg decided to contact Richard. They met a few days after his initial call at a bar close to Richard's offices. Greg filled him in on everything he had gleaned from the diaries; that it all seemed to point towards some great conspiracy: money-laundering, US dollars, the Middle East, Dubai, Saudi Arabia, North Korea, and in connection with Albright and Newson, two names: Namir and Ahmed.

At first Richard was totally dismissive. 'Listen, Greg, I appreciate you looking into this but I told Vika I wanted no part of it. Sorry but it's all a bit too cloak and dagger for me.' Richard rolled his eyes, indicating he thought it was all a foolish conspiracy theory.

'Well I understand what you say, Richard, but look, there are some loose ends here and if you could I would appreciate your help.'

'Greg, I really don't want to get into this, everything that happened, really I just want to forget it, please.' Richard was getting aggravated. Greg sensed by his body language and changing demeanour that this was going to end abruptly, so he quickly cut in:

'Okay, Richard, I understand, but listen, just do me a favour, please. These guys that are mentioned here in the diary . . .' He passed Natasha's diary over to Richard, open at the relevant page. ' . . .This Ahmed, this Namir, according to Natasha they are connected with your company. This Namir, he invests with you, right?'

Richard didn't say anything. Could it really be the same Namir? And Ahmed? Hadn't Ted mentioned meeting an Ahmed during his phone call, some connection with Mohammed Said? There were too many coincidences for his liking.

Greg took his silence for affirmation. 'Listen, please just do me a favour and have a word with him, this Namir, just ask him; if nothing comes, fair enough.' With that Greg passed his card to Richard and said, 'Call me if you do find anything you're not happy with. If I don't hear from you, well, Richard, I promise I will close this case. Really I am only doing it as a favour to my boss; it's really not our sort of thing in any event.' It was good reverse psychology. He stood up from the table and offered Richard his hand, which Richard duly shook. 'I will see you then, Richard.'

'Look, thanks, Greg, leave it with me. I will have a chat but personally, well you know what I think.'

'Thanks, Richard. Again, I am very sorry for your loss.' With that Greg left the downtown bar.

Richard stayed for a while, bumped into a few friends, then left. His instinct was to leave this all well alone but one name flitted around the edges of Richard's tired brain like a performing flea. *Ahmed, Ahmed, Ahmed.* Of course, there were thousands of Ahmeds. But it wouldn't let him go. First Natasha, through her diary, then Greg, the journalist, then Ted. So many coincidences, and Natasha had already drawn some connection between *her* mysterious Ahmed and Albright and Newson. Could it be? No, it was ridiculous. He tried to dismiss it from his mind as he walked back to his apartment. But he tossed and turned all night. What if this is what Natasha had been trying to warn him about? Is that why she had texted him to meet him at Joe's on that fateful day? Was she going to reveal her suspicions, but had been cut off en route? Had somebody discovered her investigation, somebody who would stop at nothing to silence her conspiracy theories? He had come to a decision: he would speak to Namir.

The next morning Richard spoke with his boss, Harry, but he only casually mentioned Namir. Harry looked at his diary. 'Yeah, I think he is flying into New York early next week, Richard. Well, look, I leave it with you, I guess he will be looking to do his usual round of business with us. Well I hope so, anyway . . . listen, if you want to meet with him, that's fine with me, but are you sure you are up to it at the moment?' He placed a fatherly hand on Richard's shoulder.

'Honest, Harry, I am fine, really. Thanks for your concern, but don't worry, Namir will be placing plenty with us. I hear they are really doing well out there at the moment.'

'Yeah, who would have thought that under all that sand. . .?'
Harry smiled and walked back to his office.

The week went by in a blur of business transactions and some
domestic drudgery for Richard. He was annoyed his cleaner was
on holiday but he was not going to get a replacement just for
two weeks. Then suddenly it was Friday. They met at Jack's bar
on Fifth and Lexington, a regular haunt for finance whiz-kids to
let off steam at the end of another money-making week.

'Good evening, Richard. Good to see you. How is my financial guru?' Namir greeted Richard warmly. He directed his minders
to give them some space, though Richard was well aware they
would be watching surreptitiously all the time. These guys were
absolute professionals, serious people, usually ex-special forces
types. He glanced over again; he could not tell; he certainly would
not like to tackle one of them, let alone two.

'Hi, Richard, what can I get you gentlemen?' The waitress
recognised Richard almost immediately. Within a couple of
minutes the drinks arrived and after some more small talk Richard
decided to cut to the chase, but where to start? He couldn't simply
lay Natasha's tangled web on the guy. Christ, he hardly understood it himself. But Ahmed, maybe he'd know something about
this Ahmed . . .

So, for his opening gambit, Richard simply mentioned that
Ted was in Dubai, meeting Namir's friend, Mohammed Said.

'Oh, how is he, that bastard?' Namir laughed.

'Okay, I think. Ted's seeing a friend of his . . . some guy called
Ahmed? I think it was a recommendation.' Richard held his
breath.

'Ahmed? Yes, I know him, but I can't believe Mohammed
recommended him.'

'How do you mean?' asked Richard. Christ, he hadn't expected
things to move so quickly. Of course, this could be a completely
different Ahmed, almost certainly was, but it was a start. . .

'Look, please tell your friend to be careful. This Ahmed, if we're talking about the same guy, is involved in many things. Personally, I would not take his money. It's not clean.'

Richard's stomach did a somersault. He would have to try and play it cool. 'What, drugs or something?'

'No, at least I don't think so. But the guy is into some heavy duty shit, and you and your company would be better off staying well clear. Don't get involved, that's my advice. He's up to his neck in something big; we're not talking petty crime here, we're talking big business, states, governments.'

Richard tried to stay calm. 'Go on. What do you mean? You mean the US government? Building contracts being given to US companies?'

'That's been going on for years. That's just business! They don't give a shit about that. Perhaps the British would be upset, with their ridiculous sense of fair play.' He picked up his recently refreshed glass.

'Well, go on then,' said Richard, leaning forward in his chair.

'Richard, you know me. I'm telling you this as a friend, as you have always looked after me well.'

'Okay, I'm all ears.'

'Listen, Richard, this bastard is seriously bad news. He's going to make things bad for us Arabs and we don't need to be on the wrong side of the US. Why would we? Our culture may be different but we do good business with you guys. Why bite the hand that feeds you? Only a fool, a greedy fool, does that.'

Richard felt sick to the pit of his stomach. He didn't want to know, but he had to know, for Natasha's sake. 'Come on, Namir, what's he up to?' He looked around. The bar was busy and noisy. Nobody could hear them. Namir moved closer.

'Listen, Richard, do you know anything about North Korea?'

'I dunno, a little, I guess. It's like a hermetically sealed country; largest land army in the world. A xenophobic society, supported by China and Russia, though not so much in recent years since the collapse of the Soviet Union. That's it really, what have they been doing then? Exporting drugs through China?' Richard laughed to ease the tension, but it wasn't very convincing.

Namir leant further forward, so close that Richard could feel his breath on his face. 'Listen, Richard, I've said too much.' He looked spooked. 'Just stay clear, that's all I can say. This is bad business, very bad business.'

Richard knew that Namir knew more than he was letting on. Could he trust him? Could he share his suspicions about Natasha, her death, this whole murky business with this man, who at the end of the day was little more than a business acquaintance? But then did he have any choice? Richard needed to know. He had to know. For Natasha.

So he told Namir everything: about the car crash, about her investigations and now a reporter had contacted him after scrutinising Natasha's diary and following Vika's suspicions. He'd laid his cards on the table. It was Namir's move now.

9

Namir sat in silence for what seemed like an eternity. Had Richard overplayed his hand? Had he silenced his friend for good with his confession? Richard feared he had. And then, just as Richard had begun to lose hope, Namir spoke, this time in a whisper. . .

'Richard, because of Natasha, because of her death and your terrible loss, I will tell you what I know.'

And he did. At best it was sketchy, but it all seemed to tie in with the cryptic scribbles of Natasha's investigation. Forged US dollars had been traced to an operation in North Korea. There were rumours that this wasn't just some underground crime syndicate, but that it was governmental, a sovereign state forging another country's currency on an industrial scale.

'Think about it, how much more feasible it is when you've got the resources of an entire country behind it,' said Namir.

'Christ,' said Richard. 'But how? How the hell. . .?'

'Who knows!' said Namir, 'like I say, it's only rumours; getting anything concrete out of that country is like getting blood from a stone. But it's been done before. . .'

'What do you mean?' said Richard.

'The Nazis tried to do it to the British during World War Two.'

'Yeah, I heard about that, something to do with this Jewish prisoner, master forger or something; I think there was a film about it.'

Namir nodded, and took a slug of his drink. 'Promised to spare his life if he helped them, had no choice, but the point is the notes were never good enough: the paper, the ink, the artwork, too many variables, and of course no machine to produce the notes.'

Richard cut in. 'Machine? So what . . . these guys have made their own machine?'

'Again, it's only conjecture,' said Namir. 'But the rumour mill is churning. . .' Namir elucidated as best he could, given the ragtag collection of hearsay and speculation he had to work with. Something about machine parts shipped to North Korea via China. Authentic parts too, direct from verified suppliers to the US Treasury.

'As I say, I'm making guesses here, but there's lots of talk.'

'That's all very well,' said Richard, 'getting the parts, but how the hell do they assemble the thing, how do they get the know-how?'

'The Chinese,' said Namir, 'if anyone, it's got to be the Chinese.'

'Okay, okay,' said Richard, 'let's say, just for the hell of it, that this is true, that there is some grain of truth in all this supposition, well what has this got to do with Ahmed and the Arabs? Apparently Natasha's notes mentioned Dubai and Saudi and—'

'Ahmed, yes Ahmed,' said Namir. 'From what I hear that fucker is in it right up to his neck.'

'But how?'

'Well, this is something I *do* know. The guy has legitimate money, but he was never in our league. A bit player. An opportunist. Next thing we know he's moving in the first division, so he's got to be ripping *somebody* off.'

'I guess,' said Richard, 'but who?'

'Patience, patience, Richard. We have many contacts throughout the world as you know and we discovered that he has a Swiss bank account that he sends money to.'

'Okay, but there's nothing illegal in that. . .'

'Yes, but this is just a holding account. The money then gets transferred. Guess where to?'

'North Korea?'

'Right on the money, excuse the pun; and remember these are legit dollars going in.'

Richard cut in. 'Okay, so the money goes in; what about the other direction? How does the counterfeit cash come back out and get distributed? And what's the exchange?'

'Again, we're back to conjecture here,' said Namir, 'but I could hazard a guess.'

And for the next hour they talked and surmised, and second-guessed and pinned half-truths to known facts until they had pieced together some kind of picture. A picture of hundreds of Ahmeds, setting up similar operations; of big money being laundered across the globe; the usual suspects: Iran, Libya, Cuba. Rogue regimes undermining the US economy, and at the same time helping their own flagging economies with billions of fake dollars. And at the heart of it all North Korea, a country in turmoil.

'The place is probably like Japan was at the end of World War Two,' said Namir at one point. 'Whatever the motive, whoever's behind it, no doubt it's giving them much needed foreign currency reserves to rebuild the place. They have to; it's virtually finished; many think it will implode soon.'

'And if you're right, what about China?' said Richard, 'why the hell would a country on the brink of superpower status risk such international furore if it all came out?'

'China? Do you think they want it to collapse? No, they really don't need to support a country for the next ten years, like the Germans had to when the Berlin Wall came down. So they all keep their eyes closed, their mouths shut and the train rolls on.'

They had come to a natural pause in the conversation. They both sat in silence, considering the enormity of what they had just discussed. Richard was flabbergasted; and Natasha, Natasha had unearthed all of this, and now here was Namir confirming his deepest fears. Natasha had done her job too well, and they, whoever they were, had silenced her, for ever.

'Richard, listen, you tell your man – Ted, is it? Tell him not to take Ahmed's money, it's not good. I tell you this in confidence but it will come out soon . . . it always does.'

'Namir, you said at the beginning that this guy is going to make things bad for the Arabs. What did you mean?'

Namir looked long and hard at Richard. He knocked back the remains of his drink. 'Al Qaeda,' he said, forcefully. 'Those maniacs have been accumulating money for something else. That's what I am telling you. Richard, it's something big and we don't want any part of it.'

'Al Qaeda? What do you mean? What do you mean something big?'

'Just make sure you tell your friend. These fanatics hate the US, Richard, you know that, and so does this bastard, Ahmed. It's all connected: the North Koreans, the fake dollars, Al Qaeda, I'm sure of it, I'm sure of it. So fuck his business. Those Al Qaeda bastards are up to something, maybe next year, maybe soon. I really don't know. But if anyone's up to their ears in this it's that band of brigands. Mind yourself, my friend, this thing has tentacles. Keep well clear and keep your head down.'

And with that, Namir stood and shook Richard's hand. He signalled to his two minders and headed for the exit. As he was leaving, Richard called to him. Namir paused and turned back towards him. 'Namir, do you think my Natasha. . . ? It seems as though she *had* uncovered something and, okay, it's big, but really, do you think. . .?' He looked down and ran his hands through his thick dark hair.

'It's possible, Richard, anything is possible. I told you something is in the air. Now thanks, we will speak again, please, but next time I don't want to discuss any of this. Now I must go, Richard.' The party disappeared out the door. Richard noticed that a black Maybach limousine was already waiting; seconds later it was gone. The rain was coming down hard. Richard finished his drink, grabbed his umbrella and decided to brave the weather and walk home. He knew what he had to do: he would call Greg first thing in the morning.

10

Alicia was running late. She had argued with her husband that morning. She had gone back to full-time work, and they had recently moved to a swish place out near Freeport in the Nassau area of Long Island. It had a beautiful view over the Atlantic Ocean and was only an hour's commuting distance to Manhattan. They had taken out a new mortgage and, with everything else, she was finding it all a bit of a strain. They only had the one son but Alicia was in her mid-forties, with a fifteen-year-old to deal with, and Jack more often away than she would like. Consequently, the cracks were beginning to show.

That morning she needed to be up and out really early. Her new job was in elaborate offices in downtown Manhattan. It was going to mean a few more stops on the train and longer hours, but it was more money. Noble and Black was an efficient and friendly business and she had settled in well. Jack had come home a few days ago. The weekend had gone well and Monday came and went, but Jack had waited until this Tuesday morning to tell her that he was going away again. He'd been asked to go to Argentina and assist in an advisory capacity in the refurbishment of one of the company's rigs that was on lease to another firm.

They rose at 5.30 that morning and he had made the announcement at the breakfast table.

'For God's sake, Jack. How long is it this time?'

41

Jack hesitated. 'About three weeks, maybe four. But I promise no more two-month stints.'

This is how the next half hour or so went, when finally she stopped the bickering and said, 'Look, let's leave it and talk about it tonight, and I mean it, Jack. We've discussed it before; you can find something else; we have the house paid off, money in the bank. Hell, of course you've got to work, but this is too much what with Brad the way he is . . .'

With that, before Jack could come back at her, she grabbed a few things then paced around looking for her keys. Once she had located them, she called up to Brad, kissed Jack and was out the door, making her way to the station for the hour's journey into the new offices.

At around 8.40 a.m. her cell phone went off. She was sitting at her desk going through various papers and making notes relevant to some of the larger clients that she wished to discuss with her team. Her boss had also come into work early and was sitting in his spacious office. He nodded over at Alicia, putting his thumb in the air, signalling his satisfaction with their new offices. Alicia smiled and turned away as she spoke into her phone.

'Hi, Jack. What's up?' she said rather annoyed as this was going to be a busy day.

'Hey, don't bite my head off. Listen, I've got some good news. . .'

'Really? Go on then, tell me. Hey I know, Brad has dumped those girls, the ones I can't stand, and cleaned his room?' She laughed.

'Listen, darling, I'm serious, I've given in my notice.'

'Is this a joke, Jack?'

'No, I had a think about it this morning. I rang Bill at home and told him not only was I not going to Argentina, but I was also resigning!'

'Jack is that true?'

'What, that I love you?' he joked.

'No, you fool. You're really packing it in?'

'Yes. And yes I do love you.'

A lump came to her throat. 'I love you too, baby. Look I have to go, really. Let's go out and have a meal or something. Why don't you come downtown? Hey there's a restaurant here, in the building, called Windows on the World; it's . . . Oh! Oh my God!'

'Alicia? What's up? Alicia . . . Alicia . . .? Hello?'

The phone was completely dead. Jack redialled. Nothing. He tried twice; he scrolled down and found the company's land line number. Three times he tried that. No answer. He put the phone down and mumbled to himself, 'Damn stupid phone companies!'

He walked into the hallway. 'Brad, get out of that damn bed,' he shouted up to his son. 'Come on . . . move it!'

'Dad. . . Dad. . . Turn the TV on!' Brad suddenly ran into the kitchen screaming!

'Don't you shout like that,' Jack said and stood up.

'Dad turn the fucking TV on.'

'Hey, Buster, you just hold it right there.'

'Dad, please . . . for God's sake . . . it's . . . it's Mum!'

'What are you talking about, Brad?'

Brad had reached up and pressed the on switch.

'Look, what the hell is going on?'

'Dad, it's Mum. Look. . .'

The TV burst into life:

'This is Jackie Wills. We are in the financial district of Manhattan, about three blocks from the World Trade Center. About five minutes ago a plane flew straight over our heads and has crashed into one of the towers. . .'

This was just one of many news programmes that would clog the airwaves around the globe for the next days and weeks and months. And every time Jack or Brad switched on the TV, surfed the net, glanced at a newspaper or overheard a conversation, they were reminded of their loss.

It was one of those moments that would define an era, a JFK

moment, a moment where however long you lived you would remember where you were on that fateful September day. Certainly, Jack and Brad would never forget.

Of course, there was so much speculation – theory and counter theory – that it was almost impossible to keep up. Who was behind it? The usual suspects: Iran, Iraq, the Taliban, North Korea. For one brief moment, Jack seemed to remember, the latter was trumpeted as the most likely candidate. But then their US ambassador had publicly expressed his country's regret for the great loss of life on that day; said that terrorism must not be tolerated, the usual platitudes. And presumably that was good enough because it was pretty soon concluded that they had played no part in the attack, and the manner in which they conducted themselves led the administration to look elsewhere.

No doubt many in the close circle of the joint chiefs had been relieved about that; to attack North Korea would have been foolish in the extreme and so the world breathed again. Meanwhile Saddam Hussein, who had so openly mocked the US and the unfolding events in the weeks that followed, became public enemy number one.

Jack and Brad never heard from Alicia again. Her new offices had been on the eighty-second floor. They tried to console themselves with the thought that she would probably have been killed instantly. Eventually, Jack went back to his work. He changed his mind on the early retirement; how would he cope being stuck at home without his beloved Alicia? Eventually, too, Brad met a nice young girl and she helped him through his grief at the loss of his mother.

But America's blood was up; the cross-hairs of the world's only remaining superpower were coming sharply into focus and as time went on that focus was Saddam and his tyrannical regime. As for the people of New York, they grieved, they held ceremonies, and eventually, as they must, got back to their lives while the world turned.

11

But two weeks after 11 September in New York, people were still reeling from the disaster that had unfolded. Family members and staff who had not been at work that day at Noble and Black paid a special tribute to lost colleagues and friends who had been inadvertently caught up in that terrible moment in history. And of those who had been there, none had survived. The offices of Noble and Black had been destroyed almost the moment the plane crashed into the building. There was no escape from that wretched destiny.

It was against this backdrop that Gerry, who just by chance had been away at the time, was contemplating what had become of Greg. The two men had worked closely together, and over the few years had formed a good working relationship. Gerry and his wife Tanya could only think the worst.

Gerry and Tanya were at home. It was early on a cold Tuesday morning and they were still trying to pick up the pieces and considering how to get the business back up and running with the few staff they had left. Tanya was making coffee and listening to Gerry as he talked to her from the lounge of their apartment, raising his voice so she could hear him.

'It's not looking good,' Gerry said to Tanya ' . . . and don't you think it's strange? I mean . . . it's just weird. Remember a couple of weeks before all this happened, I asked him to look into something? I'm sure I told you at the time, a young girl crashed a car, supposed heart attack at the wheel?'

'If I'm honest, no, but go on,' said Tanya.

'Well he called me and told me he had a really interesting lead and wanted to follow it up, said if it was true, it was going to make a great story, best one we have had for ages. Anyhow, I don't hear from him and then the attack; somebody thought they saw him in the building that morning, but in all the confusion who knows?'

'So what are you going to do?' Tanya said as she brought two coffees in and sat next to Gerry.

Gerry was quiet for a few moments, and then he said, 'Look, Tanya, I've called his home number, his cell phone is dead, but what does that prove? If he was in the building that day then, well I guess that's what you would expect. I actually went to his apartment. I spoke to his neighbour, the old lady that lives next door. She hadn't seen him for a week or so, but she thinks that was about a week before the attack, so who knows?'

'What was this great story anyhow? What did he say?' Tanya asked.

'He wouldn't say but whatever it was, it was going to be a real scoop. That's all he would say; you know what he can be like, he likes to play his cards close till he has something concrete, it's just his way. Then, sometime that week before the attack he had a meeting with Richard. . .'

'Richard?'

'The guy whose fiancée, Natasha, was killed in that crash. Greg just kept saying that he was going to follow it all up. Before all this, mind you, he didn't even want to take the story; I had to really twist his arm. So that's it really, darling, I don't know where he is but, you know, I just get a feeling that he is still alive.'

'That's all very well, honey,' said Tanya, 'but surely there's nowhere in the world he could be that he would not be able to get to a telephone, is there? And what about this Richard guy, Gerry, can't you get in touch with him?'

'Their whole firm, Albright and Newson, was wiped out, it was only a few floors above ours. Far as I can ascertain only a handful were left; well it's the same story as ours, darling, and God knows what will happen now! I hear some firms are never going to re-open; it's awful.'

'Have you made any firm decisions about Noble and Black yet?'

'Well I am going ahead with the temp offices as I said, but we have a meeting next week. When we've got it all up and running I'll see what the situation is; in the meantime I should try and do something about this Greg situation.'

'So what do you do now?'

'Well, I've called the people we know. He's not visiting or staying with any of them. I've been to his home; we've called and left messages. We've told the NYPD that he's missing, and he may have been at the WTC on the eleventh. What more can we do?'

It was around two weeks after they had set up temporary offices with the few staff that had survived. Gerry's secretary, Jenny, who had fortunately been at home that day, interrupted him.

'Gerry, I have an NYPD detective on the line. Can you take it please?'

'Sure, Jenny, put him through. Hi, Gerry Granton, how can I help?'

'Mr Granton, this is Detective-Sergeant Jackson from the NYPD. I understand you work with Mr Greg Sanderson?'

'Yes, that's right, sergeant.'

'Let me get straight to the point. As far as we can tell, Mr Sanderson is alive.'

'Thank God for that,' said Gerry.

'We checked with customs and the Border Protection Agency. Their passport system confirms that Mr Sanderson left the US just under a week before the WTC disaster. He left JFK on a flight to Singapore then on to South Korea. From there he went on to China, and it has been confirmed that he did land at Beijing International Airport. We have requested some more information from the Chinese and they are going to come back to us.'

Gerry thanked him and the sergeant hung up. He went straight into his outer office where his secretary was looking over her glasses at Gerry nervously. 'It's okay, Jenny. He's alive. Apparently he left the country a week before the attack and he never told us. What I can't understand is why we have heard nothing from him? The whole world must know by now, unless he has his head under a rock somewhere.'

12

Two days later, Gerry received another call from Detective-Sergeant Jackson.

'Mr Granton, it's Sergeant Jackson. I have some important information regarding Greg but I need a few more details from you. Can I come to your offices?'

Gerry looked at his watch. It was 6.30 p.m. He was going to leave the office soon. 'Sergeant, I am just leaving my offices; I am going to call into our local bar; would you like to join me? We can talk there if that's OK with you?'

'Yes that's fine, where will you be?'

'Do you know The Huston? It's just near here.'

'Yeah, sure do.'

'Okay, sergeant, how about half an hour?'

'Fine, Mr Granton, see you there.'

Gerry walked into the bar around seven. He had been there about five minutes when the detective joined him. They shook hands and the detective produced his badge. Gerry just glanced down and said, 'That's fine.' Gerry motioned to a couple of chairs in a quiet corner. He called the waitress over and ordered a beer. 'Detective?' he said.

'Nothing for me, Mr Granton, on duty. Oh, okay, just an orange juice.'

They sat in silence for a minute or two while they waited for their drinks. Then the sergeant spoke. 'Okay, look, this is what we know: Greg is okay and is certainly alive, but he's in North Korea.'

'North Korea?' exclaimed Gerry, 'what's he doing there?'

'Well that's what we'd like to know. Greg went to China then managed to get on a two-day guided tour to Pyongyang. Normally you have to go through the normal laborious process, well you can imagine, but as he is a journalist and not on one of their 'problem' lists, he was granted a few days access to the capital. He waited around in Beijing for a couple of days and managed to get his flight with no problems, but he didn't return on the due date, so at the moment he's about a week overdue. Since no one knew where he was, no questions got asked, but officials in Pyongyang have been in touch with the Chinese Embassy and asked them to report to our authorities that they are holding one of our citizens.'

'What for?' asked Gerry, not unreasonably.

'Not that they tend to need a reason, but it looks like possible subversion, attempting to bribe officials and making unauthorised movements around the capital.'

'Jesus,' exclaimed Gerry.

The sergeant shook his head. 'Anyhow there are other unspecified charges but basically that's the gist of it.'

Gerry sat with his mouth half open. 'I don't get it.'

'Neither do we, sir, but this is where we are. We get a call from the State Department. They're shitting it because of everything that has just happened, and the last fucking thing they need is a diplomatic incident! So they've instructed us to look into Greg's recent history. So, Mr Granton—'

'Gerry, please, call me Gerry.'

'Okay, Gerry, I need you to help me. Can you tell me what he was working on?'

Gerry proceeded to impart all the information he had about Greg's call to him and just that he was following a good lead.

The detective cut back in: 'Did he say what he was involved in?'

'The only thing I can tell you, sergeant, is that he was, on my instructions, following a story about a girl that was killed here in New York in a car accident. Her mother got in touch with me and it went from there. I gave her details to Greg. After that, well, as I say, I got that one call and we never heard anything again.'

The detective asked Gerry to send him Vika's contact details in the morning. They discussed the various issues for a while then the detective shook his hand. 'Gerry, thanks very much; just tell your colleagues that we've tracked him down to China and, as far as we know, he's okay and is just taking some time out. I think that's best. And for Christ's sake, please, we don't want the press, your people, getting hold of this. Let's keep a lid on it. I'll be back to you as soon as I have spoken to this Vika.'

The next morning Sergeant Jackson drove out to see Vika. They talked at length about Richard and Natasha and how they had all been absolutely devastated at what had happened to her. The detective enquired as to what she had told Greg a few weeks after her daughter's funeral.

'How did you know about that, sergeant? Is the man okay? Oh my God, was he killed?'

Sergeant Jackson cut in abruptly. 'Greg's okay. He's fine, but he's not in the US, and that's why I am here. His boss Gerry told us that he began to work on your story; it seems that he may have found something out, and next thing we know, he is a missing person.'

'I told him my daughter was on to something and she was killed for it; where is he now and what's happened?' said Vika.

'I really can't say, but I would appreciate it if you can keep this to yourself for the time being. I really don't know anything about your daughter's death and of course my sincere condolences at your loss, but with everything going on at the moment, you understand?'

'It's okay, sergeant, I won't be going to the press, they have already helped me, and as long as Greg is alive, then I will be happy to wait. As they say, detective Jackson, the truth will always out. My daughter is dead, and nothing is going to bring her back, so I am happy to wait.'

'Thank you, Vika, we do appreciate that, but if you could just give me a bit more information as to what your daughter was looking into, that would help.'

Over the next ten minutes, Vika described as best she could about Natasha's notes.

Sergeant Jackson thanked her and left.

He was back at his desk just over an hour later, when he received a call from the New York mayor.

'What's the news on this guy from Noble and Black we're hearing about from some of our people in Washington, what have you found out? I wish to speak with you before I call Senator Macgaskil in Washington. He has to report back to the State Department as soon as we get more information about what the guy was doing out there. And apparently, the President insists he is briefed by the latest tomorrow.'

'Yes I understand, sir.' The sergeant told the senator what he knew, which didn't add up to a whole hill of beans, but he gave him the gist of it: the North Koreans, the forged dollars, Ahmed, the Arab . . . all the information that Vika had memorised from Natasha's notes.

The line went quiet for a few seconds, and then the mayor said, 'How reliable is this information?'

'I don't know, but I do know that Gerry Granton and his team have a special investigation department and this guy Greg is one of the best in the business. I reckon he found out something and went looking, something to do with this alleged North Korean thing—'

The mayor cut him off. 'In light of what has just happened, imagine if these North Koreans are somehow involved, or there is a connection with Al Qaeda.'

'I know, sir, I know. Guilt by association is a dangerous presumption, but it isn't looking good.'

'I take your point. Senator Macgaskil did tell me a few days before all this blew up that even though the North Koreans are always denouncing us, we don't think they had any involvement in the WTC attacks. From the noises coming out of Washington, it's that despot in Iraq they're looking at. To be honest, sergeant, I really don't know about any of this but thanks for all your help and giving me some background to this; no doubt we will speak soon.'

With that the call ended.

13

'Please sit down, Mr Sanderson. We would just like to ask you some questions.'

Greg looked around the austere room. Its walls were battleship grey and devoid of any fixtures or pictures. He looked up at the ceiling, a grey-white colour with three fluorescent lights lined up as soldiers. The evidence of previous fittings was clear; he guessed these would have belonged to an earlier time, the kind of lights that would have hung down from a long cord, with large metal or glass shades. He was drumming up visions of old spy movies. On the opposite wall was a small wash basin with some paper towels on a shelf; next to the towels were three glasses, about the size of a large tumbler. They looked clean but certainly not as if they had been washed any time recently. It was certainly not somewhere you would wish to stay for any length of time. He put his elbows on the large wooden table. It was a smooth surface, a light wood, and marked all over with hot cup stains and general scuff marks. Opposite were two heavy chairs. He glanced round; yes they were the same as his, and were actually quite comfortable, almost out of place here, but were as worn as the table and certainly not particularly stylish.

Greg thought back to how all this had started. He needed to find out the truth about Natasha, about her death. After he'd met with Richard for the second time, only a few days ago, he was convinced. Richard himself had been unnerved by all the information Namir had imparted to him that night in the New York bar. Greg never mentioned it to Richard but in one place in Natasha's diary he'd found a reference to the North Korean capital, Pyongyang, and a building close by. She had simply written: *'looks like a factory, locals know what's going on, need to try and get a contact to photograph it, millions of dollars being produced.'* So, although at first he had dismissed the entire story about Natasha's death not being an accident, now he was not so sure. A few contacts, friends of his in the business who specialised in North Korea, had heard rumours, but nothing solid. The place was sealed and it would take a brave person to try and get a story out there.

But that was Greg, a risk taker. He'd become a war correspondent when he was only twenty-five and had been halfway round the world in his two years at CNN. Then he'd done a stint at freelancing, but he was back with his real love, the dark and sometimes murky world of investigative journalism. After meeting with Richard he knew he had a story. Richard had confirmed all of his suspicions and so he'd jumped on a plane and a day ago he'd arrived at the capital of the most isolated country on the planet.

'Mr Sanderson. Let me introduce myself. My name is Miss Woo. I am a senior officer in the People's Police, and I'd like to see if we can clear this up as we do not want a full diplomatic incident here. First, we need to know why you were trying to speak with and question our people. As you must have realised it is quite futile; most people do not speak English.'

Greg cut in: 'Well actually I did find two people who. . .' He decided not to go on.

She said nothing for a few moments, and then continued. 'Furthermore, why did you break away from your guides? You know our rules.'

'I'm sorry. I did break away, I admit that, but I did try to explain to your security people that I was asking about what life is like here, just from the ordinary citizen's perspective.'

'Yes, I have heard this story. My officers inform me that you were asking how to get outside the capital to the industrial area; why would you be interested in that?'

'I am a journalist, it's what we do. Look, I just wanted to see things for myself. Surely you understand, it makes for better reporting, uncluttered and objective, let's say.'

Miss Woo looked into his eyes and it was silent for a few seconds.

'Really and you believe that?' she said

'Well of course, what, don't you agree?'

'No I do not, even if I did you had specific instructions and you were given special dispensation to come here; normally we do not allow journalists and reporters in.'

Greg watched her face. She was deadly serious but quite beautiful. He considered a charm offensive, but then thought he would keep that in reserve.

'Yes I appreciate that, but I would not write anything bad about your country. On the contrary the capital seems such a clean and friendly place.' Greg could feel himself straining to utter those words; he did not believe them, and he was glad he was not connected to a polygraph, but he smiled convincingly.

'Well that may be, but rules are rules and this is the predicament you now find yourself in. Now let me move on.'

Greg nodded. 'Look, I just decided to come out here. I probably should have spoken to my friends and work colleagues first, but I just made the booking and came with the company that arranges all this. I was in the South for a few days, and as I wanted to get the complete picture, well I thought I should come here, get your point of view, your citizens' feelings, just tell a story really.'

'This is not America.' She looked sternly at Greg and continued: 'Mr Sanderson, we could hold you here for at least a month, possibly two. We could of course inform your government that you were attempting to subvert the people and corrupt their minds. Then your country would probably have to pay compensation to the Party. You would be deported and probably be banned from entering for at least five years!'

Greg sat back. 'This is all a misunderstanding. I agree my logic is a bit flawed, well stupid really, I guess. I wasn't thinking straight and I'm sorry, very sorry.' Greg stopped and scratched his head. This cover was preposterous, it would never stick, but then he couldn't charge ahead and accuse the North Korean government of forgery, money-laundering and murder, could he!

'Let's continue,' said Miss Woo. 'Now when you were searched by our security people you had a number of items in your possession that were taken from you.' She turned to the thick-set security guard on her right and said something in Korean. The guard leant down and began to take objects from a small leather bag and place them on the table.

'Okay let's go through them.' She looked down at the items and began to point at each one and asked him to confirm it was his. 'First, is this your camera?'

'Yes. Yes that's mine,' replied Greg.

'You were specifically warned about cameras, Mr Sanderson. Further to that I see in this report in front of me that you did hand a camera in at the airport. Strange that you were carrying two cameras and this one is quite small, almost as if you deliberately kept the more, how shall I say, the one that would be easier to conceal, do you not agree?'

Greg shrugged his shoulders. He thought it best to keep silent; she paused for a few seconds, gave another intense stare, and then continued:

'Okay, next this wallet? Oh and please check the contents.'

Greg quickly fumbled through the small Armani wallet. 'Yes, yes, that's mine, and yes it's all fine.'

'And these keys?'

'Yes they're mine.'

'Please describe the function of each key, Mr Sanderson.'

Greg looked up. 'Each one?' he asked, surprised.

'Yes, please,' she continued in her monotone.

Greg went through the entire bunch, until he got to the final key. 'And this one is for a small safe in my apartment.'

'And what would you keep in that safe, Mr Sanderson? I mean why would you have a safe?'

'Well it's quite secure where I live but . . . well, you never know.'

'Yes but you can insure goods I assume, so again, why would you need a safe?'

Greg found this line of questioning strange and didn't know what she was driving at.

'Well, yes, I mean you can of course get insurance, but for some things you can't.'

'Some things? Like what?'

'Well you know . . . personal things. I mean you can't insure mementos, those types of things.'

'And cash, Mr Sanderson. You can't insure cash and even if you could, you might not wish to tell anybody about it. You follow?'

Greg looked puzzled. 'Er . . . not really. I mean I earn good money, but not in cash.'

'No: but illegitimate money, Mr Sanderson. Perhaps money paid for information, mmm?'

Greg was totally bemused. 'Sorry, I'm really not with you.'

'Okay, let's continue. This?' She picked up Greg's small black diary, opening it at a page in which she had placed a marker. Then, pushing it towards him with the pages exposed, she asked, 'Is this yours?'

'Yes, it's my diary. I've always kept one.'

'Is this your writing?' He looked down at the page she was indicating. In that split second Greg felt as though an electric shock had been sent through his body. He went cold and numb at the same time. He sat in complete silence.

'So let's read your words, Mr Sanderson. I quote:

"Richard called after meeting Namir in Jake's . . . Namir says forged US dollars, and money-laundering on an industrial scale! Who is Ahmed? Ahmed seems to be the key . . . Namir mentioned Dubai and Libya . . . are they all implicated? And Al Qaeda!! And behind it all,

*North Korea! Must tell Gerry . . . spoke to couple of guys at W. Post
. . . only rumours, worth a look? Could be big story? Might give it a
go.'''*

She closed the diary and passed it back to the guard. 'Well,
Mr Sanderson, perhaps you can enlighten me. You seem to think
that we are involved in some ridiculous scheme to forge your
currency and that it is going out to terrorist organisations. Let's
start with this Ahmed. What do you know of him?'

Greg did not react immediately.

'Look, it's just a diary, I have a lot of notes and stories in there.'
Greg was beginning to perspire. His diary was full of notes; the
section Miss Woo had homed in on was written in shorthand in
a bottom third of the second from last page. He had not even
circled it or drawn any kind of indicators on it as to its impor-
tance. He realised that not only could these bastards read English,
they could read a journalist's slightly coded shorthand. They must
have scrutinised the entire diary, read all the eighty-odd pages,
read them all in fine detail and been able to decode his writing.
These people were smart and this woman in front of him, speaking
in perfect English, was no fool.

'So is it customary to write lies in your diary? I mean, as we
know, your country tells lies about our country, and now you're
telling me that you write lies in your own diary. Is it a lie, Mr
Sanderson?'

Greg felt uncomfortable. He would have to think on his feet.
Quick-time. 'Miss Woo, let me be entirely frank with you.'

'I wish you would, Mr Sanderson.'

He adopted a business-like tone as he continued.

'The man, Namir, is a client of this man called Richard. He
passed me the information in an informal way, which I then
told my colleague about. I mean, you understand, we have to
check these things out. Honestly, I tell you, it's a coincidence,
my brief from my boss was to do an in-depth article on your
country, well North and South. Look we don't make opinions,

I am a reporter, I report the facts, that's it. I have been all over the world, we just present the truth, we let the viewer or the reader make up their own mind. That's it really, Miss Woo, the basic tenets of journalism: get facts, not innuendo, rumour or distorted half-truths; verify and report, that's my maxim and. . .' Greg stopped, feeling he had said enough, or rather was hoping he had.

She looked at him. Her face was implacable. Eventually she spoke:

'Okay, Mr Sanderson. Now tell me the whole story: this Namir, his full name, where he lives and his business interests; about the man he told you of, this Ahmed. We must have everything you know of him. You obviously had a long conversation about it; I mean what did you tell your friend, or is it your boss, Gerry? Tell me the whole story, Mr Sanderson.'

So Greg told her the story, at least his on-the-spot, made-up, desperate version of events again and again until he began to believe it himself.

But, Miss Woo wanted details. And he wasn't giving her what she wanted.

'Again, Mr Sanderson, let's start with Namir. . .'

The next thing he knew he was on the floor. As his blurred vision began to clear, he looked up to see Miss Woo standing directly over him. 'Mr Sanderson, if you were a citizen of this country and had refused to divulge what you know, I could have had you shot. I expect a bit of respect.'

'You can't do this. I'm a US citizen and I've done nothing wrong. I demand. . .'

'Mr Sanderson, we will speak later. For now, we will contact your embassy in China. Until then, I suggest you do not say any more, unless you wish to impart the information we need.'

She left the room. Greg was picked up by two guards, taken from the room and dragged down a corridor and tossed into a cell. The door slammed firmly behind him. Greg fumbled around in the dark and found a bed. The smell was awful, like someone had been sick in it or near to it, but he did not care now. He flopped over and closed his eyes. Not thinking anything, he eventually fell into a fitful sleep.

14

In Pyongyang, the capital of North Korea, the cracks were starting to show. If ever there was a model of the abysmal failure of communism this was it. Its people were starving. As with any dictatorship, the Korean regime realised that if its people were well fed and relatively happy it could maintain the country's sealed and xenophobic existence. What it wanted was the dollar, the main international currency of trade. The Party realised that even a socialist state needed money to survive, and they needed lots of it.

Its citizens by now were finding small escape routes out of the country, making their way to South Korea. Journalists interviewed many of them and would publish their stories, stories of starvation and deprivation. All, of course, denied by the leadership.

Five miles outside the capital was a small factory; an uninspiring place, it sat generally unnoticed among other small industrial properties.

Armed guards patrolled day and night, and a small military contingent would intermingle with the factory guards. A police station had been built close by, the entire area was floodlit, and trip wires, closed-circuit television and even infrared cameras were in evidence. In short, the place was virtually impregnable.

When it had been constructed about three years earlier, it was not kept secret. Local labour had to be used and lorries were coming in at all hours pouring tons of concrete, delivering steel panels, specialist glass and all manner of construction materials. It was obvious that it was some sort of security establishment. The people were told that their dear leader was constructing a new building to hold the country's gold reserves as the old one could come under threat from a US-backed invasion by South Korea. The truth was that they hardly owned any reserves of gold, and were virtually bankrupt. Exporting little of value and with no tourist industry they had precious little in foreign currency reserves.

Around late 1997, a meeting had taken place of the highest party officials in a closed session of the Presidium. A top secret report was being given an overview by a lower official, Mr Tang, who had come up with a brilliant plan, which was going to be presented to the officials.

The basic idea was to plan and coordinate the assembly of a machine that could duplicate US dollars. Then, using various criminal elements and contacts, they would 'sell' the forged currency in exchange for 'real' US dollars, thus giving them much needed international currency to use however the regime saw fit.

There would be no shortage of takers, as Mr Tang explained: 'We have friends in Libya, who the British have accused of blowing up the Pan American flight that was destroyed over Scotland. They are willing to help us, and they also have contacts with the IRA who are also fighting the British imperialists and would be happy to help for ideological reasons. We have made contact with friends in Russia who are concerned as to the changes that may happen out there and are willing to assist us. And there is the Al Qaeda group; they are committed to the destruction of the United States; they are happy to join this arrangement and have many contacts in Saudi Arabia and Dubai. The details and logistics will have to be worked on but it can all be done through what will be seen as legitimate trade with these countries.' He paused for a few moments to catch his breath and to gauge the reaction to his opening remarks.

'The scheme is brilliant because *they* take all the risk and have the facilities, gambling houses, casinos, hotels, construction projects and the like where this money can just disappear. So, my comrades, we get what we need, hard US currency to help our glorious leader to distribute as he sees fit, and at the same time we undermine the dollar. And we help our friends around the globe to fight the British and Americans and their destructive policies: I recommend this to the Party and our glorious leader!'

Mr Tang sat down to take questions.

'How good can we get the dollar?'

Another question came almost immediately.

'Why not forge the British currency? Why the US dollar? The British are our sworn enemy.'

Mr Tang rose again. 'The British pound is one of the best quality notes in the world; we have looked into the logistics of this, there could be problems with the paper; also it has a slightly different process than the dollar. I don't wish to go into the technical issues just yet but it has been examined and we think it is not viable.'

'And the dollar?' one of the officials continued. 'Come on, how good can we get it?'

Mr Tang continued. 'Comrades, we have, as you are aware, many contacts around the world. Our agents in the US, by infiltrating certain companies, have, well, we know the machines they are using for their main production process. There are actually only three of these in the entire United States; two would be impractical but a third we believe we can clone. I say clone, comrades, as we are not going to make a copy, but an exact duplicate.'

Another official stood up, 'Comrade, your plan is brilliant. Yes, truly, our great leader will commend you just for the idea alone, but, comrade, how can we make a duplicate of an American machine?'

Mr Tang raised his arm. 'Comrade, I understand and I thank you for your remarks, but this is a machine, a complicated machine I grant you, but it is not made by the US government; it is made by a specialist company and they supply countries around the world with them. What we plan to do is purchase the individual components and then ship them here to be assembled. We have, as you know, our own specialists in banknote production; we also have made enquiries in China and the Soviet Union and they are willing to send specialists to assist. This will also be in the paper preparation process and some of the, as I referred to a while ago, more technical issues.'

Another official stood up. 'Mr Tang, please tell me, we cannot order these parts directly, so how, I mean, tell me the logistics of how we get the company to actually supply the machine parts?'

Mr Tang was enjoying the questions; he was a skilled party official and a brilliant orator. 'Comrade, let me tell you, we have contacts in Saudi Arabia, as I said. The whole area has become awash with cash. Our friends there have been asked to set up a company that is, well, this is the story. They will make an approach to the US company, the cover story being that they are going to bid for a licence to do banknote production for the Middle East. Currently a lot of it is actually done by private companies, Del a Rue, for example.'

Tang paused. He had them in the palm of his hand. He wanted to savour the moment. 'The Bank of England also produces banknotes for these countries and others around the world, so it will just look like a business that is going to bid for contracts from its own government. We shall get the company to send over the parts and these will be held in a warehouse. When we are ready they will be gradually brought here for assembly by our specialist teams.'

Another official got to his feet.

'Comrade Tang, what about teething problems with the machine? I mean, surely you will need technical support from the machine manufacturers? Assembly issues, faulty parts, damage in transit, all sorts of problems; and they may not believe this company is doing this legitimately.' The official sat down and Mr Tang rose again.

'Comrades, this is the part of my plan I think you will enjoy the most. However, before I go on to that let me just say that the reason that most forgers around the world fail is simple, and in fact it's why they forge the money in the first place. It's the cost. If any forger wanted to make perfect banknotes it could be done; the problem is simply the cost. They would have to do what we are trying to do: purchase large, expensive and technically complex machines, spend time setting them up, have large premises to house them in, pay wages to teams of specialist printers and machine minders. It's a big operation, so even the most proficient ones who set up small factories, and this is the point, comrades, they are still operating on an extremely limited budget. That is why it always fails, the best forgers in the world fail simply because they lack the manpower, scale and resources.'

Mr Tang now walked to the middle of the large room. 'Comrades, we are going to purchase two machines, yes two machines. Our contact in Saudi is a legitimate businessman, well, to all intents and purposes. He owns large tracts of land and is undertaking many construction and property developments. He is going to erect a large industrial building; he will set up the company as a separate entity, and the parts will be purchased from the US company and exported. Now, the US firm will be asked to send a team to assist in its assembly and pre-production, in preparation to full production printing. You see, they will know that the machine is assembled, paid for and ready for operation in, well, we think it's going to be Dubai. The American technical teams will go back to the US and of course report that the machine is ready to go and the owner is now waiting on the outcome of his bid. He will not arouse suspicion as the owner has told them he is a wealthy man. And if he fails to get the contract this time round he will simply mothball it. They will not be allowed to speak about this to anybody else as they all sign confidentially clauses in their contracts for obvious security reasons.'

Mr Tang paused as he drank a glass of water and wiped his forehead. Then he continued.

'Now, comrades, about three months after the machine is working, our friend then contacts the printing machine company and says that he has secured his government contract but he has had to make certain assurances regarding safety of supply. As the contract is so lucrative he is going to build further industrial premises and is going to order another machine. He will have that all delivered and stored and then he will tell the company that he will call them once it all arrives and that they must then send the same team out and assemble the second machine.

'Comrades, that will never happen. Those parts are going to be shipped via our friends into China. From there it will be delivered by train across the border to us. We will then have it delivered to a factory that is to be built, we think, somewhere near the capital. Then we shall have our own teams assemble it and test it ready for production.'

The first official who had spoken rose to his feet once again. 'Comrade Tang, I am assuming you have all the contacts dealt with and all the logistics considered? But please, three questions. First, how are you going to assemble the second unit? You can't bring the Americans here. Second, how much is this entire operation going to cost? Third, how good, and this has already been asked, how good is this US dollar going to be? I mean it has to be virtually perfect, surely?'

Mr Tang looked at him and said, 'Thank you, comrade, I welcome your questions and I will answer all three. Now, first, we are going to send eight of our people to meet with the Americans in Dubai to assist in the assembly of the first machine; they, the Americans, will be told that this is a Chinese team, which is going to be on contract to the Arab owner and wishes to know exactly how the machine is assembled and operated so that it can be done in-house. This is standard practice and it is nothing that will arouse suspicion. Our people will of course be watched; any caught trying to defect are aware that their families will be wiped out and so they will show their loyalty to the Party. Once our people, and remember these people are specialists in large-scale printing and industrial machines, are fully briefed when the components for the second machine arrive here, they will be able to set our unit up and be ready for production. We will of course then bring in all the other skilled workers that we need, most of whom are already working at our own banknote production centre. And as I said we have friends from China and some in Russia who can help.'

He walked around from his podium and stood to the side of the large stage.

'Can I take point three second?' Mr Tang nodded at the official who had asked the three questions.

'Of course, comrade, please continue.'

'Your third question, comrade . . . now once this machine is up to operational standards it will produce exact duplicates of the US dollar, in all denominations. Comrades, they will be indistinguishable from the originals.'

The room became excited. Many turned to each other and whispered and smiled, some actually clapped, but then the senior official stood up.

'Comrades, I want the second question answered before we discuss the matter.'

Mr Tang took a long breath. 'Comrades, the cost is the question you are most interested in so let me enlighten you. All, and I mean all, of the costs that are external – specifically, the machine parts purchases, the assembly of the industrial property in Dubai, the shipping costs from the US and eventually to us – are to be borne by our friends in Saudi Arabia and Dubai. All we have to do is pay for the construction of the premises, a printing works, which will be close to the capital. The wages of our own staff and all the incumbent costs from raw paper to printing ink and finally post-production costs, which include a testing and cutting machine, will be ours.'

A senior official stood up. 'They are to bear all the primary costs, in consideration for what?' He sat down looking slightly puzzled.

'Once we are in production, they want ten million dollars in duplicate notes. Now once we have reached that target, then we have to agree a rate by which we will supply the dollar in exchange for the same currency. Or sometimes we will be accepting gold, specialist cars and other goods that we may require from time to time. These will of course go to our dear leader for distribution and there may well be public utility vehicles, too, even trains and the like. The mechanics for how they will do this is yet to be arranged.'

He paused. His audience was transfixed.

'Most likely we will set up, let's say, trading companies with our friends, supplying them with goods . . . furniture, clothing . . . and they will pay for them with hard currency, with the amount they pay far exceeding the value of the goods. Then all we have to do is get our dollars to them. Various methods are being devised as we speak, but rest assured these will be innovative. We have provisionally agreed a rate of five to one.'

Another official got to his feet. 'Excuse me, comrade chairman,' he said to the senior official, 'Mr Tang, how long will all this take? I mean when would we be ready for production?'

'We estimate about two years, maybe three, to have all this actually operational, so I would say by ninety-nine, yes around late ninety-nine.'

Mr Tang then sat down and they all discussed the issues individually as they rose to take afternoon tea. After about half an hour they all sat down again. A few more questions went back and forth, and then a vote was taken. It was unanimous, the Presidium had voted to a man to recommend this plan to their dear leader.

A few weeks later Mr Tang was called in and personally congratulated by the party leader and the chairman of the original meeting. He was told to proceed with haste. Funds would be made immediately available to build the factory and cover any other internal costs. He was also instructed to start the search for personnel who would be able to operate this machine, and work at the factory.

It was a huge undertaking, he would tell them, but they would be working for the benefit of the Party and their glorious leader.

Over the next two years the plan was put into action. What was remarkable about it was not the idea – people had been forging banknotes for years all over the world – but this time it had the power of an entire country behind it, as well as wealthy business figures, who, for greed and ideological reasons, were only too happy to help the North Koreans and others fight the Americans. It was a lethal mix.

Nobody would talk, as to do so risked terrible retribution. On the North Korean side, the country was sealed and, with the Arab connection, the money involved was enough to keep people's mouths shut. Not to mention the threat from Al Qaeda themselves should anybody be foolish enough to speak about it.

Eventually the plan came to fruition and the premises were constructed a year before the printing press parts began to arrive and production of the US dollars began in earnest.

In accordance with the agreement, the financiers duly received ten million dollars, which, after costs of purchasing the equipment, paying all the shipping fees, construction of the two large premises and other incidentals, gave them a clear profit of five million dollars, eventually being laundered through the casinos and other outlets.

However, this was just the tip of the iceberg. The notes were perfect. No one had talked, and now the Dubai operation was obtaining five 'Korean' dollars for each one US dollar of legitimate currency. It went on undetected for about two years. Then, suddenly, it was out. Not because people talked, not with the discovery of the notes. No, it was simple human frailty. And greed. Because a few men flaunted their wealth, people began to take notice. Many of the old Arab families knew that riches like this did not appear overnight and tongues began to wag. First just a few rumours, then gradually stories began to filter out.

One man in particular, Ahmed. He was flash, with plenty to talk about. He began to annoy his fellow countrymen. But he had signed a Faustian pact and was going to become the master of his own downfall.

15

To the far side of Pyongyang airport was a small runway reserved for the few private jets that flew into the only really civilian airport in the entire country, the rest being all military. Some of the others were big enough to be converted to civilian use but whilst the country remained virtually closed to outsiders it would have been pointless. The tourist industry was non-existent aside from the limited 'guided' tours of the capital, and few people wished to travel there in any event. The unofficial planes that came in were usually Chinese business people who traded with the North Koreans or a small number of others who had managed to strike up trade agreements, though this was a difficult, laborious and ultimately time-consuming affair, with rigorous background checks. If you did strike up trade agreements with the regime, your brand would have to be, at least in part, sympathetic to the regime and its worn-out doctrine. Any criticism whatsoever would result in the immediate termination of contracts, and if any goods had been paid for in advance, as was usually the case, it was doubtful that the money would be returned.

Notwithstanding these problems, many people would risk it, as, given the right circumstances and products, it could prove highly lucrative. However, there were others, others who, with political connections and an ideological mindset that matched the North's hatred of the Americans, would be prepared to involve themselves in the darker, clandestine side of the regime's activities.

'Your clearance for final approach has been accepted, please come in on runway 5-2 on the eastern side. Set your glide scope to the following settings. . .'

'Roger, Pyongyang control, please go ahead with settings; making final approach.'

The pilot made the final adjustments and the small jet began its descent into the small privately reserved runway. Today, rather than being met by Korean officials, a rather different party was waiting for the occupants of the plane.

Sie Roo was sitting in his official car, with his driver, and two officers were in the rear. He turned to the officers. 'Remember what I said. Do not arouse his suspicions, but if he does try anything, shoot him in the head. Do you understand?'

'Yes, sir,' came the staccato reply.

An hour before this, Greg was woken up from his dingy cell, and taken out into the glaring sunlight, which caused him to squint. He stumbled along the corridor and eventually the two guards showed him into a large cold room, and indicated a shower unit, signalling that he was to wash himself, and dress in clean clothes that were in the room next door. Both guards, to his surprise, then left the room.

The lukewarm water was so invigorating; he felt that it was the best shower he had ever taken. He was thinking how we all take such things for granted. The soap was as hard as a brick but it did eventually lather and it smelt good. He dried himself and walked naked into the next room. To his embarrassment, Miss Woo was sitting on a small bench, next to a pile of clean clothes.

He covered himself and looked down. There was no way he was going to go anywhere near the clothes. He figured they might take a photo of him, doctor it and then send it to the US Embassy in China or South Korea, claiming he was attempting to seduce one of their female officials. Then he would be stuck here; a prospect he was already beginning to fear might be about to come true.

'Come and get your clothes, Greg.' She had called him by his first name.

'Miss Woo, would you mind moving over there?'

'You are embarrassed, Greg. I am sorry but, well, I have authority to go anywhere in this building. I am just, how you say, keeping an eye on you.'

She got up and walked over to the opaque window that was covered on the outside with blue vertical bars. A top louver window was open about halfway. The floor was red but the room had the same grey walls as in that first interview room. The usual portraits of their dear leader adorned the right wall and on the left side were two long wooden benches with clothing racks and even some lockers. It was like the changing rooms of a swimming baths from the 1950s, he thought to himself.

'Please put on the clothes we have provided, but don't try anything,' she said sarcastically. She had now turned her back to him.

For the first time in . . . Greg did not know how much time had passed . . . he felt clean and fresh, but thought he looked like one of the proletariat so often depicted in old Soviet posters. She turned round.

'Good, Greg. I will come back for you at about six-thirty or seven.' She walked out a side door and disappeared from view. Greg heard the sound of two cars starting and then what sounded like heavy gates opening. Seconds later the cars pulled out; he assumed it was Miss Woo with her staff. He wondered what her day comprised of; in his mind he chuckled to himself and thought of Orwell's *1984*. '*Yeah, the thought police,*' he mused.

Two guards came in the other door and beckoned Greg to go with them. They walked back down the corridor but this time turned a different way. One opened a heavy steel door and motioned to Greg to go inside into another cell, but it was certainly a step up from the previous night. It was clean and bright, the bed was made, there was a small table with a water jug and a glass on it, and in the corner was a toilet and a hand basin. The door suddenly slammed behind him, and he wondered what the next round of questions from Miss Woo would bring.

Sie Roo watched as the executive jet eventually taxied to a spot about fifty yards in front of them just off the tarmac. The side door opened and two minutes later a man walked down the steps and looked around. Sie Roo got out of the vehicle followed by the two officers. The uniformed driver stayed in the car.

They spoke for about three or four minutes. The man seemed confused and kept pointing around, then Sie Roo called his driver to bring the car over. They all got in, including the tall, dark man with a beautiful suit, now sandwiched between the two officers in the rear seat. He looked remarkably out of place. The car pulled rapidly out from the airport complex.

After about twenty minutes the car stopped at two massive gates. They opened within a few seconds and the vehicle went rapidly inside. There were high walls and internal fences at least twenty-feet high. The car went through another set of gates and into a small parking area. They got out and Ahmed was taken by one of the guards and escorted into the large building. They walked into an office that overlooked what looked like a newspaper-printing operation. There was a large machine, lots of noise and very bright lights. The place was immaculately clean and there were people milling about, all seemingly busy in some production process.

The men walked into the large office, the door was closed and two of the guards remained by the door. Sie Roo sat on the desk about ten feet from the doorway. Ahmed stood in the far corner, placed his hands behind his back and listened.

'So, Ahmed,' began Sie Roo.

'Look,' he cut in, 'I don't know why I'm here. I was supposed to be meeting my contact in town tonight, at the hotel, to discuss some issues we have. I have some other routes that we could use. I'm your best client, Roo.'

Sie Roo was surprised at his tone but he continued. 'Please let me go on, Ahmed. The People's Police want to ask you about something our agents in your country have warned you about before. Have you been keeping a low profile?'

The man smiled, shrugged his shoulders, turned his hands over and said, 'Of course. What's this all about?'

'Well, Ahmed, a few days ago we arrested an American, a reporter, who came here on the pretext of taking a guided tour of our great city and doing an article for a larger client on life here in the North, but he began asking questions. He was arrested after he gave our guides the slip, asking about the industrial areas outside the capital.. He unfortunately, or fortunate for us, was searched by our local police unit. He was then questioned by a senior officer, Miss Woo; she in turn called me. You see he had a diary, and we went through it. . .'

Ahmed was agitated. 'Hey, look, what's this got to do with me? So a fucking Yank keeps a diary . . . so what?'

Sie Roo got to his feet. The guards stood bolt upright.

'Ahmed, you will not use profanities in front of me! And you are lucky that those guards do not understand English. Now be quiet!' He readjusted his uniform and continued.

'In this American's diary, he has notes of a meeting with one of his clients. He knows about you and the operation. He has it written down in a *diary*! We have it in our possession and he admits it's his handwriting, it's his diary. So, what do you have to say?'

He looked at Sie Roo indignantly. 'I don't know what this is about, but I can tell you nobody has heard anything about our operation from me!'

'Ahmed, we will talk in a minute. You will go with my guards here and wait in the next room.' The trio walked out of the office, Ahmed still looking behind him as Sie Roo disappeared down the corridor in the other direction.

Five minutes later another high-ranking official entered the office, followed by two other guards. The man turned to Ahmed and spoke in English: 'Ahmed. . .'

Ahmed tried to speak over him.

'Look I have told Roo, I am supposed to be. . . '

'Be quiet! Ahmed, you listen. You are a fool. We have many sources and outlets for our operation, which we conclude are all secure. Now this has come to light and from an American. Unbelievably you stupid bastards have attacked the United States, and now the entire operation could be jeopardised.'

'Hey, the World Trade Center, that was fuck all to do with me,' he protested dismissively. 'I told you . . . I don't know any American. I was going to place some funds in an American investment house, but in the end I didn't meet the guy.'

'Ahmed, you are a complete imbecile. You were earning enough from this operation, but you can't leave it there. You want to fuck the Americans with our dollar production, and then invest the proceeds in their country, and then you mount an attack on two of their major cities. Not only that, Ahmed, you flash your money around. We know: we have agents. We watch people we do business with very closely. You are a liability and no longer any use to us. The matter has been discussed with senior members of the Presidium, now I have our orders.'

The guards grabbed Ahmed, and he was taken out of the side office and over to a large machine. Ahmed looked up and realised that the machine was a massive guillotine, cutting the dollar notes as they dropped from the final section of the printing press in sheet format. The sheets – about two-feet thick – were then sliced into perfect oblong dollar notes of various denominations. The cutting blade was enormous, about six feet in length, two or three feet in height and made of highly polished steel. It came down and sliced into the thick dollar sheets. Once it had cut all the way through it made a hissing sound, and then slowly returned to its idle position about three feet above the notes. Pneumatically driven, the blade was sharp as a samurai sword. Within five or six seconds they had taken him over to this gigantic cutting machine. Suddenly the official barked out orders to the other men standing by the machine. One man ran and threw some switches and the machine stopped.

Ahmed was shouting and struggled desperately as he was hauled over a point very close to the operating area. The massive cutting blade was suspended in mid-air, then Ahmed was pulled, screaming, over the base plate of the powerful machine. Seconds later, the blade came down and cut him in half. Blood shot out in all directions. His intestines spewed over the grey floor. More men appeared, the two separate parts of the body were put into two bags, and the other men just gradually disappeared. The guillotine stopped in its idle position; blood was dripping from it. An order to clean up the mess was barked out and people started running around with paper towels and water and buckets. The scene was horrific, macabre and brutal. He had been executed in a medieval way and those who had witnessed it would never risk encountering the same fate. An hour later, the remains of his body were taken to a local abattoir.

Back at the People's Police headquarters, Miss Woo returned from her usual day, and after going through some paperwork and laborious report filing, she summoned Greg.

'Greg, we shall speak in the morning, but tonight you are going to stay in slightly better surroundings.'

It was a short journey. As the car pulled to a halt he looked to his left and saw a large hotel, then two young women came out. Miss Woo waved them to her car and spoke briefly, ordering them to take Greg inside. As he closed the door behind him she opened the window and said, 'I will see you in the morning, Greg, sleep well.' He just looked at her amazed, turned and walked into the hotel. He was taken onto the second floor by one of the girls, who opened the door of the first room they came to. She went in, briefly showed him around the room, then, after pointing out a set of clothes in a small wardrobe, she quickly left. He walked over to the bed, lay down and promptly fell asleep.

16

A sharp tapping on the door woke Greg. He stumbled over to open it. It was the girl who had taken him to his room the previous night.

'Good morning, sir. Please come down to breakfast soon as possible. You have a meeting.' She promptly closed the door behind her. Greg looked around the room. It was the first time he had properly inspected it since arriving the night before. It was sparse and anachronistic like everything in North Korea, a veritable time warp. Even the underpants they had supplied him, everything hailed from some long forgotten era, he thought as he took them off and got in the shower. After a fairly lukewarm wash, he dried himself and looked in the wardrobe, finding a fresh set of clothes and underwear that all fitted reasonably well. He put on the jacket that had been supplied back at the People's Police building, the one that made him think he was in some Soviet propaganda film. He kept thinking Lenin was going to knock on his door at any moment and give him a lecture on the benefits of the communist system. He was having these thoughts when he opened the door. Stepping into the hotel corridor, he noticed two new security guards, smaller guys than all the previous ones he had seen, but none the less bristling with guns and quite intimidating. As he walked past them, they nodded, not cracking any smiles, but he thought that these guys did not seem so bad. He walked on to the stairs and they followed. He went down one flight and entered the reception area. As he approached the desk, a small girl suddenly appeared from a side room.

'In here please, sir, thank you.'

Greg entered a small room that had four tables all laid with simple white cloths and four chairs around each one. He smiled to himself at the perfect symmetry of it all. The floor was carpeted but had seen better days. Over to the left was a large set of windows that went right down to the floor. He could see into the garden in front and, as he got close to the table to which she was directing him, to the street beyond. She pulled a chair out for him, he thanked her and duly sat down.

'Sir, it's for you.' She pointed at the tea. Her accent was strong but her English was good. 'I bring breakfast for you soon.' With that she walked off. Greg watched her short legs taking long strides; it was almost military in style: her back straight and her shoulders pulled back. As he watched her disappear through what he assumed was the door to the kitchen; he guessed they all had to do some form of military service. He turned and looked into the main street. A few people walked by but there was no traffic, and it was quiet, deathly quiet.

He looked back out into the corridor, observing the two uniformed guards. He could not make his mind up. *Were they military or civilian?* Though he guessed that there was probably a very thin dividing line between either of these services. They were standing at the entrance to the room not looking directly at him, but he could tell that they were keeping an eye on him. Every now and then one or the other would casually look round, give him a cold, blank stare and look back. They did not speak between themselves. Then, just at random, one would walk into the reception. He could hear him speaking to the girl at the desk in Korean; then he would return. This routine went on for a while. After ten or fifteen minutes the girl emerged from the kitchen and brought a small plate of food to Greg's table.

'For you, sir, thank you.' She placed the small plain white plate on the table and with that she turned, almost in one movement

81

and walked off, this time going past the guards and back into the reception area.

Greg thanked her and turned to his breakfast. There was what looked like a kind of black pudding, just one slice, two pieces of plain toast, some rice and a tomato that had been sliced in half and lightly cooked, and that was it. But he certainly was not going to complain. He was hungry and ate the meagre breakfast quickly.

He stared out the window. What the hell was he doing here? How had he got himself into this mess? Why hadn't he just worked on all this back at the office, and told Gerry what he had found out after meeting with Richard? But it was his way, he loved the challenge and he sensed a huge story. A few guys he knew had already warned him of the difficulty in trying to gain any information, let alone getting a photo. Even if this place, this money factory, existed, how would he recognise it? Why had he not left his diary back at the hotel? Christ, he should not have brought it at all; they would have probably searched his room during the day while he was out. In all the places he had reported on around the world he'd had some hair-raising moments, some close shaves, but he began to think that this was not going well. Had he really thought that he could stroll into North Korea and carry on his investigation and find out why this girl Natasha had died so mysteriously because of what she had uncovered? It now seemed quite preposterous. But how was he going to get out of this mess? He had sensed, just the slightest inkling, that behind the authoritarian facade, Miss Woo had a humanity that he might be able to reach. Miss Woo was his only hope, but he would have to play it very carefully. He was under no illusion: he was in dire circumstance, and all of it of his own making. Yes, he would have to play it very carefully. . .

Just then, he saw a car stopping outside the hotel. Out stepped Miss Woo. She virtually goose-stepped up the steps to the hotel door and, for some reason he did not understand, he sat bolt upright.

'Good morning, Mr Sanderson, I assume you slept well?' she

said as she got close to his table. Then she sat down. 'Did you like your breakfast?'

'Fine thanks. How are you, Miss Woo?'

'Yes, well, thank you. Mr Sanderson, we have decided to be lenient with you, for the moment at least. After what happened in New York, we do not want an international incident.'

New York? What did she mean? What had happened in New York? He guessed it was probably some incident at the United Nations. He decided his curiosity would have to wait. If it was some political incident he did not want to get into some ideological debate with her. He didn't want to blow it now, just as things were beginning to look slightly more favourable for him.

'The notes in your diary,' she continued, 'are obviously some ridiculous hoax, and whoever is behind it will be sought out and punished accordingly. So we are carrying out some investigations and in the meantime you are in my charge. You are very fortunate. It is only because of the current international climate that fate has been so kind to you. Do not forget this.'

There she went again. What international climate? What incident? Greg was itching to know more but he decided silence was the best option, for now at least.

'Now today,' she continued, 'we are going to take you to see some of the sites of our great city that you did not see on your first tour.'

With that she got up. Greg immediately followed, and they went past the guards, one of whom accompanied them to the car. They exited the hotel, walking the short distance to the car. Greg noticed a clock on a building just opposite the hotel; it was 9.20 a.m.

They drove around for about half an hour and every now and again Miss Woo would point out some particular landmark or an important public building. They went past the university and a massive public library; he thought better of asking what western books were kept there; none, he assumed. They also passed the main headquarters of the People's Party and many buildings that you would probably find in any major city, except most had the word 'People's' as a prefix attached to them. The car stopped and they got out but the guard did not follow. They stood by a statue of their dear leader and she bowed down. Greg made a small gesture, thinking it would probably be a good move. They walked on to a small garden area. It was well tended with bright flowers. They sat on a bench. 'Greg, you like our city?'

'Yes, I do, I admit it's very clean, it's looked after and you certainly don't have traffic congestion like we have in New York.'

'Thank you, Greg, now we talk.' She turned round to face him. She didn't look as harsh as before, but she still had her black hair tied tightly back and wore no make-up. Her face was round and she had dark, almond-shaped green eyes and a small button nose. Greg guessed she would be around thirty-five years old; he examined the shadows under her eyes, trying to ascertain her age from the lines that had begun to appear there. He half smiled and said, 'Yes I would like a chance to talk.'

She continued. 'You were very foolish to come here . . . What you wrote in your diary could be considered treason if you were North Korean. You could face serious charges for just suggesting such a thing.'

Greg just nodded.

'However, as I said, these are extraordinary times. I am instructed to tell you that your government has been informed of what has happened to you and that you are being looked after and we are asking you questions.'

Again, Greg kept quiet.

'They have also been informed that if we suspect you of spying or any subversive activity, you will be tried by our justice system and, if found guilty, you could spend ten years in a prison here. You understand?'

'I understand,' said Greg, breaking his temporary self-imposed vow of silence. 'But I have a question . . .' He couldn't hold back any more; he needed to know what had happened in his homeland.

So she told him: about New York, the World Trade Center, the planes, the thousands of deaths, the entire story. He was flabbergasted. Was this what Richard's client Namir had predicted? Was this a consequence of this dollar-forging project? Or merely a coincidence? It was horrific. Truly horrific. Then it struck him with full force: Noble and Black . . . their offices were on the eighty-second floor and Richard's company was only a few floors above that. His heart raced, his mouth dry.

'I can't believe it, God, it's madness, you say both the towers collapsed? Did that happen immediately? Did people get out of the buildings?' He was firing questions at her like a verbal machine-gun.

'Mr Sanderson, really I am not willing to discuss this any further, I should not have informed you but, well, we had information that your company is, was, resident in this, sorry these, Twin Towers. All I know is what I told you, both the towers were destroyed, so as you can appreciate the international situation is volatile at this moment. However, I am sure your government would not be so foolish as to think we had any involvement in this.'

Greg did not know what to say next, all he wanted at that moment was to get on a plane back to New York. His boss, Gerry, and all his friends at the office, they would have all been there. Miss Woo told him it was early in the morning; most of the small contingent of staff were always in early, even the secretaries, and what of Richard's firm? He hoped now he could turn all this around, persuade her that the diary was just a loose story that he had heard, that he had made a mistake, that he needed to get back, to give what help he could. This story was unimportant now. If he could impart this to her, if he could win her over, convince her! He would try his best charm offensive. He went to speak, but sensed this precise moment was not quite right. There was silence.

After what seemed like an eternity, Miss Woo continued. 'So as you can see, these are very complex circumstances. We cannot afford to be dragged into this political turmoil, so our glorious leader will consider returning you to the United States, but it will not be for some time yet. Therefore we have decided you will be kept under house arrest. You must obey all my instructions, only go where you are told, and you must not go anywhere unescorted. Is this understood?'

Again, all Greg could do was nod silently.

'You will not question our people or say anything about your country, or how different it is from ours. You will respect our system. If you give me your word then you will stay at the hotel, which is normally reserved for foreign dignitaries. Do not try to use the phone or post letters or anything of that nature.'

She looked at him for some sign of affirmation, but he just looked down at his feet. He realised there was no point in engaging her at this moment; she was making her position clear, and this was time to be a conformist. Every bone in his journalistic skeleton ached to argue his position, but in this place, he realised it was probably futile.

'If you break that promise, you will be sent to one of our labour camps, which is not like prison in America. You will work all day and will have little food, nobody will speak English, well you get the picture I am sure. Also, if you break this promise, I will be in trouble and, in our country, Greg, I would be well punished.'

Greg held out his hand to shake hers. To his surprise, she responded and, even though it was formal, something passed between them just for a second or so, and then it was gone. With that she said, 'Good, now we must go, I have work to do. You will return to your hotel, and I will try and find you some reading material in English.'

Greg nodded and with that they walked back to the car. Moments later it accelerated away.

17

After his briefing from New York's mayor, Senator Macgaskil had to report back to the State Department. First, there had been the terrible events of September and now it looked as though a serious diplomatic incident was blowing up. They had only just agreed that the North Koreans were not going to be in the US line of fire as no direct connection had been made between that strange closed country and the attack on the world's greatest superpower.

He was contemplating this as he got to the first sets of security guards.

After several security checks, the senator made his way to the third-floor room. Its large wooden double doors were flanked by immaculately turned out marines in full regalia, who saluted and opened one of the doors.

There were about twenty people inside: senators, security chiefs and two of the President's aides. One of these, Bill Travis, who reported directly to the President, walked quickly to the head of a large table.

'Gentlemen, can we all be seated, please. First off, thank you for all coming here at such short notice but I have news for you that we must discuss. Frank here is going to give you some more details and then, well I guess it's just going to open for discussion. But, gentlemen, I can tell you the President is aware of what you are about to hear, and has asked us to meet and come up with a solution by today, tomorrow at the latest. So we're here all day and night and all of tomorrow if need be.'

The room was silent. Outside the two marines could be seen through the net curtains standing either side of the large doors. The trees swayed slightly in the light breeze on that Washington morning.

'My friends, we have a serious problem, as if we need any more! What is that quotation? Something like: "when problems come, they come not as single soldiers but as battalions"? Anyhow, let me get straight to the point. Two days ago we had a message from the Chinese Embassy in South Korea that they had been contacted by a senior official of the People's Party of North Korea to inform us that an American citizen, a reporter, has been arrested whilst on an official – note I say *official* gentlemen – an *official* organized trip to the North Korean capital, Pyongyang. He has been held for about a week, has been questioned and is being treated well, although I would not like to say what their definition of well is!'

He had the room's attention. He took a sip from a glass of water, gathered his thoughts and continued: 'However, he is alive. They have not laid any charges on him, but he is suspected of . . . well basically this guy walked off, lost his official guide and started asking questions. Next thing, he was arrested and well that's what we know so far. Now Frank is going to fill you in, but just before I go on I have logged a complaint, via the Chinese, with the North Koreans, and have asked for contact with him. As usual with these people the official message we got back was: *"your concerns and requests are noted . . ."* I'll now hand over to Senator Macgaskil.'

'Thanks, Bill. Gentlemen, this afternoon I had a long discussion with the Mayor of New York who has some background on this guy. His name is Greg Sanderson. He's a New Yorker, thirty-one years old, and works for Noble and Black, as one of their investigative reporters. It's a well-known – well, relatively well-known – organisation in the newspaper world. Anyhow, a few weeks before all this, a young woman was killed quite tragically in a car crash.' Senator Macgaskil scanned his detailed notes and continued:

'Then, sometime before he left, Sanderson's boss told an NYPD detective that Sanderson had been working on some story that related to this girl. She was a freelance reporter supposedly working on something big, but he didn't know what, he had simply passed the lead on to Sanderson and left it at that. After her daughter's death, the mother had got in touch with Noble and Black and insisted that they look into it. She was adamant that her daughter was killed because of what she had found out. This NYPD detective then talks to the mother and she spouts some kind of conspiracy, about a massive counterfeiting operation in North Korea. And that's just the start of it. Dubai, Libya, Iran, you name it. Anyway it seems that Sanderson had some reason to believe that there might be some veracity in all of this and was trying to check it all out. Apparently, according to his boss, Sanderson met the girl's fiancé, but we can't get hold of him; his office was in the World Trade Center.'

There were murmurs around the table.

'Gentlemen, if I may? One of the names that the dead girl's mother remembers from the diary and papers is Ahmed. Of course we've done our own investigations and we've tracked our man down. It seems that in the two or three years that he's been operating, he has got into the big league. And the reason?'

Senator Macgaskil stopped, took his glasses off and placed them on the polished teak table. He exhaled, and then sat back.

'Gentlemen, this guy is involved somehow with the North Koreans. And it seems that this girl, this Natasha, was right. These bastards are forging our money! They're forging US dollars. I don't know the extent of it, but what we've got ourselves here is a situation.'

'And the girl? You think they got to her? Whoever they are?' asked one of the aides.

'As I said, she had unearthed something that had she exposed it would have been the scoop of the year for her and would have been an international incident, no doubt about the ramifications of all this. So, one minute she's beginning to piece everything together, making connections, drawing conclusions, and the next she's dead. It doesn't take a genius to figure out that maybe the girl's mother was right. Which is obviously what our Mr Sanderson has concluded, and taken up her baton. But instead of going through the usual channels, and alerting us to the situation, he's shot on down to North Korea like fucking Superman . . . now, gentlemen, I must throw it back to Bill now.'

'Thank you, senator, look, gentlemen, that's all the information we have for now. Obviously we are keeping all this under wraps at the moment; last thing we need is CNN getting hold of this, so, gentlemen, ideas please, comments?'

One of the senior advisors to the Treasury got to his feet. 'Gentlemen, I have been working very closely with a specialist team at the Treasury, as the President is aware. Over the last three months, we have suspected that the dollar was being forged on a massive scale by the North Koreans. I can't go into the technical details of how it was first picked up, but we realised two things. Firstly, whoever was doing it was doing it on a massive scale; and secondly, the fake dollars are virtually indistinguishable from original notes.'

He opened his jacket pocket and produced two one-hundred-dollar bills and placed them on the table. 'One of these was produced by our Treasury, the other one is a counterfeit. I'll pass them round. See if you can tell the difference.' After about five minutes the notes were passed back. A few made guesses but most were wrong, or if they were right, when questioned, they could offer no conclusive evidence as to what the fundamental differences were in the notes. It was agreed by all that these were perfect copies and it was clear that the forged notes were so good that only experts would be able to accurately identify the differences.

The Treasury advisor continued. 'We have speculated as to

why one country would forge another's currency. North Korea is in serious trouble, and is basically bankrupt. I guess this idea came along and they ran with it.'

One of the senators cut in. 'How long do you think it's been going on?'

'Our best estimates are around two years. They're running a massive laundering operation. The Koreans can't use the money directly as the forgeries would eventually be detected. Steps have already been taken and we are now able to identify many of the notes. Our agents suspect the money is coming via a number of routes: Libya, Saudi Arabia and Dubai. The problem we have is how we shut it down. The WTC disaster came along and if the President finds any link between these bastards and Al Qaeda well. . .'

'Do you think there is a link?' asked another senator.

'There is a strong possibility. We've managed to trace this Ahmed guy and it seems he might have Al Qaeda connections, and what's more, he was recently known to be in North Korea.'

The meeting went on for around six hours. By 10.30 that evening a decision was reached to be recommended to the President. The brief read as follows:

Dear Mr President,

After due consideration and in light of all the factors, we have conclusive evidence that the US dollar is being forged, and all said evidence now points towards the North Koreans as the primary perpetrators. They are involved in its large scale production and it's obvious that we have to stop this as soon as possible. If we do not act promptly, our currency could be undermined and lose its international status. A possible connection has been made to some Arab countries, but so far it seems more financial than ideological. However, Al Qaeda cannot be ruled out as using this to finance its operations.

We therefore recommend that our embassy in South Korea arranges for the ambassador and two aides to meet secretly with the three high-ranking North Korean Party officials on neutral ground, in the Chinese

Embassy in Beijing. They will inform them that we are aware of the dollar production and want it stopped. In return, we will start an immediate aid programme of food and raw materials and offer technical assistance in other areas. They will also ask for the return of our citizen, Mr Sanderson. However, we will probably have to agree with them that he will be under a restraining order not to speak about his time there. Finally, we will agree that we never mention that we ever suspected the Koreans of being involved in this and that our focus is on the perpetrators of the 9/11 attacks.

The communiqué was signed by the two senior aides.

The next morning, the President was presented with the document. He called in the Vice President and a few other close people, then, after about two hours, he agreed to the plan. A few hours later a phone call was placed to the US ambassador in the South Korean capital, Seoul, and the ambassador was instructed to make contact with the North Koreans via the Chinese.

18

It was about 10.45 a.m., and the sun was streaking through Miss Woo's office window. She was speaking with two of her officers about a problem they'd had from the night before. The highest ranking of the two was explaining that they'd had yet another report from one of the many small housing estates close to the edge of the city. A neighbour of a family that lived in the flats was bringing boxes in late at night and he was concerned as to what they contained.

'Well, Miss Woo,' the senior officer began, 'we went straight to this apartment, and we asked to see these boxes. At first the man denied it, then we warned him that to lie to us was tantamount to lying to the Party and our dear leader, and that he would be severely punished. Anyway he still said nothing, but his wife then spoke up. She went out to the kitchen. I followed her, then out to the balcony. I can tell you, Miss Woo, that the boxes were concealed under blankets.'

Miss Woo was getting impatient. When was he going to get to the point?

'Anyhow, we opened the boxes and inside was fresh fruit. We questioned her and she admitted that she had been selling the fruit at a small market nearby. She told us that it was just some extra money to help the family; her husband had been out of work, well his wages had not been paid but he was still going to work every day and. . .'

Finally, Miss Woo had had enough. 'That is irrelevant, what happened then?'

'Well, the food we have confiscated, and both husband and wife have been arrested.'

'They have children?' she enquired.

'Yes but all grown up and left home now.'

'I want the woman and her husband released, you will tell her if she is found doing this crime again, making money privately, she will be arrested and sent to prison. Tell them I am being lenient.'

'What about the goods, Miss Woo?'

'Take them over to the orphanage. . .'

A few minutes later Chan, her deputy, knocked on the door. 'Come in, Chan, how's things?'

'Oh, the usual, sorry I did not have time to deal with that this morning but I have just got back.'

'Sit down, Chan, let's talk.'

'Thank you, Miss Woo.'

She sighed. 'Chan, what is this job coming to? Do you really think that arresting people for having illegal markets is real police work? That is the fifth time this month. I did not see these people but the last couple you lot brought in, they were visibly malnourished. Most of them, in fact all, Chan, I have refused to prosecute. I know it will probably give me a problem soon, but I can't justify locking people up for trying not to starve; how can you?'

Chan nodded in agreement.

'It's a serious problem, Chan, and I don't mean in a legal sense; this is a humanitarian issue. These are just people trying to feed themselves but, as usual, we never question it, do we?'

Chan nodded again. 'I know, I know. A lot of us feel the same but we have to put that aside; I mean, we have to do our jobs; I mean, that's right isn't it?'

'You know, Chan, I once read about the Nuremberg war trials when I was at university; do you know what that established?'

He shook his head.

'It established that a man, more specifically a soldier, is responsible for his own actions; he can no longer rely on the premise that he was merely acting under orders.'

Chan's eyes grew wider. 'You are in a philosophical mood today, I don't think Sie Roo would concur with you, although I would not even discuss it with him, but I agree. Sometimes I wonder what will happen to this country eventually. Things are bad outside the city, everybody knows that; well you saw what happened just then and, as you say, it's getting worse. People setting up illegal markets, it's happening all the time now; people have to eat.'

'Chan, I don't know what will happen, but you understood my analogy with the Nuremberg trials? I mean, you can't just treat people like animals. It's like choosing between your duty to the State and your responsibilities as a human being. That's my point, Chan. We have a duty as officers and duty to the Party, but surely higher duties to humanity, do we not?'

Chan nodded. 'When you say it like that, yes it's true. I know it's wrong what goes on, especially now at this time, and really it depresses me, but as you say, what can we do?'

'I don't know, Chan, but it doesn't sit well with me, not at all.'

Chan agreed. They talked for half an hour or so. Chan realised that she, like him, was becoming disillusioned with many aspects of life in the North, but as police officers they had little choice but to do their duty. Too many people watched; he could trust her and she likewise but they both had doubts and it worried them both, her in particular.

'Well, Chan, I suppose we should get on; let's talk in the week; I like our chats. Don't worry, it's just between us.'

'Yes, me too, but as you say, just between us.' With that he got up and left.

A few moments later her phone rang.

'Miss Woo, it's Sie Roo.'

'Yes, Officer Sie Roo.'

'Miss Woo, I have spoken with members of the Presidium at

some length about this American you are holding. Can you get any more information from him?'

'Sir, he refused to say anything further about the notes in his diary; he still insists that he came here to write an article on life in the capital, he claims objectively. His name is on no lists of banned journalists and he is sticking to his story about the diary notes, but, well, we can all draw our own conclusions.'

'And what are yours, Miss Woo?'

'I think what he has written in the diary is his ulterior motive. It may be true that he started out with a legitimate assignment, but I think he came across this information through this Richard man who got it from a business client originally from the Middle East. Do you, sir, think that he has imparted that information to authorities in America? Is any of this true, sir?'

'I cannot say anything on this matter. I am more concerned with what you are doing with him.'

'Sir, he is under house arrest at the Yanggakdo hotel in the centre of the city and I've told him that he will be here for some time. I've also decided that I will speak with him once or twice a week and shall gain information in this way. As you know, the Party will not allow us to torture foreigners, unless it is suspected or proved that they entered the country illegally, or work for agents of a foreign power, sir.'

'Or disguised themselves in an attempt to pass off as a citizen of our great country, or are carrying weapons, or involved in subversion. You see, Miss Woo, I am well versed in our extensive regulations so please do not quote them to me.'

'Yes, sir, however, I was merely pointing out the situation: if what he says is true it would be a difficult situation for us internationally would it not?'

Sie Roo was becoming aggravated by the flippancy in her tone and he resented her questioning of matters that did not concern her.

She carried on in the same vein.

'I thank you for your extensive knowledge of our regulations and laws concerning the treatment of outsiders,' she said, now with a dry sarcasm in her voice.

'Miss Woo,' said Sie Roo, ignoring her tone, 'ensure that you are, let's say, very vigorous in your interrogation; do not be soft with the Yankee bastard. I expect concrete results. Don't be taken in with any of the American Hollywood shit. Furthermore, I will be discussing other matters with you soon. These illegal markets must be cracked down upon. People tell me you are being very lenient these days, is this true?'

'With respect, sir, I think we need to examine closely whether these people are actually profiteering or simply trying to get themselves over a particularly difficult time for some families at this juncture; what do you expect me to do, lock them all up?'

'I expect you to do your fucking job, Woo, that's what I and the Party expect, no more and no less.' With that he terminated the phone call.

Miss Woo was completely unaware of the fate that had befallen Ahmed, and had previously known nothing of the US dollar-forging operation, although she had her suspicions. But she had done her duty and passed the information on. This was another part of the Party's mantra: only tell people things on a need-to-know basis, and even an officer with her ranking would still not be considered significant enough to warrant being privilege to information such as this. It was only when it got to Sie Roo's level and above that the distinction between the military and the police began to blur. She was aware of the high security establishment outside the city, but had been given the same story as everyone else: it was used to hold gold and currency reserves.

A car pulled into the airport complex at around 11.45 a.m. The driver was instructed to park next to the airport control tower. Two officers and Sie Roo entered the building and, after speaking to the control tower manager and informing him of what was to happen, Sie Roo went directly to the overnight rooms, looking for the two pilots of the private jet.

'Good morning, gentlemen. I hope we have made you comfortable?' he enquired.

'Yes thank you. We thought we were going back today. Where is Ahmed?'

'Unfortunately, gentlemen, he has had a dispute with our security police and they are unhappy with some questions he has asked. He is going to see some of our people further north. I'm sure it will be sorted out soon and you will probably have to return at some stage to take him home, but for the moment I am instructed to tell you that he must remain as our guest. However, you can return today.' He smiled and went to walk off.

'We don't understand. We have a duty to our passenger and, well. . .' He did not complete the sentence.

'No, gentlemen, I am telling you that you *will* return today. That is what we require. Do you understand?'

This was no time to argue.

'Well if you insist then of course we will leave; do you know what time we are supposed to depart?'

'I believe around fifteen-thirty hours, but check with our flight operations manager.' He pointed down the corridor and to the small elevator at the end that led to the control tower. With that he bid them a safe flight and left, the car passing out of the airport gates and back to his headquarters.

Later that morning Miss Woo left the station in her official car. She had a high level meeting the other side of the city. As her car passed through the city, she was thinking about the woman selling the fruit at the market. She began to wonder how her own family was back home. She rarely saw them now and knew things were difficult. Her mother had not been well and her brother had written to her once saying that things in their home town of Chongjin were getting progressively worse. Her father had died a few years ago and her brother had divorced some time back and had gone back to live with their mother. He had two children from the short marriage and was depressed. She had written back and said she would visit but it was difficult: she had an important job and they would have to manage somehow for the moment. That said, she did feel guilty about it all; there they were in increasingly difficult circumstances and here she was living well in relatively prosperous Pyongyang.

She had clean clothes every day, an apartment in the city and good government wages; she would be earning about three times what one of her ordinary officers would be making and that was good money. She had the use of a car and was feared and respected at the same time. She had few friends and no partner or husband, not even a boyfriend, because few people wanted to get involved with her. Not because she was unattractive; in fact the very opposite. She had been a gymnast in her youth and had nearly represented her country, but her career had got in the way. Consequently she had a good figure. She was intelligent and her command of English was excellent with just the hint of an accent. The irony was it had a slight American twang.

Her real problem was that all the men who wanted to date her were too frightened; they figured if they fell out with her then bad things would happen to them, not in any physical way but their career prospects would be damaged. It appeared that she was married to her job and would never want children, so effectively she was ruled out even by men who were superior to her in rank. That is, all except Officer Sie Roo. He had made a few thinly disguised approaches to her, but she was not interested in him. Apart from anything else, for all her training and disciplined manner, she was unhappy with the environment in which she lived: it was a closed country full of closed minds, but some like her had begun to have their doubts.

Later that day, on her return from her meeting across town, she instructed her driver to make a short detour to the Yanggakdo hotel. Her car pulled up outside and she sent the driver in, who returned to tell Miss Woo that Mr Sanderson had gone to the main shopping area, accompanied by two guards as instructed. She told him to go back into the reception and tell them to inform Mr Sanderson she would call on him this evening at 18:30, and they would take dinner in the hotel.

At the airport, the pilots had been given their instructions by the control tower and boarded their aircraft. They were still unhappy about leaving without Ahmed, but thought better of making noises about it. They spent the next hour in the cockpit making preparations for departure.

'Stand by for final clearance, which will be in two minutes.' The headphones in the pilot's ear crackled; they were glad they were leaving. They were well paid for these flights but hated the place, like most South Koreans. The entire place was anathema to them. Life in the South was good, but they had got jobs with this small private company operating out of Dubai, and flying wealthy clients around the world was well paid and quite glamorous. The occasional trip to North Korea could be tolerated, but now they were glad to be leaving.

The final order came and with that the pilot pushed the throttle controls to full power and the small jet aircraft accelerated down the short runway. Then forty seconds later they were airborne. Their flight plan had been changed as they were told it might interfere with the flight of an official plane that day; so they were instructed to fly north for some one hundred miles, then they could make a turn to take them back over China and then on to Dubai. About half an hour into the flight they began to make the required turn. They were flying at eighteen thousand feet and at four hundred and fifty miles per hour as they had been instructed. Once they had made the turn they could accelerate to full speed and full cruising altitude. The co-pilot went to get up and make some coffee after the turn and could feel the plane climbing and accelerating gently. Suddenly he heard the pilot call him from the cockpit.

'Look, get back in here, can you? Have a look at this.' When the co-pilot returned he could see that the on-board radar was bleeping. It was a warning that they were on course with another plane. They feared they had made some mistake and this was the official delegation that had been spoken about by the airport manager. The bleeping intensified and the co-pilot looked over to his pilot: 'That thing is really moving, it must be a military jet, are these guys fucking paranoid or what? I bet we are going to get an escort now.'

A military fighter jet was about twenty miles down range from the small executive plane. It was flying at eight hundred and fifty miles per hour, and taking into account the speed differential of the two aircraft, in just less than three minutes it would have visual contact. He was approaching fast from the south. The pilot flicked the black flap back on the right of his control lever to reveal a red button. A buzzer sounded and a light flashed on the control panel directly in front of him. As a double safety measure he was required to take his right hand off the control stick and press the yellow flashing button marked '*arm*'. He did so and the light went to red and stayed permanently on. The buzzer stopped, he put his right hand back on the control stick and placed his thumb over the red button. He glanced down at the left display: another light flashed red with the word '*armed*'. A switch below that was in the up position, marked '*ready*', with the down position marked '*engage*'.

He moved his left hand to flick the switch down. As he did so a sharp electronic bleep pierced through his ears. He waited another minute until he had visual contact; ten seconds later he pressed the red button on the right-hand side of the stick with his thumb. He felt the plane kick slightly to the left as the missile released, pulling away fast from the underside of the wing, its jet trail spitting orange fire. A few seconds later the missile hit its target and a spot in the sky gave out a bright flash then disappeared both from his visual contact and the internal radar screen.

Switching the left switch back to '*ready*' and closing the flap on the red right button, he banked sharply to the left and accelerated hard by pushing the two thrust levers forward until the afterburners engaged. He saw his air speed go past one thousand miles per hour. Punching in some numbers, he watched as the guidance computer gave him directions and a course back to his military base. He looked at his watch; he expected to be landing in about twenty minutes and was looking forward to seeing his wife and children later.

19

Senator Macgaskil was in his office when he got a call from the American Embassy in Beijing.

'Ted, it's Frank, Frank Hanson, look this meeting we are trying to set up with the Koreans, well you know the Chinese are brokering it for us. Anyway, I have told them I don't know all the details but I am waiting for that to come over the secure document unit. But, listen, I am aware one of our citizens is being held out there. Look, this meeting will get sorted, that's not the problem. The Chinese are really good at this. I think they enjoy being the guys in the middle and, well, it certainly seems like we always get a bit more from these North Koreans if they are involved in the discussions. But, listen, I think we have a problem.'

'Problem? What kind of problem? The last thing we need is more problems. . .'

'A guy has been sniffing around here from *The Washington Post*. He's got information from a reliable source that the North Koreans have got one of our citizens out there and, apparently, he wants to know if it's anything to do with something he's been working on for a while. He says he has information from sources back home in the US that the North Koreans are involved in some kind of counterfeit operation, involving the dollar, and perhaps other currencies. And he would like a statement.'

There was a stony silence on the other end of the line.

'I can fob him off for a while, but you know how these people work. Either you give me a statement, or at least your comments. I just thought I'd run it by you.'

'Let me come back to you tomorrow,' said the senator eventually. 'Hold this guy off till then. Promise him an exclusive. He'll wait, and let me see what the State Department says.'

An hour later the senator's phone rang.

'Senator Macgaskil? This is William Orson, *The Washington Post*, Beijing. We have been in touch with your embassy out here, and I've been trying to contact some of your press officers but I can't seem to get hold of anybody. I've been working on something out here.'

'Yes, Mr Orson, what can I do for you? I am a busy man.'

'Sure, sure, I'll be brief. You are aware, of course, of the refugees that occasionally manage to escape from North Korea.'

'I am a well-informed man, Mr Orson.'

'Of course. Anyway, I've interviewed some of these people myself. Some time ago I was doing a special assignment in association with *America Today* and our company concerning the plight of these people and what life is actually like out there at the moment. Well the article was done and published a few months ago; you may have read about it, it was in one of the Sunday editions?'

'I am sorry, Mr Orson, I am afraid I did not but, well, yes, it's an ongoing situation out there and we are aware of these people who manage to get out. Please continue.'

'After that assignment I came back here to Beijing but I get a call one day from another reporter for the *Los Angeles Times*. He was in the border area for some time; he actually managed to cross over and got inside the place, spent about two weeks over there, bribed border guards, that sort of thing. So, anyway, he met up with two refugees and crossed over with them, helped them to a safe house in the area. Before he left to come back to the US he interviewed them at length. He was told by them that somewhere near the capital the Koreans have a factory that produces banknotes, lots of them, the US dollar included. His paper was not prepared to run with the story so he passed it to me.'

'So what makes you think I am going to tell you anything?'

'Because, sir, we have also heard that one of our citizens is being held for "security reasons". Can you comment on any of this, sir?'

'Mr Orson, I really don't know anything, but give me your number and I'll get back to you.'

'Okay, sir, but I'd appreciate it if it could be as soon as possible.'

The senator wished him good day and immediately buzzed his secretary. Can you get Frank Hanson in Beijing back on the line, please?'

'Yes, sir, immediately.'

'Look, Frank, I've just had *The Washington Post* on the phone, a guy called Orson.'

'Yeah, that's him.'

'He seems to know quite a bit.'

'Did he say if he knows the guy's name, the man who is being held by them?'

'No, I don't think he knows, but we can't have any of this coming out yet. We need to be in discussion with the North Koreans. You know how jumpy these people are. We'll probably be forced to give him an exclusive along with one of the channels in return for them keeping it under wraps, so we can get that meeting with the North Koreans going ASAP. Tell them, as a gesture of goodwill, we will release some limited food aid if they agree to meet as soon as possible. Tell them we are so busy here what with the attacks that we just want to get our citizen back.'

'Do we mention anything about this counterfeiting business?'

'No, hold off. We can wait till we are in talks before we confront them with that particular can of worms.'

Afterwards, Senator Macgaskil called two of the President's advisors to apprise them of the situation and seek their advice. Frank Hanson called William Orson and spent about fifteen minutes trying to prise from the reporter what he actually knew, and then said he'd call him back in two days.

It was 6.30 exactly. Greg was already sitting at the solitary table, but tonight it held another place setting. As Greg sipped his fresh water Miss Woo strode in with her usual military gait. She wore no hat and her ink-black hair was tied severely back. She was in uniform but Greg had not seen this uniform before. The usual light green had been exchanged for a smoother material of grey in colour. She had all the usual accoutrements and wore epaulettes on her shoulders. Her name was clearly displayed just above the right top pocket. She looked very official and as she pulled out the chair opposite Greg to sit down she did not smile but just looked at him.

'Good evening, Mr Sanderson, how are you?'

'Yes, Miss Woo, I am okay, thank you, yourself?'

'I have had a busy day, but yes I am fine. But as you can see, I am still working.'

Greg just smiled. A few moments later a meal was served. Not much talk went on during the meal and after the girls cleared the plates she put her hand into her jacket pocket and produced a packet of cigarettes. She flipped the top back and pointed the packet at Greg. 'Would you like one, Greg?'

'No thanks, really.'

She removed one from the packet and, pulling a lighter from the other pocket, lit the cigarette. She placed the packet and the lighter on the table. Suddenly a girl appeared with an ashtray, quickly placing it down then scurrying off. If Greg needed any more evidence of them watching them he certainly had it now.

'Mr Sanderson, please, we must talk. Now look, you are being treated well; would you say I would be treated any different if the roles were reversed, truly?'

'Miss Woo, I am being treated well and you are right, if this was America and I was you, well I would like to think we would treat you in a similar way.'

'I think we have treated you better perhaps?'

'Well I would not quite put it like that.' He slightly averted his eyes.

'Ah yes you refer to when my guard hit you? Well I am sorry for that and for that cell we put you in, but look, if we had not done that, really, would you have agreed to do as I ask now? Are you not now free to go around our great city?'

Greg was not going to argue. 'Miss Woo, I am happy with how I am being looked after. I would like to forget that incident. I want to cooperate with you and I respect your country and what I want more than anything else is to be able to get back to America soon.'

They talked for about two hours, and then she abruptly announced she had to leave.

'Thank you for joining me, Miss Woo, good-night.' He nodded as she walked out. He noticed her boots were highly polished. She was wearing a tight skirt that just covered her knees and her whole uniform fitted perfectly, not like his shirt, he thought. And with that she was gone. The place was deserted now and deathly quiet. Then suddenly all the lights went out. It was black as midnight. One of the girls rushed in with a torch, shining it in Greg's direction.

'You go bed now, sir, I show you up.' After negotiating the flight of stairs, Greg closed the door to his room. It was black, and he gradually worked his way over to the window and looked into the street. What amazed him was how dark it actually was and how quiet. He looked up and down the main street: no car headlights, no sounds, and no people; this was a strange place indeed, he thought.

20

Frank Hanson put a call through to Senator Macgaskil in Washington.

'Sir, I spoke to Orson yesterday, and his sources seem pretty reliable. He reckons *The Washington Post* would run with the story. They think they know who the Koreans are holding. He wouldn't say but you know how they find these things out . . . probably someone at Interpol or in the Chinese passport office . . . anybody. He wants to know where we are on this and is looking for an exclusive. The deal is, they keep quiet about the dollar story, completely, and get the guy's name and his story once we get this meeting going. He won't wait more than a week, sir.'

'Then, that's what you've got: a week to pull in the North Korean ambassador with his guys and the Chinese ambassador. Try to get some sort of deal in place. I don't want them to think that they've got us over a barrel. Anything else you can add, Frank?'

'Well I think we should also agree with them that once we have a deal in place we will release it to our press, but we give it to Orson before it goes out on the official wires. That way *The Washington Post* will get an exclusive with this Greg Sanderson. We'll allow *The Washington Post* to see him as soon as he is taken to our embassy in Beijing, obviously in return for playing ball with us on this.'

'Okay, Frank, that's fine. I am speaking to Bill Travis directly after this call, so I'll confirm all this with you within the hour.'

A few days later the diplomatic phone lines were hot with activity. Various diplomats began arriving at the Chinese Embassy. Frank Hanson and his two aides made their way to a formal reception room. The Chinese ambassador was waiting, with the North Korean ambassador and a small entourage. The room was cool, and light flooded in from the windows. The massive ceiling fans span slowly, almost as if to set the tempo of such a high level meeting. This was going to be tense and difficult, Frank thought, as he offered his hand to the Chinese ambassador first, who then introduced him to the Korean party. The Chinese ambassador, having directed the six of them to their respective seating positions at the square table, then pulled out a chair and sat at its head. The two parties now sat opposite each other.

'Gentlemen, now first please,' he pointed to the water jug and glasses sitting in the middle, 'please let us all be refreshed before I begin.' They could all speak perfect English and one of Frank's aides was a specialist linguist in Korean and Mandarin. They all filled their glasses, and looked at the Chinese ambassador.

'As you are all aware, we have a problem,' the Chinese ambassador began. 'I of course sincerely hope this can be resolved amicably and to the benefit of both your governments. We are willing to assist in the role of arbitrator and advisor in our capacity as a conduit between two very different, but respected cultures. For after all, gentlemen, what would our tiny planet be like if all our countries were the same and I do believe that each has its own merits, advantages and disadvantages. There have been times in the past when matters seemed insurmountable between yourselves but we have always found common ground and this only helps to bring us all closer over time. . .' Eventually closing his preamble, he then turned to the Korean ambassador.

'Now perhaps you could give Mr Hanson some more

information on the American citizen who is being detained by your security people pending investigations.'

'Yes, we have detained this man. He came to our country on an organised three-day tour of Pyongyang. As you are aware, he is a reporter from New York, and particularly in this regard we have rules that we expect members of that somewhat dubious profession to follow. He strayed, again after being specifically informed to stay with our guides, intentionally we believe, to gain information; the content of that information we are still trying to ascertain. None the less, we have not charged him with any offence and he is being held under house arrest.'

Frank Hanson informed him that Greg was absolutely in no way connected to the security services and went through the whole story as it had been passed to him. The Korean ambassador waited a few seconds.

'Mr Hanson, yes we have heard all this from Mr Sanderson, but these notes we discovered in his diary, this is a serious matter. I have a transcript here.' He passed over a piece of paper. 'Clearly he is making suggestions as to the integrity of our great country, serious accusations of criminal activity. We wish the United States to publicly and categorically apologise.'

Frank interrupted. 'Could my colleague now address you all?' The Chinese ambassador nodded to one of the American aides, who stood up.

'Sir, I have in my possession a number of US dollar bills, which have been certified by the US Treasury as counterfeit.' He placed a number of dollar bills on the table.

'We have been investigating this for three months or more now and have incontrovertible evidence that these notes are being produced in North Korea. The man, Ahmed, whose name is referred to in this transcript, is known to us. We have photographic evidence of a printing press that was delivered to Dubai and has never been used and another one that investigations confirmed was taken to your country.'

He paused to let this information sink in. 'Sir, we suspect this man to be an Al Qaeda operative and, as you are aware, this group is directly linked to the WTC attack and other targets on that day.'

Frank cut in. 'The point is, gentlemen, if the US agents find a direct link between this Al Qaeda group and this currency counterfeiting it is going to cause a major incident, which the United States wishes to avoid. We remain resolute and focused on apprehending these people, who were responsible for the death of so many, an attack on the very fabric of our society.'

The Chinese ambassador knew the Americans were on to the Koreans, but they had to find a way out. Greg Sanderson would be part of it. He looked at the Korean party. 'Your comments, gentlemen, please.'

Over the next hour, the Koreans continued to flatly deny any knowledge about the counterfeited dollars and continued on about Greg and how the United States always attacked North Korea at every opportunity. Then they broke for lunch. After which the Chinese ambassador requested the parties go to separate rooms to see whether they could find a 'compromise' that would be satisfactory to all concerned. Around half an hour later they all filed back into the main room.

'Mr Hanson,' began the Korean ambassador, 'We, North Korea, do not recognise any of these accusations in respect of this story of forged currency.' He rambled on for another five minutes about the integrity and the probity of the one-party state and its goal of a pure, uncorrupted country, untainted by what he described as the yoke of capitalism; then the bombshell.

'However, we now have information that this man, Ahmed, did in fact visit our country. Internal investigations have concluded that, whilst he did have legitimate business dealings with us, recently he attempted to bribe certain officials. I am informed that he was expelled a few days ago from our country for this very reason.'

'Where is he now?' interrupted Frank Hanson.

The Korean ambassador cleared his throat and continued:

'Apparently his aircraft developed technical problems and crashed in a remote area to the north of our capital. Our search parties discovered the remains of a small jet aircraft but there were no survivors.' He paused.

'We do believe he may have been linked to this Al Qaeda group, although we have no direct evidence. Perhaps you could tell the President that his unfortunate accident was welcomed by us as a fitting end for a criminal. We are, of course, investigating the circumstances of the crash and will let you know our findings.'

Frank could see the deal in front of him. 'Can I assume then that this man's unfortunate accident will deal a blow to whoever was involved in counterfeiting our currency? If so, I am empowered to tell you that, provided we get our citizen back, the aid programme will begin immediately. Half the original quota to be released, then delivered immediately. The rest on Mr Sanderson's return.'

The Korean ambassador nodded and said, 'This seems satisfactory, however, we will probably insist that Mr Sanderson has to remain with us for three months; we cannot move on that really.'

Hanson looked to his aide and to the Chinese ambassador a moment. They conferred quietly together. 'Okay, as you wish, if it will satisfy your people over there, and send out the right signals to others. I will apologise for his actions with regard to not observing your regulations. We would of course urge you to release him as soon as possible, realistically within the next month.'

The deal had been done. A day later Frank contacted William Orson at *The Washington Post*, and told him most of the story but the US dollars were not mentioned. Only that their citizen would be coming home at the latest in three months' time, and food aid and other essential items would begin to flow into North Korea again.

Senator Macgaskil passed the news on to Bill Travis and the wheels in Washington turned another notch.

The next day the story was all over the front pages of most US papers and CNN had it as an early morning exclusive:

US CITIZEN HELD IN NORTH KOREA TO BE RELEASED.

21

Greg was pleased to no longer be incarcerated but was beginning to think perhaps it would have been better if he were. There was nobody to talk to at the Yanggakdo hotel. Apart from a few staff, it was deserted. At night, he had to go to bed as soon as it got dark as the power would go off and he would look out of his second-floor window into a sea of darkness.

It was at this time, in the dark hours, that Greg tried to reconcile his situation. He knew he was lucky, very lucky indeed that things had not gone worse for him. But it was a double-edged sword. The only reason he hadn't been locked up for good, or possibly shot, was because of the atrocities inflicted on his beloved New York. As far as he could glean, North Korea was in the clear on that front and it was a case of damage limitation. The powers that be, his captives in other words, couldn't throw away the key because if they did then that would jeopardise the fragile hold they had on any form of diplomacy with the US. To be implicated in the September attacks would mean full-out war, and everybody wanted to avoid that, especially with nuclear proliferation in the deadly mix.

So Greg was inadvertently a pawn in this game. What had started out as an impromptu decision to try and make some sense of a young woman's death had turned into something quite separate. He was sure it was all connected, her discoveries, her car crash (though of course as yet this was just speculation), the counterfeiting allegations, Ahmed. But what about the World Trade Center attacks? That was a different story altogether. He wanted no further part in all this. He had made a mistake. He would do anything he could to get out and get home and, if he could, he would investigate Natasha's death through the proper channels. NYPD to start, then who knew?

One thing he did know, and one thing he kept reminding himself, was that Miss Woo was his meal ticket home.

When he wasn't brooding like this, he listened to the radio, but of course it was just welcome background noise. He couldn't understand a word. . . There was no TV apart from the one in the reception which seemed permanently fixed to one channel. The food was bland and he could feel that his body was really not being nourished sufficiently. Though he exercised in his room and would often go for long walks with his usual two minders, he did not feel fit.

He had lost weight, around eight pounds he figured, as he had no scales to weigh himself on. His lean, muscular frame was feeling the effects of the poor rice diet and lack of real exercise.

Miss Woo had been over a few times, always in the evenings. She had softened her questioning of him and they would have discussions on a wide variety of issues. He was impressed with her knowledge of international affairs. They would eat dinner then chat for an hour or so, and then she would look at her watch, bid him good-night and leave. When she did not come over he missed her company; he realised that her visits were becoming one of the highlights of his day as things were generally predictable. He also knew that if he could keep her on his side, then his chances of getting home were ever greater.

Gradually, his frustration grew. The city's people were not friendly, never returning a smile, and in the shops (the ones that were open) there was little interaction, if any. It seemed that shopping was just a functional necessity with no social aspect to it. He began to hate the place and could not believe he had got himself into this. He could not wait to leave.

Walking back from the park early one afternoon, with his 'over-seers' trailing behind him, he heard the sound of a car approaching. Eventually it pulled alongside him. Turning his head, he could see Miss Woo in the rear seat. She beckoned him over to the car. Greg opened the door and climbed in.

'Mr Sanderson, they told me you were out walking, so I thought I would meet you and give you a ride to the hotel.'

'Thank you, Miss Woo, how are you today?' he enquired.

'Yes I am my usually busy self but I have some time so I wished to bring you up to date. I have some good news for you.' She motioned to the driver and told him to go to the hotel. The car accelerated away leaving Greg's 'followers' just looking on.

'Let's have coffee.' She ordered the car to turn next right and they proceeded down another main thoroughfare before the car came to a halt.

'Come this way, Mr Sanderson.' She got out of the right side and Greg opened his door onto the kerb. In a few short strides she had walked into a shop. Greg followed her inside.

Inside, there were eight tables with two chairs at each. Two couples sat over in the far corner; he noticed they had both stopped talking as soon as she had walked in. As she was in full uniform he guessed they knew exactly who she was. She called Greg to the counter.

'I assume you will take coffee with me?'

'Well . . . yes. Thank you.'

'You will, of course, have to pay as it cannot be seen for the State to pay for people under investigation. He will appreciate your American money.'

Greg duly paid over the two dollars. They took the coffees and went to sit close to the window. By this time the two couples in the corner had swiftly left. Greg noticed them scurrying out as he and Miss Woo stood at the counter.

'Now, Greg, I can call you by your first name when my staff are not around. Most do not speak English but I must not be seen in any way that could be construed as being too informal with you. Greg, there has been a meeting between our countries' ambassadors and the outcome is that we have agreed to speed up processing you and if everything goes well and you cooperate then I am at liberty to say that you will be considered for repatriation to the United States very soon.'

'Thank you, Miss Woo. That's good news.' He smiled at her and ran his fingers through his hair; he exhaled hard then leaned on the table with both elbows.

'Greg, you do not have to thank me, but I accept. I must say I have been enjoying our dinner conversations. We disagree fundamentally on the differences in our respective systems but no society is perfect.'

Greg sat back; he was beginning to feel relaxed. 'I know,' he said, 'I have learned a lot, too, and I must say that North Korea is not all I imagined. Though there is a fundamental difference: people here cannot come and go as they please.' He regretted it almost instantly. He was supposed to be playing it carefully. That was the trouble with being off-guard.

'Greg, please, I am doing my best for you, more than I should really, please this is my country; our system works for us.'

'Yes, sorry, I am not judging you.'

'Just our system?' She said dryly, though with enough openness that he felt compelled to continue their conversation. He wondered how frank he could be with her? He needed her on his side, but he also wanted to get to know her, and perhaps if he could get through to her, if they could somehow find a shared humanity, then who knew what could happen?

'Can I be frank with you?' he asked finally.

'Yes, Greg, tell me what is on your mind.'

'It's just that, I mean, I have to say that it does not seem a very vibrant and happy place . . .'

'I suppose New York is then? You have your problems, too, Greg, be honest.'

'Yes, of course we have problems, like any society, but I would not change any of it.'

'Why not?' she retorted.

Greg glanced down at the table and then back, setting his gaze directly into her eyes.

'Because we are free to go where we want, free to see who we like, make our own choices, we—'

She cut in. 'What is freedom? You think you are free but really you are enslaved; it is easy to control a society when they believe they are free.' She smiled and sat back.

Greg continued. 'You may well be right. I am enslaved in the sense that I have to go to work and pay my bills, but I am free to think.'

'We are free to think.'

'Miss Woo, truthfully, I don't think you are; tell me, can you leave here, this place, if you wished?'

'Greg, why should I? I am happy here.'

'Miss Woo, look, my system isn't perfect, we have crime, drugs problems, healthcare costs, immigration and education issues, it goes on. I would never deny that, but we are an open society. If you say you are free, come and visit New York. Then make your mind up.'

'*Freedom*, Greg, please, you are wearing the word out.'

Greg continued. 'I am just saying: wherever you live in the world, whatever a particular country's ideology, its form of government, that doesn't matter, but when you have real freedom its tangible; you can almost touch it.'

She sat for a while in silence; then, she said, 'Greg, you will get another coffee for us.' She called out to the small man sitting behind the counter; he jumped up and began fiddling with what appeared to Greg a rather antiquated coffee machine.

It was about 3.30 when they eventually left the coffee shop. Her car appeared and they proceeded back to the hotel. She dropped Greg off and just as her car went to pull away, she called to him. 'I will be back here at 1.30 tomorrow; we will talk some more, goodbye, Mr Sanderson.'

He called back. 'Miss Woo, just one other thing I meant to say.'

'Yes, Mr Sanderson?'

'I wanted to thank you again for what you have done for me.'

'You're welcome, Mr Sanderson, but, Mr Sanderson, you are wrong on some of the impressions that you seem to have formed of my country.'

'Well perhaps so, but remember this, Miss Woo, you can imprison a man, but you can't imprison his mind. Still, perhaps freedom is slavery?'

'Very good, Mr Sanderson, I have read the book too.'

'Good afternoon, Miss Woo,' he smiled sardonically. She looked at him for a few seconds, and then her car pulled away.

The next morning Greg did his usual routine (he had begun to do a regular set of morning exercises in his room before he went down to breakfast). He was feeling better and hoped that soon he would be going home and could get his life back on an even keel. It was close to 1.30 p.m. when he stepped out of the hotel and waited by the empty road. Five minutes later her car pulled up; he stepped in and they drove off.

The car made its way to the People's Park, eventually pulling up at a spot about two minutes from the main entrance. They got out and walked through the large iron gates, past the usual statues, mainly of their leader, Kim Jong-il. Greg just glanced over. They walked around the park for an hour or so, the conversation this time lighter, although she still made a point of reminding him of the contradictions she perceived in American society. They had just rounded a large section of garden, which she was telling him was dedicated to war heroes of the Korean War, when he noticed three men approaching them, almost marching. The man in the centre was clearly a high-ranking officer, dressed in a dark khaki; he seemed to have a similar uniform to Miss Woo. He got within three feet of them and Miss

Woo stopped dead. The man spoke first. Greg did not understand what they said as they spoke in Korean.

'Miss Woo, you have been colluding and are over familiar with this man, I am instructing you to return immediately to your station where you will be further questioned by me!'

Miss Woo looked shocked. 'Sir, this man has been in my custody and I was asked under the provision of our rules governing the treatment of—'

'You will go with me now, and one of my men will take the American back to his hotel. Then I will decide what will happen.'

Miss Woo interjected again. She reminded him that she was working on her own initiative but with his general approval. She had been asked to use her discretion and treat him how she deemed appropriate. But now for some reason he had changed his mind and was directly accusing her of some form of fraternisation.

But he was in no mood for listening.

'Go now, Miss Woo.' She stepped forward slightly.

'On whose authority do you do this?' she demanded.

The next few moments were to have serious consequences for Greg. The officer stepped forward and, without warning, struck her around the face with a short stick. She bowed her head, and she asked again:

'I just want to know, sir, who has the authority to take me off my duties?'

The officer went to strike Miss Woo again, but Greg grabbed him by the throat and threw him backwards. The man turned on Greg, but Greg had had enough. He grabbed the man's arm holding the stick and threw him over his shoulder, crashing him to the ground. The other guards went towards Greg; he kicked the first one in the groin and the next one he punched straight in the face. He turned round: the officer was getting to his feet. Greg stood over him.

'You bastard, leave her alone!' He went to have another go at him when suddenly he felt a pain in the back of his head. As he fell to the ground, he realised that Miss Woo had hit him with the butt of her gun. She looked at him as he passed out. Just before he went under, he realised she had probably saved his life: and by reacting as she had, probably her own.

22

Greg awoke with his head thumping. The room was dark and there was one small window. He looked round to see a toilet and hand basin. He rushed over and immediately vomited. He looked to his right and could see a towel. He wiped his mouth, ran the tap to clear the sink, then cupped a few mouthfuls of water. Whether it was okay to drink or not, he did not really care. He went back over and lay on the bed. It was rock hard and with just one blanket. He got in and pulled the blanket over him and lay there, dazed and feeling nauseous.

Down the corridor in Miss Woo's office, Sie Roo was apoplectic with rage.

'What has gone on here is unacceptable. This American attacked me. I will deal with him later. In the meantime. . .'

'Sir, I really—'

'Don't argue with me. I am relieving you of your duty for four weeks with immediate effect.'

She tried to protest. He silenced her with a look. 'It's the only way; I will make a report up and the matter will be investigated. You will of course give up four weeks' pay and will have to leave your uniform and weapon here. I have no more to say, now get out and report back here in four weeks to the day. Personally, I think you should leave the capital. Go to your mother's if you wish, but I advise you, in the strongest terms, to stay away. When you get back the American will probably be gone so we can get back to normal I hope.'

She had been humbled in front of her staff, as had no doubt been his intention, and now she was to leave the city for four weeks as well.

As far as Sie Roo was concerned, she was getting her just deserts. If she had designs on the American it would have never amounted to anything anyway. The American would be gone soon, then he would try with her again. He wanted her and was getting fed up with her constant rejections. Now the reports he had been receiving from the minders assigned to watch him, and even from her own driver, gave him the opportunity to put pressure on her, to make her vulnerable, and then she would be in his control. Then he would make his move.

Miss Woo changed in a small back room of her office, took a few personal things out of her desk and presented her station keys, security passes, her identification badge and gun to her deputy, Chan. He looked at her on the way out, holding her arm just as she went to leave.

'Miss, I am sorry.'

'Don't be, he has done this deliberately. As you know, my record is unblemished, but it does not matter. I will see you soon.' With that she walked from the building and would now have to take the bus back to her small apartment about twenty minutes' ride from the police station. She felt depressed on the bus ride home. Why had Greg done that? She could not get the words out of her head: *'leave her alone, you bastard!'* She also realised that a man she hardly knew had tried to protect her and, in doing so, must have realised the consequences. For all Greg knew he could have been shot.

She started to admit to herself that she did like him. He had kept his word and not done anything wrong in his time at the hotel. He was intelligent and open in his admission that his country had many shortcomings, and his remark about freedom had cut into her: about how freedom was not a word or a state of mind, but it exists. As Greg had said, *'It's tangible, you can feel it, you know when you have real freedom.'* On and on it went; over and over in her head. *'You can imprison a man, but you can't imprison his mind.'*

She walked into her apartment and, after making some food, she continued to dwell on his words; perhaps it was just him. She tried to put her thoughts away for the night as she went to bed. After about an hour she woke again, restless and unable to sleep properly. She had to admit to herself that there was something about this man: his quiet spoken manner, the way he accepted all his country's frailties and yet still believed in it. With her country, you could never criticise anything. Yes, like Greg, you loved your country, but surely you must question from time to time the decisions it made?

She also thought about how she had been treated, and the strange thing was she was glad the American had come. Would she have done the same for him? Stood up for him like that? She hoped that she would have. Yes, she liked to think so.

She got up and made tea. On returning to the bedroom, she began to realise and accept that she had a problem; sitting there in the dark on the edge of her bed, she wished that the American was here; she wished Greg was here.

It would have been impossible to get through to her mother as the phone system was showing its age, and it was sporadic at best. Added to that, her family did not even own a telephone; there was a communal one in the military-style blocks of flats where they lived but most of the time it was out of order, and as a letter would take for ever she decided to leave this morning. She got a small case together and made her way to the central train station. This vast building was impressive but, as usual with the North, it was all on the surface. To get a train to her mother's place could be a two-day affair for a journey of only two hundred miles. Many of the trains were out of service, the tracks had seen better days and there would be the inevitable derailments, but it had all become the accepted norm and people adjusted.

Miss Woo had not left the capital city for three years now. The small apartment that came with the job was an improvement on her previous one and in a better part of town. Life was good. She was earning good money and all the other benefits commensurate with her position.

This was a long way from her life as a young girl growing up in Chongjin. Her father had died when she was only fifteen and her mother worked many hours to make sure her daughter would be able to go to the main university in Pyongyang and make something of her life.

Stories were beginning to circulate about how bad things were getting outside the capital, what with the food shortages. She, like many others who lived in the city, simply hadn't realised the extent of the problem; she was in for a shock.

Two days later, in the early hours of Wednesday morning, the meandering train finally arrived at Chongjin station. Woken by the sound of the sharp whistle and the guard striding along the narrow corridor shouting for all to depart, she looked at her watch. It was 6.45 a.m. and just getting light. She stood up and stretched, turning and picking her bag from the assortment that had accumulated on the journey. She made her way to the carriage exit and stepped down onto the platform, passing through the open barriers that had stopped working.

Her mother's house would be about an hour's walk. No buses were waiting so she resigned herself to it. As she turned left down the main street she was shocked at the number of children begging. This was a rough place, an old industrial town that had seen its share of factory closures in its time, but nothing like the chronic scale she now witnessed. The children were clearly malnourished and some of them were practically naked. Kids no older than ten or eleven were actually scouring bins for food; others just looked and held their hands out with a pitiful look on their faces. A small girl walked behind her trailing a doll in the muddy broken roadway, her hair filthy and mud on her hands. She was calling to Miss Woo.

'Food, missy; food please, missy.'

Miss Woo looked around but kept going. To help just one would probably start a mini scramble. There must have been at least fifty children like that. She was shocked and picked her pace up, the wheels of her small case bumping along the muddy remnants of what was once a concreted road.

She wondered how her mother was coping, how her brother was? Would his children be okay? She prayed none of them were the scavengers she had just witnessed, but she had money on her and was going to help as much as she could.

As she rounded the last corner she could see the housing estate in front of her, its bleak grey façade with its autonomous blocks standing like sentinels against progress. Uninspiring and dull, it reflected the mood of the town, old, decaying and in need of attention. The concrete buttresses spaced out at thirty feet intervals were crumbling and now the reinforcing rods were beginning to show through. Stained water marks streaked down from many of the broken drainage pipes. She looked up to the flat in which she had once lived, up to the third-floor window. She could see the window open to the lounge, and the kitchen window at a similar angle; they were certainly in need of cleaning. She remembered as a young girl she would spend her Saturdays washing them. She guessed her mother could not be bothered any more; but if her brother was here why was he not doing them? She considered that perhaps things were so bad here that even cleaning materials were in short supply.

The final set of stairs to the third floor was littered with paper and general rubbish. She turned at the top and walked the last few feet to the door. Just as she got level with it, it opened; her brother came out with his children, and his face lit up when he saw her.

'God, it's so good to see you, what a surprise.'

They just hugged for a few moments, then, hearing the voices, her mother came out. Miss Woo practically screamed and she held her mother tight for a minute or so.

'You know it's been three years.' Her mother was wagging her finger and showing her displeasure at the length of time that had passed since she had seen her successful daughter. 'Come on, let's all go in. I was just taking the children for a walk but now you are here I suppose I'd better go later.' They all went into the tiny apartment and sat around the kitchen table and talked.

She noticed how old her mother looked. Her brother's clothes looked worn and faded; he was always a smart man. His children, the two boys aged eight and ten, did not look as bad as the ones at the station or in the town, but she could not deny this place was not what it had been.

She spent the next few days walking around her old town. She realised that the entire fabric of the place, the infrastructure, was literally falling apart. During this time her mother and brother told her the stories.

'It started about three years ago,' her brother began. 'In fact not long after your last visit. First it was the electricity, then a few of the factories closed, including the one where I was working; well we went down to three days a week, now it's two and that's all I am doing at the moment. They blame it all on the Americans, but, sis, it's rubbish. Then some government people came and took away all the useful and operational farm machinery so our people here, they had to go back to using horses, horses I tell you!' He was standing now and clearly annoyed.

'Then food supplies started failing, the shops closed and the animals, well they just died; sis, we were eating their food.' He would not hold back now, he knew what his sister did but he did not care. 'Listen, did you hear? We are eating the fucking horses' and pigs' food. For all that we are supposed to thank the dear leader, the man is a fraud!'

She looked shocked but she knew; she knew and was starting to really see the truth of what was becoming of her country. She had noticed the deprivation from the train window on the way here, but now it came sharply into focus. This was her family telling her, this was her home town. She could see it with her own eyes, and her brother knew she could. A few years ago he would not have made that kind of statement in front of her like that, but times had changed and the cold winds of reality were blowing through the country and into people's minds.

She just looked at him and nodded. She put her arms around him, and told them she was sorry. She had not realised the situation was so chronic. She had money and could help. Her brother thanked her but said, 'Sis, we know you want to help but even money, that's no good here, the shops are empty.' He just laughed. 'Listen, sis, there's only two things money is good for here.' He sent his two boys out of the room for a minute. 'One is buying a prostitute . . .' She was shocked and gave him a questioning stare. 'No of course I have not but I am telling you. Listen, one is buying a prostitute and the other, a ticket out of this hell hole.'

'Would you?'

'Yes, sis, if I did not have my children and mum I would go; this place has nothing left. Look, they keep saying how terrible life is in South Korea, but, listen, one of my friends, he knows about electronics, and the other night we retuned a TV to pick up South Korea TV. Sis, you have to see it, it's wonderful, there are cars, people have beautiful clothes, they have freedom.'

She just nodded, but that was the loop closed. Greg came straight into her head; it was what they had argued over. Perhaps he was right.

She only stayed for another three days, telling her family the story of what had happened with work and how upset she was. She told them about the American, though she did not mention his name. But they had heard on State TV that a man had been held by the security forces for minor crimes and they were speaking with the Americans about it. So she told them that although she was suspended for a month, she was returning to the capital, and was going to appeal against this and would speak again with her superior.

She left them money and that evening took her case and got the train back to Pyongyang, feeling very different from how she had in the week before meeting Greg. Looking out the window as the train lumbered back towards the capital, she wondered whether she would see Greg again? She knew why she was going back; if she could persuade Sie Roo to lift her suspension then it could be possible to see him again. For one of the few times in her life she wanted to be near a man, but he was different and he was an American.

She arrived back late Thursday evening. It had been just over a week she had been away, but it seemed like a lifetime. She could sense something was in the air and she had an uneasy feeling come over her. It was nothing like she had felt before. It was not just Greg; no, it was more fundamental than that. It was like she was fighting with her very soul; everything she had believed in was now in doubt, but she was not a quitter, she did not wish to run away, she wanted to argue and fight, to do her bit and get her country back on its feet. The system was only being questioned because people were hungry. If Greg could be returned quickly and the food aid programme started (she had heard rumours through the powers that be that this was something the Americans were likely to offer) people would soon be well again, and with full stomachs they would be happy. She just wanted to put it all right, but still those doubts were there and thoughts of Greg persisted.

She walked from the station in the pitch black night. Only one police car went past her, its headlights the only light she saw on the entire walk; it took just over an hour to her apartment.

Greg was taken out of his cell. It was 9 a.m. He was told to go and wash and then he would be allowed to use the small yard to walk around for an hour. Greg's face and body had clearly taken several beatings and he was limping as a result. He had been walking around for about half an hour when the door opened and Miss Woo stepped into the small courtyard. She was not in uniform.

'Good morning, Miss Woo,' he said formally and respectfully. 'I haven't seen you for about a week or so.'

'Yes indeed, Greg, look I am just letting you know that I have not been around. I have been to see my family, and I just came to say I wish you well. I am led to believe that you will be going home soon, so I wish you luck.'

She leaned forward and shook his hand; they both knew in that second. Something went between them. Greg thought: '*Well if nothing else I have perhaps made a friend and I don't blame her for what she did.*' She smiled at him, nodded and then disappeared inside.

'Don't ever ask me to do that again,' said Chan, 'if that bastard had turned up we would have been fucked.'

'Thank you for that, Chan. Listen, please just put that call through to Sie Roo. Tell him I just called in and requested a meeting. I have returned from my mother's and I will await his call. I am going to appeal that my suspension is lifted.'

'Yes, miss, and I do hope so. He is only doing this to you because . . .' He looked down; she tapped him on the shoulder.

'I know, thanks, Chan, you are a good friend, I'll leave now and thanks for letting me see the American. I just wanted to make sure he was okay. I did hit him very hard and, well, we don't want any problems. By the way, did a doctor look at him?'

'Well no, Sie Roo refused, but then he had a phone call and the next thing the doctor was summoned.'

'It doesn't really matter now as he seems okay, but I guessed that bastard would not have had him looked at, if he had his way. Listen, I had better leave. Don't forget to tell him I expect a call.' With that she left the police station by the small public access door and went into town.

23

A week later, Greg was taking his usual exercise in the small courtyard. He continued his slow circular walk, occasionally holding his damaged arm. It was getting better now; the pain was gradually subsiding and the ache in his legs was beginning to diminish. A few days before, a doctor had visited him in his cell and, to Greg's surprise, had checked him over very thoroughly. Perhaps they were just doing that in order to know that he could take another beating? He went over and over it in his mind: why had he been so stupid, why had he fought with the officer, Sie Roo? Had he reacted instinctively or did he think something of Miss Woo?

He discounted it, and a few moments later he was led back to his cell.

In the evenings he would get a reasonable sized meal that consisted of rice and some cooked vegetables, occasionally meat, but what it was he had no idea. It was tough and not very palatable but he had lost so much weight now he had to eat whatever he was offered. The solitary cell was cold and he had been told not to deface the walls, as that was also a crime. It was one of the things that had struck him, every cell he had been in: no graffiti. The kind of small philosophical scribblings that the more literary prisoners would set in stone. No, there was absolutely nothing. He would have been unable to read it anyway, but just to have had the knowledge of others that had been there before him, well, it might have given him some sense of hope.

As these thoughts drifted through his mind, the door opened and out came the Chief of Police, Sie Roo. He looked impressive in his uniform. He was accompanied by a man wearing a rather ill-fitting suit but who was introduced as some party official. The official spoke a very basic English with a heavy accent.

'Mr Sanderson, I have good news. We speak today with high officials in the Party and our negotiations with your country go good, so our dear leader decree today you be released. He wishes you safe trip and says you may return some day but hopes that we forget the problems that happen before.'

Greg looked up at him; he couldn't believe what he was hearing.

'You will be handed over to Mr Sie Roo. I think you have misunderstanding, but he wants to forget that and take you to airport, where you will be boarding plane, this take you to Beijing and the Chinese Embassy, where you will meet with officials from your country. I wish you goodbye.'

With that he shook Greg's hand, turned and walked back through the door. Officer Sie Roo stepped forward and looked at Greg with a cold stare.

'Come this way.' Greg was led to his cell. As he walked in, he could see his original clothes, all washed. His personal effects were all there: watch, keys, wallet, and, of course, the offending diary.

'Put your clothes on, wash and be ready. We are to leave in one hour.' Sie Roo pointed to his watch 'So we leave at eleven, okay?'

Greg nodded, then sat on the bed for a few moments, taking a few deep breaths. He thanked heaven that his nightmare was soon to be over. He thought to himself that he would never take anything for granted again.

It was 11.05 when they set off. Sie Roo turned to him.

'You are a lucky man; Miss Woo is in serious trouble. It's okay for you; you're going home now, but for her, it's a very big problem. She's got no job, I suspended her.'

Greg looked puzzled; he turned and said, 'Why?'

'She was discussing matters with you and acting in a manner that is not considered appropriate for a person in her position. These talks with you, she will have to discuss in detail all the things she spoke about; it could be a big problem for her.'

Greg did not know what to say. He was unsure of Sie Roo's motive. Was he trying to get him to allude to the content of their conversations? Was he just trying to provoke some sort of reaction, and by his reaction make matters even worse for her? He had already guessed that she was probably in some sort of trouble but figured that by smashing him over the head it would have demonstrated that, however chivalrous his actions were, she would never deviate from her loyalty to the Party and her fellow officers. Though secretly he hoped that she had appreciated what he had done, albeit that it had been a spur of the moment thing.

Greg pondered for a few seconds, then, in a glib manner, said, 'Look, I really just want to forget the whole thing. I just need to get home. I mean it's her problem, not mine.' He said it in such a way as to indicate no concern whatsoever. He looked straight ahead, glanced at his watch, occasionally looking out the car window. Nothing more was said until they pulled into the airport. The car drove to the small airstrip, and as they rounded the corner Greg could see the small aircraft that he was told later was sent by the Chinese government as they were acting as arbitrators in the entire dispute.

Greg greeted the Chinese diplomat waiting at the steps of the plane, and they chatted briefly. Sie Roo nodded his head and said a curt 'goodbye' and with that he turned and went with one of his soldiers over to the control tower. Greg and the Chinese diplomat boarded the waiting aircraft and within ten minutes were airborne. As the plane banked, Greg took his last look at Pyongyang airport and the surrounding area. He thanked God he was finally going home and his nightmare was over. He had a few last thoughts of Miss Woo but he was on his way home and just wanted to forget it all. The aircraft climbed and Pyongyang gradually became a small speck, until it eventually disappeared in a mist of low cloud. It felt good.

24

Miss Woo had heard nothing from her request to meet with Sie Roo; it had been just over a week. She was unaware if Greg had finally left or if he was still at the police headquarters. She had been trying to suppress thoughts of him. She had to concentrate on getting her career back on track. Sie Roo was going to try his best to make things bad for her but if she could straighten things out and reason with him then perhaps she could inform him of her plan, which was another reason for her return.

She had been seriously considering the idea of asking for a transfer to Chongjin to be with her family. Everything she had seen there on her recent visit had shocked her to the core, and she also felt enormous guilt about how she was living while her family were practically starving. Her conscience weighed heavy on her mind.

It began to feel like she was getting her focus back again. She knew the transfer would inevitably be a lower position with less money but she had some savings, and she would still be earning relatively good money. Perhaps they could all live together and refurbish her mother's apartment; maybe she could get her brother a job in the civilian section. At least it would give him some pride back and much needed money for his children.

At around 11.30 she was considering calling her station again. This suspension was not sitting comfortably with her and all the while she was getting agitated. She was about to leave her apartment and go into town when there was a knock at her door. It was Chan. She looked surprised. 'Chan, come in.'

'No, look, I am not stopping. I just called in to tell you that Sie Roo is on his way here later.'

'How do you know this?' asked Miss Woo.

'I overheard him talking to someone really high up; I think it was one of the party officials. Anyhow, I think he has been told it's up to him how he deals with you. Basically they have given him *carte blanche* to do what he thinks is best.'

'So they are washing their hands of me?'

'With the entire flap over the American, the food shortages and everything else, they are not interested. I don't think you're the problem but he has twisted it all. He told them you were fraternising with the American.'

She wasn't sure what to think.

'Well, look, I am just warning you. Sie Roo is going to turn this to his advantage now. He wants to fuck you up; they are all laughing at him.'

She looked shocked. 'What do you mean, Chan?'

'Look, everyone knows that you rejected him, and all he has now is that other woman, you know the one that works at his station; she is older than him and fat, not beautiful like you.'

She blushed slightly, and then laughed.

'Chan, that is kind of you, but, honestly, I did not know. I mean he asked me a few times, but, well, he is an arrogant bastard. He has used violence many times on people. I think he likes it; I could never have trusted him. I didn't know it was common knowledge; I mean about me and him.'

'Yes, it most certainly is, and he knows people talk about it behind his back; it drives him mad. I don't know what he's planning but I reckon he will suspend you for a bit longer, that's all.'

'Thanks, Chan, you know he is a piece of shit, but as you say, what can I do?'

'Look, just keep cool, that's all I am saying.'

With that Chan left. She watched out the window as he jumped in the police vehicle and left. She looked at the clock; it was just gone twelve.

It was around three hours later that day. Her door was tapped very harshly. She guessed who it was but feigned surprise when she opened the door.

'Officer Sie Roo. This is a surprise, please come in.'

'Thank you, Miss Woo.'

She closed the door and he went into her small dining area.

'Well, Chan told me you had returned and requested a meeting so I am here. What do you want? You were suspended for a month as you know and were told to leave the city for that period. Now you return, why?'

'Sie Roo, look, you know my record. I came from the military to the police. I have worked my way up and been a loyal officer. This thing with the American, it was my decision to act the way I did but, well I was trying in my way to get information from him. It was obvious we would have to release him. All the information I found in that diary I sent on to you, which I assumed you passed on. The rest of his story checked out so I could not see any point in treating him badly.'

'Then why did he attack me when you were being disciplined by me, why would he do that for you? I think you were having close, intimate conversations, it is not our way.'

'Don't be ridiculous, I was just doing my job,' she retorted.

'You see, the way you even speak to me, no fucking respect!' He was getting angry now.

'Officer Sie Roo, I was doing my job, I am respectful; please, I just want my suspension lifted and this matter to be put behind us.'

'No, Miss Woo, you are arrogant, a fucking arrogant bitch and, further, I know you came to see the American. You have no shame. What did you want to do, hold hands before he left?' He was pacing up and down now. 'Due to your gross insubordination and this fraternisation, which you still have to answer for, I am suspending you until further notice, without pay. So now, perhaps you will realise not to cross me.'

She walked over to the apartment door and opened it.

'There is nothing I can say, Officer Sie Roo, you have given me no choice. I have nothing now; I will return to my mother's. I can only accept what you say but I wish it recorded that I have always done my duty, am a loyal party member and police officer and I wish to apologise for a mistake I may have made. But I honestly believed I was working in the country's best interests. . .' She went on until Sie Roo walked over to her. He stood about a foot away.

'All noted, Miss Woo, now, off the record. . .' He pushed her door closed again and the lock clicked into place. 'Listen, I can forget all this, but I wish something in return.'

She looked straight at him, but he came a step closer.

'I want you and me to be together,' he continued. 'Look, I have asked you before; you are foolish; you are getting beyond child-bearing age; you have no husband; no one is interested in you. I have a good job, one of the best in the city. With our salaries we can have a good life. Look, just give me a chance; I am asking you, please, I can help you.'

'Sie Roo. . .' She paused for a few seconds, looked around the room, then, looking back at him, said, 'Officer Sie Roo, I don't care what you do to me, but I would rather share a bed with a pig than you, now if you don't mind. . .' She indicated for him to leave.

There was silence for a few seconds, then suddenly she felt her head being wrenched backwards. She started to fall then managed to regain her equilibrium. He pulled harder, dragging her backwards. Then he got her into her bedroom, and forced her onto the bed. Next thing, he had his hand round her throat and was standing over her.

'You are a stupid bitch and now I am really going to fuck you; you won't ever be coming back, your career is over, you stupid bitch.' He put his other free arm into his uniform pocket and pulled out the short stick he had used on her before. Two, three, four times he struck her face. She did not cry out, but she felt the agony of every blow. Then just as quick as the blows came they stopped. Then he grabbed her blouse and tore it off. He was tearing at her clothes and she fought back. Eventually, somehow, she got him off her.

Then, realising what he had done, he tried to compose himself. He stood up, pulled his jacket down and, replacing the stick, he turned to walk out of her bedroom. Getting off the bed, she followed him out. He was just reaching for the front door catch when she called him.

'Sie Roo, wait, okay listen.'

He turned. She was holding her face; it was bleeding heavily as she walked towards him.

'Well then?' he said. 'Last fucking chance, what's it to be?'

He never even saw it coming. She kicked him straight in the groin. He screamed; his testicles felt like they were in his stomach. He felt sick as he doubled over. She then smashed his head with a glass ornament she kept on the table; he crashed to the floor, cracking his forehead as he collapsed in a heap. She stood back, her mind racing. *How could it have come to this? My life, I have really done it now.* She stumbled back to the edge of the bed, and sat down.

Sie Roo was stunned and began groaning. Eventually he brought his hand up from his groin and felt the back of his head. Blood was starting to ooze into his hair. She could see it on his fingers as he rubbed his head. He rolled on to his side. She put her head in her hands and was going to cry, something she never did. Then, as she went to get up, She saw him go for his gun. Then things all started to appear in slow motion. Her brain was saying, *he is going for the gun, but he won't shoot you, let him take it out, it's the best way, just let him arrest you.* Each frame built on the last, and she could trace the path of the gun on its way up to her face. Her brain flicked another switch: *he's going to shoot you; he's going to shoot you!* She was back in real time; she dived on top of him and

139

grabbed the gun with both hands. They struggled for a few moments. He was trying to force the gun from her hands, but she kneed him again in the groin. He cried out but still he was twisting the gun towards her. She kicked him again, then just for a few milliseconds, he relaxed his grip. She twisted with all her strength, and it seemed to pop from his grasp. Now she had the weapon in her hands, her mind was made up; there was no way out now.

She gave him a perfectly aimed glancing blow to the side of his head with the butt of the gun and he lost consciousness. 'You are lucky,' she said to the silence of the room, 'I was going to shoot you just like you were going to do to me, you bastard.' She sat down at her table just looking at him. She could not quite take in what had just happened. It was surreal. She had to think. Looking down at the gun, for a moment she contemplated killing herself; perhaps it was the only way out now.

She thought of her family, how they would feel, her nephews, her brother and mother. Over and over, round and round it went in her mind; she knew if she did not kill herself then her night-mare was only just beginning.

25

That was it, the moment he had been waiting for: the small jarring as the plane touched down at Beijing. Greg shook hands with the Chinese diplomat and thanked him warmly.

'We'll get you through customs, Mr Sanderson, and into the VIP area from where I understand you will be sent directly to the American Embassy.'

After all the usual formalities, Greg was ushered to an open area and asked to wait. Five minutes later the American ambassador arrived.

'Mr Sanderson, welcome to China. I'm Frank Hanson, the American ambassador.' He shook Greg's hand with a vice-like grip. 'It's good to see you, sir. How are you feeling?'

'I feel like I've just got out of prison.'

Frank laughed.

'Come on, let's get you to the embassy, have something to eat and get you a change of clothes. Then we can have a chat. Look, tonight you will stay here at the embassy, then tomorrow evening, from what I understand from our admin and logistics people who handle all this, you should be on a flight back to the US.'

'Thank you, Mr Hanson, and thank you for getting me released, I guess you need the whole story?'

'Hey, call me Frank. Yeah, listen, we know most of it.'

'You do?' said Greg, surprised.

'Yeah but come on, let's get a move on, soon you will be on

American soil, albeit the subsoil is Chinese, but well, you know what I mean.'

Greg just smiled; he couldn't believe how quickly things were moving.

'Now listen, the press are outside. I'm afraid to say you are a bit of a celebrity now, and they all want a piece of you. Airport security will escort us out. Get straight into the car. I am just waiting for our guys to join us.' Frank smiled and with that they walked out of the VIP holding section and into the corridor. As they neared the doors two secret service guys who were standing inside joined them. Greg could see the hordes of press outside. 'Okay, you ready?' said Frank, 'Don't say anything, just look ahead or down if you wish.'

The secret service detail got on either side of Greg and the doors opened. Airport security had formed a human corridor for them to pass through the flashing cameras to the ambassador's official car. Journalists were shouting:

'Greg, Greg, how was it? What happened?'

'Mr Sanderson, did they torture you?'

'Mr Sanderson, what did you do to be arrested?'

On it went, and then the door slammed shut. It was the first time he had sat in an American car for weeks. The security man got in the front and they moved off. Frank slapped Greg on the leg. 'You okay, Greg?'

'Thanks, Frank, yes really I feel good. Hell, Frank, what a place, it's like, it's like just crazy.'

Frank just smiled. 'Save it, Greg, we will talk soon.'

Inside the embassy Greg was shown to a room; there were clothes and a shower room. Greg's day was getting better all the time.

Half an hour later Greg heard a tap on the door.

'Greg, it's Frank, are you ready?'

Greg opened the door and said, 'Hey, thanks again, it all feels good, but I am so hungry.'

'Come on, Greg, let's get you some food.'

They went to a small room and the two of them lunched together and chatted briefly. After they had eaten, Frank said, 'Listen, Greg, when you get back to the US you know that you will be interviewed by the CIA; it's normal practice.'

Greg just nodded. 'Sure, whatever you say; I'm just glad to be going home.'

'Good, in the meantime I have my secretary coming here now to take a few notes.'

'Fine by me, like I said, I'm through the worst. But what is it you want to know, exactly?'

'The thing is, Greg, and I guess you probably don't know the extent of this, but you've had a profound effect on international relations over these past few weeks, since the attacks on the Twin Towers.'

'I couldn't believe it when I heard,' said Greg. 'I missed the whole thing; and it was only because, well, anyway, let's just say a little bird gave me some privileged knowledge.' He wasn't sure what he should or shouldn't say about Miss Woo; he would have to play it by ear.

Frank gave him a strange look. 'Okay, well, it's crisis time as you can imagine and President Bush was looking around the world for answers, still is; of course we don't think the Koreans are involved but, well, things were tense.'

Frank's secretary entered the room and began to take notes.

Greg spoke at length. He told him the whole story. First, how he had been asked to investigate the death of this Natasha, then how he had been alerted by her mother, Vika, to the papers that Natasha had been working on. She'd found them in her own apartment, hidden away. Natasha had obviously been scared to leave them in her own apartment, or at Richard's in case they were discovered. Vika had stumbled across them, and Richard had given her the diary. And then Greg became involved after Gerry insisted he look into this woman's death. Apparently that was just an accident, but after reading the diary and papers then meeting Richard that second time after his meeting with this Arab client Namir he knew there must be something in the story, something that took him to North Korea and seemed to spiral in all directions. And this crazy counterfeiting business.

'And you put two and two together and decided that Natasha's death was no accident.'

Greg was looking down at the table. At this, he looked up. It was the first time that anyone had actually articulated this. 'Yes, now you say it, that's exactly the conclusion I came to. Well it was just a suspicion back then, but when I spoke to Richard, Natasha's fiancé, what he told me convinced me that there was enough to check it out. It seems stupid to you perhaps, but that's the world we work in, we take big risks. If I had not gone there somebody would have beaten me to it and from what I hear now the story had been doing the rounds. Anyhow, I went and, well, you know the rest.'

'Listen, Greg, I don't know whether you are aware that Richard and his firm were wiped out in the attack on the Twin Towers?'

Greg nodded. 'I guessed as much, poor bloody guy!'

'And your firm, well it's only Gerry and a few people left I'm afraid to tell you.'

Greg just shook his head and paused for a few seconds. 'God, what a way to go!'

Frank went on to explain how many people had simply jumped to their deaths just to avoid the searing heat, how the day panned out and eventually the realisation that over three thousand people had lost their lives on that September morning.

The conversation continued in that vein, then Frank said:

'Now, Greg, I have to tell you something and I want you to promise that you will not go off on one again, that you will leave this in our hands, let us take the reins, it's what we do, it's what we're good at.'

'What?' said Greg.

'I need your word, Greg.'

'Yes, yes, of course, whatever, just tell me.'

'It's about the woman, Natasha.'

'Yes?'

'We've done our own investigations in your absence, since this whole thing came out, and we have evidence, and let's just leave it at that, that just as the girl's mother, and indeed you, suspected, her death was no accident.'

Greg sat bolt upright.

'She was murdered, Greg, because of what she knew, because of what she was investigating. Her death, as you supposed, was planned and ruthlessly executed.'

'But how? The autopsy reports said it was a heart attack; how can you fake that?'

'We don't know, exactly, but she was injected with something that affected her heart, no question. How they got her to drive the car, that's the bit we can't understand, unless she was trying to get to a hospital or something. But we checked it out: the route she took, the way witnesses say she seemed to drive on that morning; it's strange, almost as if she was just having a normal day.'

'What do you mean?'

'One witness, a pedestrian who noticed the car beginning to weave around, said she seemed to have a glazed look on her face. Look, that's it really, but please leave that with us. I promise we will keep in touch, but for now, I suggest you get home and see what the situation is with your old company. We hear that Gerry is working from some temporary offices; we hope you guys get it up and running again. Over the years, Greg, we know you have produced some great stories, even if it's upset some of the diplomats and politicians.'

'Thanks,' said Greg.

'Hell, we need guys like you; if you had not gone out there this thing might not have blown so quick. We reckon you have probably saved the US Treasury a fortune, and restored the reputation of the dollar. As I told you, it had been suspected for some time, but, well, that's it so far.'

Greg shifted on his chair and exhaled. 'So how did it actually start, I mean with the suspected dollar production?' he asked.

'Rumours were starting to leak out, a diplomat from their embassy had passed some information to a reporter. Now we know it was Natasha. She had actually contacted someone close to our Treasury people. They had suspected it for some time, but we had no concrete proof. Next thing we know, the diplomat, who we were prepared to give diplomatic immunity to on the condition that he defected to the US, that guy then suddenly disappears. Soon after, the girl is dead. Then your boss, Gerry, is approached by the girl's mother, who is going around demanding an inquest into her daughter's death and claiming that we had not told the truth on the original autopsy.'

Greg opened his hands, saying, 'And did you? Did you cover it up?'

'Don't be ridiculous, Greg, of course not, the days of Watergate have long gone; no, no, it was simply that we did not give the story enough credence. But then all this blew up with you, and subsequent to all that we had the body re-examined; that's when it was picked up, she had been drugged.'

'So where does it all go from here?' Greg asked.

'Look, the main problems have been resolved: the North Koreans have no connection to Al Qaeda; the dollar production will stop now, although our Treasury agents suspect that they will just mothball it for a while; and we got you back. Even the North Koreans are happy: they are getting some much needed aid, so it's all going the right way.'

'Except you have a woman who was killed, a US citizen, what about her?' Greg was annoyed, his journalistic instincts kicking in. The truth still needed to come out, someone should take responsibility; someone should tell the truth to her mother, Vika.

'Greg, look, I know what you are thinking, we have asked a small contingent at the NYPD to look into the whole thing including the missing Korean diplomat, we—'

Greg cut him off. 'You mean dig around for a while, find fuck all and then let it wither on the old vine.'

'Come on, Greg, look, I can assure you—'

Greg was aggravated. 'Frank, I am sorry, but I have been around diplomats and politicians a long time, I know how you guys work. You got what you wanted. As I said, you will go through the motions, ruffle a few feathers, and it will all blow over and be forgotten.'

Frank looked flushed. He was a man of his word but clearly he could see Greg's frustration, and part of what he said did resonate with the truth. The government had got North Korea where it wanted it, the President wanted to move on, he wanted someone to pay for the attacks, and, well, Natasha was just a small cog who got caught up in it. Frank stood up, then said:

'Greg, you are a good man, you've been through a lot; look, go home, please leave it with us; I promise I will do what I can, but, well, Greg, as you say, the wheels of government and all that.'

Greg shrugged his shoulders but accepted Frank's hand. He thanked him for what he had done for him and the meeting was over.

'Well, Greg, I'll hand you over to my admin staff and they'll brief you on your flight and all the details, but I'll see you before you leave. There's a guy from *The Washington Post*, William Orson, you may have heard of him, who I've said can speak with you for about half an hour before you leave.'

'Why should I speak to him? Christ, I'm the one who's been through the mill here. I'm a journalist too, and it's my story. I'm not going to just hand it over to another hack.'

'You have to,' said Frank, more forthright than he had been until now. 'It's the deal. We jumped through hoops to get you out of the mess you found yourself in, and this is the price you have to pay. No negotiation.'

Greg sat brooding, but he knew Frank was right. He would have to let the story go. He was lucky to be out, he was lucky to be alive. Natasha was dead, Richard was dead, and he'd had a lucky reprieve. What the hell, Orson could get the glory, good luck to him. . .

'What do I tell him?' said Greg at last.

'Don't give him your whole story, please, just the basics of how you were treated in North Korea, that it was all a terrible mistake and that you're glad to be back on US soil, so to speak. The North Koreans will make the usual noises but we'll just blame it on the price we pay for having a free press. Anyhow, listen, I must go, and Greg, thanks again. Oh and good luck with Orson.'

The next morning, William Orson called and they spoke for nearly an hour. When the ambassador arrived, Orson thanked them both for speaking with him. He reckoned he had a great story. Greg had agreed to do an exclusive. In the interim, *The Washington Post* was only going to release the main points; the details of Greg's two months in North Korea would come out later, and would probably be serialised. Greg didn't know how great the story would be. He was going to play his cards close to his chest, and he was certainly not going to endanger Miss Woo in any way. He would keep his own counsel on that matter.

As Greg waited at the airport for his flight he felt like he had aged five years. The flight took off on time. He was going home, but the world had changed and so had he.

26

Looking out the window, Greg beheld a beautiful sight. Manhattan Island was coming into view, the bold skyscrapers with their gleaming windows reflecting the winter sun. It was almost surreal; perhaps it had all been a dream, but he knew only too well the truth of it all.

Natasha was dead, murdered by unknown forces, Miss Woo was gone to God only knew what fate, and New York had been violated in the most barbaric of ways. Frank Hanson had told him all about Noble and Black, how the offices had been obliterated in the attacks, and how nobody who had been there that day had survived to tell the tale. His first thought had been Gerry, and he had been relieved beyond words to discover that he had escaped that unimaginable scenario. 'Thank heaven for small mercies,' he thought, as he took in the scene below.

He stared out, not wanting to take his eyes away for even a moment. He imagined that in that split second, in the act of looking away, it would all be gone for ever. Part of it had and that seemed almost beyond his comprehension. Perhaps he felt guilt that he had not been there on that fateful day with his fellow New Yorkers. He speculated as to the thoughts that must have gone through the minds of his friends at Noble and Black. . .

Once they had landed, it took an hour to negotiate the press pack inside the terminal building. Eventually, aided by the NYPD,

Greg and the embassy aide who had accompanied him on the flight got into an official government car bound for City Hall and a meeting with the mayor.

The mayor and Greg spoke at length, for around two hours. Then, finally, it was time to go home.

The apartment was dark. He remembered closing all the blinds before leaving. It smelt musty. He guessed his cleaner had not been round; he assumed she knew he had gone missing and just not bothered. 'Guess she figured she may not get paid,' he thought as he walked over to the balcony windows. He slid the blinds all the way back, opened the doors and walked out. It felt good to see that view again. For now, he was just glad to be home.

Over the next couple of days, he had the apartment cleaned and went through all the mail that had mounted up. Gerry and his wife Tanya called over. They talked about how both their experiences had shattered their lives. Greg relived his story. He explained how he still had not resolved everything to do with the story he had been working on and all that had unfolded in Korea, but for the moment he wanted to get his life back on track, he wanted to get back to the firm. Noble and Black had to rebuild their business and Greg and Gerry would be at the forefront of that long process.

The next day he received a call from Vika. He contemplated going to visit but then changed his mind. What could he tell her: that her daughter had been murdered but that he had no proof? No, he would leave that particular revelation to Frank and his cronies.

Over the next few days, he took calls from various television networks anxious to get an exclusive on his story, but he politely declined as he had agreed a deal with Bill Orson, with whom he would be meeting later in the month. November was coming to a close and New Yorkers were preparing for Christmas; their first without the Twin Towers and a special time to remember all those families affected by the events of what had become known as 9/11 in the public consciousness.

He decided to take a walk to ground zero, the former site of the Twin Towers. He stood there for a couple of hours watching the clear-up operation. It still did not seem possible but there it was, America had suffered an unprovoked attack on its own soil. In his mind he realised how the events he had become unwittingly entangled in could have played out so differently. He was glad to be home, and looking forward to going back to work albeit at temporary offices. He craved some form of routine, getting back to a semblance of normality, but he just didn't feel himself. He felt restless and unfulfilled and strangely alone. Sonia had found another guy while he had been away but it was not that, it was something else, something that was unresolved. Not just the story of the girl's death by some unknown forces; no, something else lay at the back of his mind, just a strange feeling.

One day, soon after his return, he visited Natasha's grave and placed flowers there. He had only met the girl briefly, it now seemed a long time ago, but all this had started because of her. And he knew in his heart of hearts that it could have so easily been him; he was simply paying the respect due to a member of his difficult and sometimes dangerous profession. He felt better, but he discounted visiting Vika. He knew she would ask questions. He felt guilty, but in the end he decided that he would wait and see if Frank was true to his word, if he really would try and keep the pressure up to come up with something. Perhaps the NYPD would unearth something, bring some justice for Natasha and some closure for Vika.

Soon after he got back Bill Orson called and said that he was returning home soon and wanted to interview Greg personally. They tentatively agreed on Sunday. Orson said he would call back and confirm within the next few days, but cancelled at the last minute, saying he had to visit South Korea for a few days and could they make it the following Saturday?

The following week, Bill arrived as planned.

They talked for about two hours. Part way through the conversation, the fellow journalist brought up the subject that Greg had been trying so hard to keep under wraps. Miss Woo. Orson had done his research well. He knew all about Greg's captivity, and that he had struck up some kind of friendship with an enigmatic female police officer who had gone out of her way, at considerable risk to herself, to help him. It was dynamite as far as the journalist was concerned, real human interest story, but there was so much he didn't know, so much he wanted Greg to fill him in on.

Greg had agreed to speak. After all he didn't have any choice, Frank Hanson had spelt that much out quite clearly. But on the subject of Miss Woo, no deal. He would talk off the record, but there was no way he was going to put Miss Woo at further risk. Without some kind of guarantee, that was as much as the journalist was going to get from him. Take it or leave it.

And of course, he took it. Bill Orson wasn't going to let this one slip through his fingers. . .

27

As Sie Roo lay unconscious, Miss Woo made up her mind and packed as quickly as possible. The whole place was so unusually quiet. It was winter now and she would need warm clothes. She crammed as much as she could get in her suitcase, eventually forcing the lid down and struggling to close the zip, having to readjust the clothes several times. She opened a small drawer under the base of the bed; she took out her cash tin (she had enough stashed away to get by for a while) and her personal papers.

Wiping her mouth, she began to perspire; her heart was pumping hard and adrenaline was flowing through her body. Her mind was set on its course. She ran to the bathroom and wiped her heavily perspiring face with a fresh towel. She tidied her hair and tied it back in a black ponytail.

She searched Sie Roo's unconscious body, taking his car keys and gun.

She tried to compose herself. Glancing out the window she saw that Sie Roo's car was beginning to draw attention as hardly anyone in the North owned a car; generally they would be either military or police vehicles.

Ten minutes later, she emptied the water from her kettle over his face, and he began to come round. Still dazed, he slowly got to his feet, holding his bleeding head. He circled round and saw her pointing his gun directly at him.

'You've done it now, you stupid bitch. You're fucked!'

'Listen. We are going downstairs and we are going to get into your car, then we're going to drive off. If you try anything, I will shoot you, but I won't kill you. I'll blow your testicles off and leave you here. If you don't bleed to death, the rest of *your* life will be fucked. Do I make myself clear?'

'Don't be stupid. You can't get away.'

She walked closer to him, holding the gun higher. 'Take me out of the city as near as we can get to Rasan station.'

He looked at her in amazement. 'That American, he has turned your head; your loyalty is to the country, the Party.'

'What? A party that presides over the starvation of its own people? Imprisons people for misdemeanours? Why are we building nuclear weapons when people can't feed themselves? How does it justify how our citizens are living? Or should I say "existing"? Because that's the truth. We all have a right to live, the right to life. You are well-off, Sie Roo, it has not hit you; but you have eyes, you should open them. People have even forgotten how to think.'

'We are strong together; you know that we suppress individual thought to enable the whole to be stronger.'

'No, Sie Roo. No, you are a misguided fool just as I was. Yes, perhaps the American did make me think, but I have seen it with my own eyes. Go outside the city, go and see what it's like.'

He was becoming agitated and he was beginning to get his senses back. 'Look, I will forget this; please, you know what I want.'

She cut him off. 'No more discussions, we are leaving now; and I have told you what I will do, make no mistake, I don't make idle threats, do you understand?'

He glared at her but realised she was serious. Thinking they could talk in the car and then he would be able to persuade her on the journey, he decided to comply for the time being.

'Okay, but I think you're being foolish.'

She threw him a towel. 'Clean your face and put your cap

back. Let's go.' She took a last look at her apartment and, throwing a spare jacket over her arm to conceal her gun, she opened the door. He was still a bit shaky on his feet and was having difficulty carrying her case. She closed and locked the door behind them. Slowly they both walked down the flight of stairs into the lobby. A neighbour of hers was standing there talking to a friend with two young children; it went quiet. 'Good afternoon, how are you all?'

They just nodded then her neighbour said, 'Oh, Miss Woo, are you going away?'

They both stopped and Miss Woo turned to her.

'Yes, just a few days. I have already been once, but I decided to go back to my mother's for a few days; my friend is dropping me at the station.'

'Oh I think the trains are not running till tonight, Miss Woo,' said her neighbour, enjoying the prestige of speaking to two senior officers; it was impressing her neighbours and she was revelling in it.

'Oh it doesn't matter; I'll just read for a while, probably get something to eat.'

The woman tried to re-engage her. Sie Roo was looking ill and Miss Woo noticed that blood was running down the back of his head.

'If you could open the other door, please, we really have to go.' She indicated to one of the women as she stood close behind Sie Roo. Her neighbour and the friend obliged and in a joint effort they worked the bolts, swinging the other door open.

'Thank you,' Miss Woo said as they passed through the doors. Sie Roo placed the case in the trunk then closed it.

The women were still watching. Then Miss Woo looked back around and said, 'Thanks again, I will see you soon. Now if you don't mind.'

The women finally got the message; they quickly closed the door and then pushed the other one shut.

'Get in,' said Miss Woo as she opened the passenger door for him.' She waited as he climbed in, moaning slightly; he had concussion and was feeling nauseous. 'I feel sick,' he said.

'Not yet, you can throw up in a minute, shut that door and don't move; remember I don't give a fuck.'

'All right, all right: I won't do anything; you are completely mad, Woo.'

She swiftly walked round the other side, keeping a watchful eye on him.

Two minutes later the car had pulled off the concrete frontage onto the road and then turned right onto the main street.

'I think I am going to be sick.'

'Then open the window,' she said quietly, concentrating on the road and using her peripheral vision to make sure Sie Roo was not going to try anything.

He wasn't; she had a gun in one hand and he realised that she was physically able to overcome him, particularly in his current state. She had proven that back at her apartment. He was shocked at how fast she was; he was not a small man but she was practically all muscle and determined. He threw up, closed the window and sat quietly. The unmarked car continued its journey.

She glanced down at the fuel gauge; it was reading a quarter tank. A quick calculation gave her a range of seventy miles, maybe only fifty, but that would do.

They were heading out of town, but not to the station: there was no way back now. As they crossed the next junction her mind began to race. She had the skeleton of a plan, a disjointed idea, but she realised she had no choice. She knew the system, she knew how it worked. She'd be locked up for a month or so, and then the military would take over her entire station. The others would be allocated to new stations, probably outside the capital, and she would be sent to a labour camp, probably executed.

Once Chan had told her that Sie Roo had been making reports on her, she knew her fate was sealed. The authorities would not care that he had tried to rape her. Sie Roo was a bastard, but a bastard who was highly respected and had friends in the right places. She would never be allowed to return to duty; at the very best she would be demoted all the way back to an ordinary officer and that would be at some godforsaken small village outpost in the north somewhere. She had made her mind up at the station; now there was no turning back. She pushed the accelerator down hard and headed out of Pyongyang.

If any suspicions were raised and the truth was discovered they would realise that a defection was underway by a high-ranking policewoman. It would be crushed with unremitting force. She would be a dead woman walking. Occasionally pilots would try and defect, most of the time in vain. If they deviated a fraction from their authorised flight path orders were given to shoot them down. Often mistakes occurred: pilots did make genuine errors. But in North Korea it was fatal, there were no margins. Life was lived out to the mantra of party discipline; mistakes were not an option, it was as simple as that.

She had to get close to the first station after Pyongyang going towards the north. South was out of the question; that would only lead to the demilitarised zone, the most fortified border in the world, but at Rasan station there was a chance. It was one of the stations that did not appear on any international maps, like so many other things in the North.

Rasan station was an ex-military terminus where main passenger trains had been stopping for some time. Gradually, the station was becoming popular. However, the level of security was still fairly low and if she waited till dusk it should be easy to get on a train for Chongjin, to persuade her family to come with her.

She was aware of the escape routes. As a senior officer, she had often read reports of how people escaped. She would need to get to her home town first, then prayers and a lot of luck.

After about twenty minutes she pulled off the main highway, driving on for ten minutes, before deciding to stop on the crest of a steep hill.

'So what are your plans then, Miss Woo? I assume you have one?' Sie Roo stared straight out of the windscreen. She got out the car and walked round the other side. Opening his door, she used the gun to indicate that she wanted him to step out. Slowly he got out of the car and stood by the bonnet. She was about three feet away from him.

'Sie Roo, I have crossed the Rubicon. Now there is no way back for me thanks to you. Now, here's the deal: you will accompany me all the way to Chongjin. I intend to pick my mother up then I am making to the border. Okay, it's not much of a plan but it's all I have got: help me get there and you can just say I held you hostage. Get me there and that's all I want.'

He laughed. 'Don't be ridiculous. I would be charged with colluding in your escape. They would never believe I did not make any attempt to disarm you. I am not assisting you in this farce, so what are you going to do now?'

'I don't know really but first you are going to get on that radio and tell them you have been to see me at my home, informed me I am suspended and you have dropped me off at Pyongyang station. I am going back to my mother's until I am called for. You are coming out here as you are taking personal charge of this illegal farming investigation.'

'You're crazy!'

'Maybe I am, maybe I'm not, but if you don't do what I ask, you'll find out either way! So get on with it, make that call and make it now.'

He turned his back to her and looked over into the valley below; the banking fell away sharply and in the distance the main rail line could be seen snaking its way across the landscape. A few run-down farm buildings were dotted around. The brown soil was untended and produced little of any value; fertiliser was in short supply and crop treatments virtually non-existent. He saw broken farm machinery and, in the far distance, a farmer using horses to plough a field. Miss Woo came alongside him. 'Look at it, open your eyes, man,' she said.

'Miss Woo, you make a run for it but I am not helping you.'

She pushed the gun into his groin. 'You are going to radio in and tell them that I have been suspended until further notice, and that you are going out to the Rasan area to meet with local investigators and won't be returning tonight.'

He looked into her eyes; seconds later he made the call.

Contemplating her next move, Miss Woo walked to the rear of the car and leaned against the trunk, pulling a packet of cigarettes and lighter from her trouser pocket. As the nicotine entered her brain it helped calm her. She smoked rarely and noted that the last one she'd really enjoyed was at the hotel, the evening she had spent speaking with Greg. How different now her situation was; now she was in more danger than Greg ever had been.

'Are you satisfied now?' he asked, replacing the radio. She was suspicious that he had left it on transmit.

'Move away from the car,' she ordered, covering him all the time with his own gun. She leaned in and glanced away from him for a few seconds to check. He slammed the car door on her legs. The pain tore into her. She tried to get out but he threw the door back open and made a grab for the gun.

They struggled for a few seconds then she shot him in the chest. Blood spurted from his jacket, and he slumped motionless, a small amount of blood dripping onto her chest. She pushed him off and his lifeless body fell onto the dusty road, the blood now flowing copiously but absorbed by the reddish dust of the roadway.

She leaned down to check for a pulse. The body twitched but she already knew. Thoughts flooded her mind: '*I will finish this then my life is over; I wish I could have just seen my family one more time; I wish I could have told my mother how much I have missed her; I hope she was proud of me as a daughter.*' The gun was on the driver's seat. Moments passed, then she was ready; there was no alternative. The entire military and political machine would hunt her down, but she felt calm, almost serene. She'd had a good life; she wished she had been married and had a good man but, well, she accepted how it had all turned out. '*I'm just going to pick up the gun, count to ten, then put it to my forehead and pull the trigger. It's for the best.*'

She reached for the gun, but something held her back. She knew it was just nerves. *'You coward! Get on with it! Just pick it up!'* She had crossed one threshold, this was only another. *No turning back*, that had been the mantra she had always lived by; well now she was going to die by it. Yes that was it: *'once I pick that gun up it's all over, not going to count to ten now, just do it do it do it!'*

She was perspiring now, taking short, deep breaths . . . trying to overcome her survival instincts; pitting the pure logic of the hopelessness of her situation against her inbuilt wish to live. *'Stop it, stop it!'* She was breathing harder and faster now; she was ready to go, she was ready, she would look down, pick the gun up and just fire, now all that was stopping her was picking it up . . . She knew it would be over in two or three seconds. Her hands were twitching, her whole body felt heavy. She looked up at the sky. . .

'*NO!*' she screamed. 'My life is not going to end like this. I'm going to fight. I owe it to my family. I'm getting out of this place.'

It was nearly dusk; she was running out of time. Her focus came back. She had a new plan and this plan could just work. She was going to turn Sie Roo's foolish actions, which had ended in his death, to her full advantage. It was crazy but it had a chance. Dragging his body onto the rear seat and closing the door, she jumped back into the driver's seat. Driving as fast as she could, following the steep upward gradient, she kept looking out the side window, and keeping the railway track in sight. She was high up now, the drop would be about two hundred feet into the valley at this point. She went round two more bends then, as the third approached; she turned the car towards the edge of the road and skidded to a halt. The car rested two feet from the edge, and beyond that was a steep bank with the valley floor way below.

She jumped out and went to the trunk, praying that it was there. Owing to fuel restrictions, all police vehicles were required to keep a spare gallon of petrol in the trunk. She crossed her fingers and saw the canister sitting just to the left, tied to the spare wheel.

Releasing it, she took it round the driver's side; then, opening the back door, she pulled his body out. She was struggling now; he was heavy and her legs were painful where the door had hit them, but this was the only way.

It took her about five minutes in total but eventually she manoeuvred Sie Roo's lifeless body directly behind the steering wheel. Then, taking the fuel can, she poured the entire contents over his body then over the fabric seats, which soaked it up like blotting paper. She returned the can to its original position in the trunk, even tying it back down. Then she closed the trunk and went back to the driver's side.

Leaning in, she started the engine and turned the wheels on full lock. Looking round on the dusty road, she needed something, a stone a branch, anything to hold that car for a few moments. She paced up and down; there was nothing. She had to go back to the trunk and retrieve the jack. That would do but she would have to make sure it was hidden when discarded. Placing the jack under the outside front wheel, she leaned in and opened the driver's window slightly, making sure, in case the windows did not break, that the fuel would have enough air to feed the flames. She released the handbrake. The car moved momentarily, checked by the jack under the wheel. She flicked her lighter and held it to the seat, which ignited immediately.

She jumped back, slamming the door shut and tugging on the jack. The vehicle rolled backwards; first the rear inside wheel dropped over the edge, then she ran round the front and pushed hard. It had enough momentum now and seconds later the car went crashing into the valley below.

She watched it as the fire took hold, then waited no longer and made her way back down the roadway. It took about twenty minutes, eventually reaching a point where she could navigate her way down the banking. The drop was shallow now and only about thirty feet to the floor of the valley. She made her way towards the train line about a mile away.

The holes in her plan were too many to count; there were too many variables. Would the fire go out? If it did continue burning, would it be enough to not arouse suspicion? She wanted it to appear that he had simply been driving too fast, come off the road, crashed and the vehicle had caught fire. Would it remain undiscovered long enough for night to fall?

If she could get on a train tonight she could be in Chongjin by early morning. By then, hopefully, the car would be completely burnt out; his body would be unrecognisable. Only upon a close examination would the truth be known.

She felt her pocket. She had considered putting his gun back in the car but it would be a welcome safeguard on the journey. If her plan unravelled and she was cornered, she would put a bullet in her brain. There was no way these bastards were going to put her in a labour camp, rape her, probably break one of her legs so she could never escape, and disfigure her face. That gun was her insurance policy. She was going to do her best to get out and she wanted to take her family with her, but if she failed they would not take their revenge on her.

She had turned against it all now: the system she had once believed in; the torture she had witnessed first-hand; the poverty that was afflicting the country. It was crazy, the whole place was defunct; it belonged to another decade, maybe another century . . . She was getting out: it was do or die.

Her plan was to get to Rasan about fifty miles outside Pyongyang, where the security would be much lower key than in the capital. She was about five miles away now from the crash scene. Her luck had held: the vehicle had burned ferociously for about twenty minutes; she continued to track the flames as she walked. Sie Roo's body would be nothing but ash and bone. Then the vehicle suddenly exploded.

Then she heard it: a military helicopter flying low over the area on its way back from a routine flight to Pyongyang. She had been shadowing the main rail line. Keeping out of sight, she darted into the undergrowth.

*   *   *

Officer Chan was reading reports when the radio suddenly crackled into life:

'This is Unit 515. We are approximately forty-eight miles north-east of the city centre and ten miles from Rasan station. A car is on fire just below us and burning intensely. We are about sixty feet above it and are going down to investigate. Please stand by for further information.'

The radio cut out and Chan and two other officers who had just entered his office all looked at each other.

Ten minutes went by.

'Five one five to Police Central. This is not a military vehicle. We have managed to partially extinguish the fire; please confirm the vehicle is one of yours? The identification number of the vehicle is PGN 125. There is a body in there, burnt beyond recognition. The vehicle appears to have left the roadway some two hundred feet above here, rolled over and caught fire.'

Chan grabbed the radio. 'Deputy Officer Chan here. That vehicle was being driven by Officer Sie Roo. He called in some time ago to inform us he was heading to that area on routine investigations. He was due back tomorrow, that's the message we had from him just over an hour ago. Do you wish us to get out there tonight?'

'Stand by, please; we need to contact our central control.' Chan and the other two just stood opened-mouthed.

'Well, looks like the bastard has fucked up this time.' Chan half smiled. 'Perhaps Miss Woo told him that she would never get involved with him and he drove off that ravine. It's the right place; wait till she hears of this.'

The other officer cut in: 'How do you mean, Chan?'

'Oh that bastard went to see her today to discuss her suspension. I bet he offered her a deal. Anyhow next thing I know he calls in saying he is going up the Rasan area and that Miss Woo has been sent, well ordered, to Chongjin and has been suspended indefinitely.'

The radio burst into life again. 'Unit 515 here. We have been advised by central control to leave two soldiers here. They will be relieved at first light. Can you please meet us here at around that time to investigate the matter, and recover the vehicle and the body?'

Chan, still holding the radio, said, 'Yes, we understand. We will meet you there at first light. Please forward the exact coordinates.'

A few minutes later Chan received the exact location and they agreed to meet the military relief helicopter there by 6.30 the next morning.

Five minutes later the helicopter departed leaving two soldiers on guard. Miss Woo heard it fly close by again; she was sure it had seen the burning wreck and reported it. It sounded like the helicopter had gone down to investigate. But it was dark and the car must surely be completely burnt out by now, she thought.

She had made it to a spot about ten yards from the main railway line, crouching down against an electrical box. In the distance she could see a trackside hut but she was not going to move for a while. Places like that were occasionally searched and if a lock was broken off it could trigger a search of the area. People had been stealing all sorts of things from the railway; even the copper wires of the phone cables would be cut down and sold for scrap just to buy food. So she waited for the cover of darkness.

Finally night fell and it was dark proper. It was now about eight o'clock, pitch black and deathly quiet. She could not even see her watch but was not going to chance using her lighter to illuminate its face. But she needed to move, so she got between the train rails and started walking as fast as possible. *'They would have found it by now, definitely,'* she thought, *'too late and dark to do anything now; if I can get a train soon, I should be in Chongjin by early morning.'*

She knew that once they found Sie Roo's gun was missing they would have their suspicions, or the body might not have burnt enough and it would be obvious by first light that Sie Roo had been shot. She knew they would eventually make a thorough examination of the body and then they would start a massive investigation. *'All I want is one night and part of a day. I never prayed much but I am praying now, God help me. . .'*

She had walked for around three hours and was now about ten miles from where she had joined the track. Chongjin was another two hundred miles. She continued for another twenty minutes then spotted a tiny light in the distance. Her heart raced and she began to breathe a bit faster, hoping she was nearing Rasan station. She picked up her pace. Another fifteen minutes went by. If her plan worked there would be no soldiers at the station. She felt in her trouser pocket for her gun.

It came as small pulses at first but then the unmistakable sound of an approaching train. She started to run as the sound got closer. She turned and there was the single beaming light of the train, Cyclops-like, slicing into the darkness.

The station platform was very dimly and inadequately lit but it was a pleasing sight. She got about one hundred yards from the start of the platform then darted behind a signalling panel and waited. Gradually, it came into view in all its magnificence; she had never been so happy to see a locomotive in her life even if it was an old rusting hulk. This decrepit beast might just be her last chance. She crouched down and waited. The train hissed and creaked as it passed her hiding place. The sound of the air brakes coming on and off intermittently broke the silence. The station lights seemed to have brightened now and a dim glow permeated from some of the carriage windows. As she peered out from the trackside panel she noticed most on board were asleep. She waited until the last carriage had passed. Normally at the back was a guard's van. If she was in luck it would be empty, or she could bribe the guard to take her on. She could not risk going for a ticket.

Two minutes later the train ground to a halt; the final blast from the air brakes locking on indicated that it had finally stopped.

She waited and watched. A few people got off. Suddenly twenty or thirty people appeared from a waiting-room and began the boarding process, all with heavy bags, some with small children, but mostly on their own and mainly men, travelling around from town to town seeking work. She noticed how ill they looked, how thin, and how dishevelled all their clothes were. She knew with even greater certainty now that she wanted to get out. She had closed her eyes to the reality of her country's plight long enough. Her brother was right: their dear leader was a liar and a fraud. She was ready to make her move.

There were no soldiers, only one policeman at the far end, talking to the driver. Suddenly, a hand went round her throat. She did not react. Then she felt another hand on her shoulder, forcing her to turn round. She looked straight into the man's face.

'What do you want?' she asked quietly.

'I need to get to Chongjin. Give me any money you've got.' His face was weather-beaten and dirty, his clothes had seen better days, but it seemed that under different circumstances he would have been a kind man. She spoke again, trying to reason with him.

'Please, I need to get on that train as well. If you help me, I've got a bit of money.'

He squeezed her throat. 'No, just give me your money. I could really hurt you.'

'Look, maybe we can help each other.'

'Forget it! Just give me that money. I'm warning you, I'll. . .' He never finished the sentence. She had in an instant spun round, yanked his head back by the hair, pulled her gun out and pushed it straight into his open mouth.

'You call out and I'll blow your head off. So, you understand? Just nod . . . slowly.'

His eyes had grown to twice the size they were and he could not even nod, so he just grunted.

'Now, go and knock on the door of that guard's van. If anybody is in it ask them for a ride. Tell them we are husband and wife looking for work. We need to get to Chongjin but don't have transfer papers. Tell him we'll pay him if he lets us ride in there.'

He stumbled back. 'Okay . . . okay,' he said, then turned and walked out into the half-light towards the rear of the guard's van. She followed him, staying in the shadows. He climbed the steps and tapped on the door. A few seconds passed. The door swung open.

'Oh, here we go, another tramp. Go on . . . clear off!' He was about to push him from the top of the steps when the man said:

'Listen, we have money and just need to get to Chongjin. They wouldn't give us transfer papers. We just want some work.'

'How much have you got?'

Miss Woo quickly emerged and jumped onto the steps. 'I have got the cash, here look.' The guard looked around at the other man.

'Well that's usual, the wife's got the money, so what you got?'

'Two thousand won.'

'Fuck off. I'm not losing my job for a month's wages. Forget it.'

Miss Woo was considering grabbing him and pulling him down from the top step but it would be pointless, so she accepted his superior bargaining position 'All right then, three thousand won. That's all we have.'

'Don't lie! Make it six thousand and you can come and travel in the warmth. I've got a bit of food. Come on, it's a good deal, but don't take too long. The police will be along soon, they always give me a knock just before we leave, to make sure everything's okay.'

He waited a few seconds then made to go back in.

'All right . . . all right, I've got six thousand here. Look!' She pulled it from her pocket. He snatched it from her, counting it quickly in the half-light.

'Okay then. Come on . . . hurry.'

The man and Miss Woo hurriedly entered the van and closed the door behind them.

'Right, get over there and keep quiet. I'll keep the lights off. He'll knock that door soon.' A few minutes went by then a bell sounded in the interior.

'It's okay . . . looks as though they aren't checking tonight.' He reached up and pressed a button. They both assumed it was some signal to the front of the train to proceed. Seconds later, the train began to depart. As it cleared the station he switched the single light on. It was dim but at least they could all see each other now. The van was warm and even though the seats were bare boards it was the most welcoming place she had been in the last five hours.

'Well, you two look like you are starving, especially you,' he said, peering closely at the man.

'Have you got any food?' he asked.

'I've got something. It's not much but you know how it is. To tell you the truth I don't even like taking your money, but even we don't get our money on time from the railway. It's incredible how many people are doing this. Look, I know you're not searching for work. You two are looking to get out, am I right?'

Miss Woo and the man remained silent.

'Hey, don't worry. I ain't bothered. Why do you think I risk doing things like this? I do it loads of times. Listen, I'm saving all this money to do the same one day. Good luck to you. Oh, by the way, you aren't husband and wife, but I really don't care.'

'How did you know that?' she said, realising there was little point keeping the pretence up.

'I don't know but, well, I think *you* are in the military, and if I am honest, when I saw you back there you looked like you were going to pull me out of this van. I don't know, it's just something about you, but as I say I really don't care and I don't care if you point a gun at me and arrest me and say you are both undercover, but there again, I know *he* is not.'

He pointed to the man with her. 'You are starving, you can't fake that, but you, miss, you look well fed . . . lean but well fed.' He smiled and turned back round. She stood up and walked over to him and looked him directly in the eyes.

'Well perhaps it's you who is the undercover officer?'

He turned and looked at her. She knew he was no agent, but she wanted to be sure. She stared at him for a few moments, then she could see it: he had fear in his eyes. Seconds later he looked away. Not wishing to continue the interrogation, the guard went to the small stove in the corner. Miss Woo looked over. It was pitiful. He had a small bowl of rice and some beans and a few vegetables. It would not really have fed one person.

'Listen, you two, eat that food. I'll just have coffee.'

'Thank you, miss,' said the guard.

The other man got to his feet. 'Yes, thank you, miss. I am starving and I'm ashamed of what I tried to do to you back there.'

The guard cooked what rice there was and made coffee. As the train trundled on they listened and swapped their own stories. She realised that they were all victims of circumstance. She was surprised how educated the man who had apprehended her was. He told them he had been a teacher but the school had closed because they could not pay the salaries any more. His son had escaped and promised he was going to return for him but there had been no news from him for some time. He travelled to Chongjin when he could afford to, then on to a border town called Musan where he got letters from his son through a woman he knew there. He wanted to get out but had never had enough money. His wife had died two months ago and then his life just spiralled out of control.

She listened intently and was sure her decision to get out was the right one. She just prayed that she could persuade her family.

As the train continued on its journey she mentally crossed her fingers; she had been lucky, so far. . .

28

She was trying to stay awake but could feel herself drifting off. She sat by the rear door looking into the darkness, contemplating her plight. The sound and tempo of the train wheels drifted into her mind. She started to think of her family. Could she persuade them to leave? Her brother would go. He could give his children a better life, but her mother? Would she leave? Her eyes felt heavy. The warmth of the guard's van felt good after her long walk in the cold. Her eyes closed.

'Miss, have this.' She looked up. The guard was holding out a cup of coffee. 'That's the last cup I can give you, so enjoy it.'

She got to her feet and took the cup gratefully, noticing that it was only half full but welcome none the less.

'Thanks. How long was I asleep?'

'About an hour.'

'How long before we arrive in Chongjin?'

'Well, should be about five-thirty, I reckon. They fixed a few of the old rails the other day and it's been getting a bit better; amazing isn't it? We are all starving but they find money to fix up this old decrepit railway, anyhow about a couple of hours or so.'

The guard busied himself cleaning the plates. Miss Woo and the man sat next to each other. She whispered to him, 'I never asked you your name.'

'It's Chi Ha,' he replied, 'and yours?'

She leaned in close. 'Just call me Woo for the moment. When we get out I am going to use my full name again, but for now that's fine.' She realised for the first time in a while she had actually smiled. Then she told him about her family and that she wanted to get them out. She had money and if there was enough, she could take Chi Ha with her.

'Listen,' he said. 'We need to get to Musan soon as we can. That village, it's a real hotbed of corruption, but I know a lot of people there. Maybe we can help each other. I have no money but I do have some good contacts and I know a safe house.'

'Chi Ha, it sounds a fair arrangement. I will pay for you to come with us; then hopefully tomorrow we can get across. Once we are in China, we can make contact with the people your son told me of; but I must get to my mother's first. I will persuade them all to leave, they have to.'

They could feel the train slowing. Chi Ha went to the window and the guard called to them.

'You need to get off here. I can't let you travel any further. Keep away from the tracks. Get into the woods and make your way to the town that way. And, miss, you need to dress down.'

'Dress down?' she enquired.

'You look too well. You both need to look a complete mess, and make yourselves smell of shit. I'm serious!'

'Thanks for the advice,' she said. 'I would say I enjoyed doing business with you but that would not be true; I think you must be a rich man now?'

'Hey, you got a good deal. Look, come on, you need to go.'

She nodded at him then turned to Chi Ha, saying, 'Come on, when it's doing about ten miles an hour we can jump.' She grabbed her bag and Chi Ha picked up his few belongings.

About a mile from the station they both jumped off the train, landing either side of the tracks. They crossed into the wooded area that would take them close to the town, making their way until eventually they were parallel with the station but about a mile to the north. This was a back route into the town; armed with the rail guard's advice, they knew what to do.

Before emerging into the town they passed intentionally through one of the old farms then onto the main road. Miss Woo had ripped most of her clothes and deliberately stumbled a few times in the muddy fields. They had rubbed animal excrement on their clothes, and now both looked and smelt like authentic tramps, wandering about, appearing desperate for any scraps of food. As they approached the station area, they really blended in. She was surprised how bad the situation was getting. They reached the other side of the station. It was shocking to see how quickly things had deteriorated even in the short time she had been away.

Like before, children were walking around aimlessly, almost in a trance, their faces ashen, clothes practically rags; they were malnourished and filthy. Men and women picked scraps up from the pot-holed and muddy streets. She even saw a woman picking up dog excrement and finding bits of undigested food in it. That's what it had come to. She turned away in utter disgust then looked up. There it was, a larger than life picture of their dear leader, Kim Jong-il, looking down on his failed Stalinist dream: a utopia for him and his elite but to the ordinary people just a crumbling mess.

It was an interesting paradox that the country presented to the outside world: a shimmering, gilt-edged façade, but scratch the surface, pull the curtain back, and it was all smoke and mirrors. They walked on.

'Come on,' she said. 'It's about half an hour to my mother's. Hopefully she'll have some food. Are you okay?' She could see that Chi Ha was suffering now; he coughed and was stooped over, looking like a man twice his age, which she guessed was around mid-forties.

'I'm okay, thanks. I can make it. Don't worry.'

She rubbed his back. 'Okay, come on then, we'll soon be there.'

*   *   *

She tapped lightly on the glass panel: there was no sound. It had just gone six o'clock in the morning and was getting light. She tapped again, then, hearing someone stirring, she stood back, with Chi Ha behind her. The door opened. At first, her mother did not recognise her; she just stared.

'Oh my God, it's you! What happened to you?'

'Just let us in. This is a friend of mine.' She turned and pointed at Chi Ha, who duly nodded.

'But what has happened and who is this?'

'Mum, we can't talk out here; quick, before the neighbours see us.'

She backed into the hallway and called them both in, Chi Ha closing the door behind him.

'What is that smell?' Her mother pinched her nose.

'Mum, I will explain it all in a while. We obviously need to clean up. This is Chi Ha; he is a friend of mine. We're helping each other.'

Her mother nodded at Chi Ha then said, 'Oh I see, you are both undercover.'

Miss Woo rolled her eyes and Chi Ha smiled. 'No, Mum, this is serious, let Chi Ha have a wash and ask To San for some of his clothes. They're about the same size. Oh and don't bother with his old ones, just burn them. I'm okay, I have my own clothes with me.'

The old woman nodded and showed him the way to the small bathroom. 'Oh, Chi Ha was it?' she said, unsure.

'Yes, madam, that's right.'

'Chi Ha, there is hardly any hot water but, well, if you are a friend of my daughter's then you are welcome to what we have.' He touched her shoulder.

'Thank you, madam, and that's a whole lot more than I have got at this precise moment.'

'Look, go and have your shower. I will wake my son and get you some clothes, go on,' she said, indicating for him to go into the bathroom. Then she went back to the lounge. Miss Woo was sitting down by the window. 'What the hell happened to you then, darling?' said her mother.

'Mum, look, let me get these clothes off; even I can smell them now. Can't believe I was actually getting used to it.' They began to talk as she took off all her clothes. Her mother went to the balcony, returning with an old sack and placed them all inside. Then she passed her daughter a towel to put round herself. She then went to wake To San, who came into the lounge.

'What the hell is going on?' he said.

'Look, sit down while Mum makes some tea. I will tell you the story, but in the meantime have you got spare clothes for the man with me?'

'Yeah and who the hell is that?'

He was getting agitated and pointing toward the bathroom.

'Look, listen and calm down, sit down and wait till Mum comes back with this tea. We need to talk; oh, how are the boys?'

To San sat next to her and looked down at the bare floor of the spartan room. 'Well, sis, if I am honest with you, not good. I am worried; it's getting worse every day here. You know a few days ago there was no food, and I mean no food.'

Miss Woo looked alarmed. 'What did you do? How did you manage?'

'Mum and I had to go without for two days just so the boys could eat and that was only enough for one really; it's horrendous, a horrendous fucking joke.' He wiped tears from his eyes: they were the tears of a proud father who was watching helpless as his two young sons were beginning to show signs of serious malnourishment. She put her arm round him.

'Listen, I am going to tell you a story in a minute when Mum brings that tea in, but let me tell you this, we're getting out. That man was like you, To San, a proud man with a family and a good job as a teacher. He'll tell you his own story, but the point is, he knows Musan very well and has contacts there. He wants to get out.'

'What do you mean?' asked her brother, incredulously. 'What, how, when?'

'I'll explain later. . .'

'But it costs money, you have no idea how much. . .' he argued.

'I have money,' she said. 'I've brought all the money I have. It is enough.'

'For whom?'

'For all of us. Bad things have happened, and worse things are to come if we don't get out. My family is the most precious thing I have, and we are going to have a better life, all of us.'

Her brother turned to her. 'Really? You're really going to take all of us?'

'I am. I think I've got enough to at least get us across the border and spend a week or so in a safe house. After that, well . . . we'll figure it out.'

Over the next ten minutes, she told them the whole story. Her mother nearly fainted when she told her what had happened to Sie Roo. She was going to lie but decided there was no point. They would all have to make a break for it now; she was sorry but it was the only way.

Chi Ha appeared round the lounge door. 'Is it okay to come in?'

'Yes, come on, have some tea. I'm afraid that's all I can offer, sorry,' said Miss Woo's mother.

'Thank you again, madam.'

Miss Woo's brother shook hands with him and they chatted briefly. Chi Ha told all of them about his situation. They talked for another twenty minutes, eventually agreeing they were all going. Miss Woo's mother would go into the town and see if there was any food available, especially now Miss Woo had brought a substantial sum of cash with her. They would then eat and wait till it got to about four o'clock. It would take about two hours to get to Musan. Miss Woo's brother knew of a farmer who would, for a fee, take them by truck.

Miss Woo, in the meantime, got herself cleaned up. The shower was cold. The boiler was practically broken down; nobody ever came to service it, let alone carry out repairs. The same was true of the electrical system: half the sockets in the apartment were not working and it should have been rewired over twenty years ago. In the 1950s it had been state of the art but now, like most things, it was held together with parts cannibalised from empty apartments and a few prayers.

Her mother left for the shops about two hours later, taking her two grandchildren with her. Her brother, To San, left half an hour later to find his friend, who knew the farmer, but time was running out and they had to get out tonight. With the apartment empty Miss Woo began to worry what was happening back at the crash site. It was nearly nine o'clock.

29

Chan had arrived at the scene at just gone 7 a.m. having been taken by helicopter. Two other officers were sent by car. A recovery vehicle had been called for but would not arrive until 10.30 a.m. Also, the position of the car was going to make things awkward, as it was stuck at the bottom of the steep banking, on its side, completely burnt out and surrounded by ploughed fields.

Chan looked into the car. It was as black as coal in the vehicle and the smell made him want to retch. All that was left of the body were odd bits of flesh. Parts of his skull could be seen and some teeth were visible. Chan looked away, just confirming the vehicle's identity and that the body was probably that of Sie Roo, although he could not confirm that from what was left of it. A cursory inspection led him to conclude the obvious: just a simple accident.

'Can you get me up there please?' Chan said to the pilot.

'Well, yes, but you will have to jump the last few feet; the roadway is just too narrow at the point to set down.'

'Okay fine, let's go then.'

Ten minutes later Chan jumped from the helicopter, telling the pilot he would wait there once he'd looked around. The other officers had called and were ten minutes away. Chan went over to marks on the roadway and ran his boot over them. It had rained in the night, only lightly, but there was some evidence of heavy braking close to the edge. He walked up a bit further, looked down into the valley, then came back down to the spot where the car had clearly gone over. Peering over the edge, he noticed something about three feet down the bank. He lay down carefully and tried to reach it. He tried twice, then a third time. It was precarious and he was going to leave it; then he gave it one last go using his other hand to hold on to a small jutting rock. He clasped it and dragged it up. He was surprised to see he was holding a jack and one definitely from one of their cars, presumably from Sie Roo's car. He was puzzled. Maybe the car had had a puncture and had toppled over the edge. But if it had what was he doing inside?

Turning and walking down the steep incline, he kept looking over the banking, and then he noticed it: a cigarette butt lying barely visible under some bracken about a foot down the bank. He picked it up. Sie Roo did not smoke and that jack was definitely from that car.

He was thinking of possible scenarios when he heard a vehicle, guessing it was his two officers approaching. Just before they rounded the bend he threw the jack back down into the valley and did the same with the cigarette butt, then cleaned his hands by slapping them together. Seconds later the police car appeared around the bend; they stopped and called. 'Is it him, sir?'

Chan walked a few steps until he was alongside the vehicle. 'Well, yes, it's his car all right, and the body inside is burnt to a complete cinder, so really I don't know, but who else would it be?'

'Everybody is talking about it now, once the morning shift came on. Sir, to a man and a woman, everybody is pleased.'

Chan wagged his finger at both of them. 'Okay, let's have no more of this talk now, I am serious, I don't want it, you understand?' They both nodded. 'Come on, I am finished here. I've looked around and all I can see is what's left of some witness marks at the top of that bend, and the banking is just crushed where the car obviously went over. The recovery vehicle will not be here until ten-thirty so we may as well go back to Pyongyang.'

'What about the body, sir?' asked one of the officers.

'It's all just too badly burnt, it needs a forensic team to thoroughly examine it.'

Back at headquarters Chan put a call through to a local police station in the Chongjin area, about three miles from Miss Woo's mother's house. 'Yes, that's right. I want you to send a car round. There has been an incident here with our chief officer and she was probably the last person to see him. I just need to talk to her, to confirm a few things; that's all. Send someone out and just get her on the car radio.' The officer at Chongjin said he would send a car within the next ten minutes; Chan looked at his office clock. It was ten past nine.

She was in the bathroom when Chi Ha tapped on the door. 'Woo, get out here quick. There's a policeman at the door. I can see his uniform through the glass.'

Checking her pocket, she felt for her gun and opened the bathroom door.

'Right, get in there and keep quiet.' She shoved Chi Ha in, then, straightening herself up, she walked to the door and opened it.

'Yes?' she said abruptly.

'Are you Miss Woo?' asked the officer.

'I am. What can I do for you?' She noticed he was on his own but her right hand was at her side all the time just making contact with the gun and feeling its shape through her trousers.

'Miss Woo, Officer Chan from Pyongyang called us. There has been an accident involving the Chief of Police. Apparently he crashed his car and has been killed. Officer Chan wants to speak with you. Can you come to the radio in the car?'

She closed the door behind her. 'Well that's terrible! When did all this happen?' As they walked down the flight of stairs he turned to her.

'Sometime last night; apparently you may have been the last person to see him.'

'Well he dropped me off. We were going to the main station, but I asked him to drop me off just before as I needed to get some things for my family. I never saw him after that.'

The officer nodded. 'The car is just there.' He pointed over to the corner of the road.

'Hello, Chan, what's this I've just heard?'

'Miss Woo, we can't formally identify the body yet but it's his car; there is a body inside, although it's completely unrecognisable. In the last communication he made, he informed control that he dropped you off and was making his way to Rasan. Can you confirm that?'

Miss Woo confirmed that he had been to see her, and told her that she was to be suspended for a while, pending an investigation, but he had agreed to take her to Pyongyang. Again, she made a point of saying that she had been dropped in the main shopping area and spent some time there before going to the station. 'That's about all I can tell you really. What is to happen to my situation now then?'

'We have to wait until all the forensics gets sorted, but then I think it best you come back here. I will let you know. You know what?'

'What's that, Chan?'

'He was talking about jacking it all in as well. Never smoked, never drank. He was a good officer and that happens. Well, I'll keep you posted.'

'Okay, thanks, Chan.' She handed the radio back to the officer. 'If you have any more news, please let me know.'

He saluted her then closed the driver's door and pulled away. She nodded and walked in the opposite direction, but she knew . . . *'talking about jacking it in . . . never smoked . . . that bastard never smoked and he would never have left that job, he loved it . . . I know the bastard never smoked, so what? Why mention . . .'* Then she got it! *Thanks, Chan, thanks . . .'* Chan knew and had given her the best coded warning he could. He'd guessed what had happened and he figured that she was somehow involved.

They all had to leave and leave now. She walked as fast as she could back to her mother's apartment. Chi Ha let her in and she explained what had occurred. Together they grabbed all the cases they could find and set to work packing. Soon after, her mother and the two boys arrived back with food. Hopefully it would be enough. Ten minutes later, her brother got back. She informed them of the situation and they looked at the packed cases.

'But the truck won't be here till four. That's what I agreed.'

'How far is his place?' she said.

'It takes about an hour to walk from here; his farm is just at the edge of town.'

'Right, we leave now. Come on.' They looked like a family going on holiday, only in the North there were few people who could afford to do that. But many of her mother's friends and neighbours knew Miss Woo had a high profile job and would assume that perhaps she was taking them back to the capital for a while. So as they walked they nodded a few times, smiled and looked as innocent as they could.

Arriving at the farm, To San told them to all wait at the entrance.

'No, I'm coming with you. I need to speak with him. He needs to take us now.'

'Be quiet. I'm sorting this out.'

Miss Woo walked straight past him. 'To San, if you want your boys to have a new life then please come with me, but then leave the rest to me.' To San continued to argue as they got close to the small farmhouse.

Reaching the door first, he knocked. There was no answer. He continued a few more times. Miss Woo looked in through one of the windows. It was a ramshackle place. What was left of the curtains partially obscured her view into the room; that and the filthy window. The frame had almost rotted away. She figured that if she pressed on the glass it would fall through, probably taking the frame with it. She stood back and looked up. Many of the roof tiles were missing and others seemed precariously balanced and without any symmetry. No wonder he had taken to smuggling people to the border, his farm was not earning any money, she thought.

She called to her brother: 'To San, come on, let's look around, he must be around somewhere.' They looked over to some outbuildings and as they were making their way there the farmer suddenly appeared.

'Hey, what do you want?' he shouted. Then, recognising To San, he mellowed slightly. 'Oh, you were here earlier. I thought we agreed four o'clock?'

Miss Woo strode past her brother: 'I'm sorry, but our plans have changed. We have our family with us. They are waiting outside and we need to leave immediately. Where is your vehicle?'

'Just hold on a minute. You can't come in here making demands.'

'Okay, how much extra is it going to cost?' she countered.

'Twice the agreed amount, as you're obviously in some serious trouble.'

She nodded. 'Let's go over there and negotiate.' She indicated one of the buildings. Her brother went to follow.

'No, To San, go and get Mum and the boys. Bring them here, quickly now.'

She walked with the farmer till they got just inside the shed. 'Where's your truck then?' She looked round. Over in the far corner a few underfed pigs were searching for food. There was a tractor against another wall with no wheels. The entire place was hanging on to commercial viability by a thread.

'Give me the other payment now.'

She looked at him. 'My friend, I can see how things are here but I appeal to you as a fellow citizen and a human being. I can't afford any more, so will you help us, please?'

'If you come back as we agreed earlier then it's no extra but right now no. I've got other things going on, so you have to pay. It's that simple.' He held his hand out and half turned to walk out of the open building 'Well, are you paying?'

How she had done it he could not figure out, but in a second or two he was lying on the muddy ground, slightly dazed and with a gun pointing at him.

'Now, I tried to appeal to your humanity, but it seems as if that has deserted us all in this godforsaken place, so I am now appealing to your common sense. Go and get that truck or I will drive it myself, leave you here tied up with your pigs and will inform the local police about your clandestine activities. It's up to you. But no more cash.'

He was not going to argue. She did not look the type to cross. 'Okay, all right. It's round the back here. I've got to put some fuel in it and you'll all have to get under the silage that I'm taking to Musan, so it's a genuine trip. I never get stopped.'

She pulled him to his feet and put her gun away.

'Come on then, but I will sit next to you. If anybody stops us I am your wife, lover . . . I don't care.'

He cleaned himself down and they walked around the building. His truck was like everything else, long overdue for replacement but, with luck, this was going to be the last mode of transport Miss Woo would see in her country. She imagined that just across the border were farms that prospered, free from the yoke of totalitarianism. She kept that picture in her mind. *'I am always going to remember this old truck, as our final lifeboat,'* she thought.

She watched as he filled it with diesel then loaded the silage. She jumped in the front and they drove back past the other outbuildings to where all the others were waiting. They got under the mound as best they could; the smell was high and penetrated the nostrils like smelling salts. They wanted to retch, but the price was low in comparison to what they were leaving behind.

A few moments later, with Miss Woo in the front, they pulled out onto the dusty roadway. It had just gone midday.

It was about fifty miles to Musan and with their agreed route, avoiding main roads, and keeping to the dusty farm tracks, it would take them about three hours. Chi Ha had been there many times, but mostly by train, to look for his son. He had got to know a safe house, where they, for a deposit fee, would collect letters sent by former citizens now on the Chinese side, and pass them on upon further payment.

In Musan life was much more liberal than in the south of the country. It was something akin to a wild-west gold-rush town of nineteenth-century America. Occasionally there would be the investigative journalists, who chanced crossing the border to get a glimpse of life in this secretive land. Bribery and corruption were endemic and brazen; people would often be seen with cell phones, although they were strictly banned in North Korea. Prostitutes could offer their services virtually out in the open, goods were traded on the street and markets operated late into the evening, albeit with the light of Chinese-made generators smuggled across the border. The spirit of capitalism was thriving in this far outpost of the extremist communist state.

Occasionally there would be a crackdown and the military would take the place over for a while. Most of the local police would be removed, charged with corruption and assigned to other duties if they were lucky. Mostly they would be sent to labour camps. Prostitutes would suffer a similar fate. Younger girls would be sent to work in factories, market traders would have all their goods impounded and other property confiscated.

The biggest problem was the border. China was the other side of the town, just separated by the Tumen River, which at certain points and at the right time of year, could be waded across. Or if you were a good swimmer you could cross it in just under one minute. But at these points, guards were always milling about. However, it had been a few months since a crackdown; sometimes it could be over a year.

These guards could be bribed. A guard posted there for three months, who was prepared to take money from people desperate to get out, could make three, sometimes four years' wages in that

time, and would still have their military salary. But they also had
to be careful. Sometimes, secret military police posing as escapees
would attempt a bribe. If the guards accepted, they were taken
away and quietly shot.

There was also a special unit that would occasionally be deployed
along the remote border; an elite team who would infiltrate the
refugee gangs or even threaten them. They were rumoured to be
the most dangerous and feared people in the country. Only a
handful of people knew of their real existence and, generally,
they dealt with more clandestine security issues that the State
would not tolerate. It was a useful ploy by the regime; it engendered
fear into potential escapees and fear was the regime's weapon of
choice. Men would be found, either shot or with their throats
cut, lying by the banks of the Tumen River or floating in it. That
was the chance you took, but many did. It was worth it for a new
life and that was the gamble.

All this – the illegal commerce, prostitution, vice and general
corruption that went on – gave the whole area a highly charged
atmosphere. It was vibrant and exciting and one of the most
dangerous places in the country. For some it was an intoxicating
mix. Anything could be bought or sold; there was no morality,
just cold hard cash, and that was the only game in town. You
had to be on your guard, living by your wits all the time. But
people would flock there, some never wanting to escape, just to
have a different life for a while, make some money, then go back
to their normal life. So there it was: a small island town of
capitalism completely out of kilter, land-locked by the most isolated
country on the planet.

It had just gone three o'clock as Miss Woo looked at her watch.
The journey seemed to go on forever. The farmer pulled off the
track into a small clearing. She jumped out, tugging as fast as
she could at the rotting mound. Her nephews were crying and
her mother wanted to go back. She did not want to go on now;
she'd heard stories of what happened if you were caught, but

Miss Woo was in no mood for dissent. She argued with them and said that this was their last chance, telling her mother and brother that if they stayed they would probably starve to death. The farmer, although still aggrieved with her, concluded she was right. He turned to her mother.

'Your daughter is right: listen, I have a farm and what are we producing? Well I tell you, nothing, virtually nothing. There is no fertiliser, no machinery, I can't even pay people to work for me; we don't even have fresh seed to plant. It's going to collapse. I don't know when but, well, it will.' They all just looked at her.

'But what if we get caught?' said Woo's mother. Then the farmer went to wish them luck and said:

'Listen, I don't know you people but I tell you, with this woman with you, you stand a real chance.' He then turned to face Miss Woo.

'I am not happy what you did to me back there, I don't know what you did in your former work and, well, I don't want to know, but I think you are a very clever and resourceful woman; there is something about you. . .' He cut the conversation and wished them good luck, telling them to wait here now until dark and then they could make their way into the town.

Chi Ha nodded and confirmed he knew the way from here. They shook hands and the farmer jumped back in his truck and headed off.

Her brother looked at her 'What did he mean? What did you do to him back there? You have antagonised him now. Look, he may just drive into the town and give us away. You are mad, come on, what did you do?'

'To San, listen to me, he won't do anything; look, if he does his lucrative illegal business will be over. Added to that he is still not sure if I was working for the State, a double bluff. He knows that even if I am we are not after him, so he will keep his mouth shut.'

'But what did you say to him? Did you have to pay more money?'

'To San, I will get you out, you understand?'

Before they made their way into the town, Miss Woo called Chi Ha over then whispered to him.

'Here is my gun. Don't let them see that I've given it to you. If anything happens to me, promise you will get my family out.'

He looked down at the compact weapon. 'Well that's the second time I have seen it and it still frightens me. I have never even held one let alone fired one.'

'Listen, don't worry. Just take it, please, and promise me that, will you?'

'Yes but I have never used a gun.' She turned the gun on one edge, explaining the operation of the safety catch. He looked at it again then put it in his trouser pocket.

'Okay, Woo, I promise.' She held his hand.

'Thank you. Hopefully we will all make it.'

After about an hour the town came into view. It was just getting to dusk and Chi Ha shepherded them to the old market area where they went unnoticed amongst the crowd seeking food and goods. Women looking for men, plying their trade, some openly; some perhaps seeking to find redemption. They were close now. A few dim lights hanging from the market stalls, people milling around. As they got closer the sound of small generators punctuated the evening air, humming away. The sound of barter and chatter was clear now.

They entered from a side street, Chi Ha guiding them. Traders sat on the floor with their wares. There was food everywhere; it was tempting to buy whatever they could, but Miss Woo had told them no more money was to be spent now. So they pressed on through the scrum of market stalls and street traders.

Miss Woo was really shocked. Officers were always being told to shut these sort of places down in Pyongyang but in reality she and Chan would turn a blind eye to it. It was only Sie Roo who would insist on breaking them up and confiscating the goods. Yes she was shocked but she did not care at all now; they were leaving this place. A few ladies of the night came into view but disappeared into the shadows as they all walked on. Then eventually they all turned down a side street. Chi Ha approached a door and knocked. A few seconds passed. The door opened slowly, and a woman appeared, but it was dark inside and she was just visible. He spoke to her for a minute. She looked out, had a good look, then called them all in.

Once the door closed behind them, the lights were switched on. Now the place was bathed in light but that was not discernible from the outside as her curtains were so thick it was impossible for light to escape. The room was clean with a large table to one side and chairs around the edge. Miss Woo could see it was clearly set up for business. She noticed there was another door that was closed. She assumed that this would lead to the rest of the house where she reasoned that normal family life might take place. This was more like a doctor's waiting-room.

Chi Ha spoke. 'Do you have any letters for me?'

'Yes, I think your son has written again,' she replied, going to a cupboard next to the table. She opened it, exposing a pile of letters. It was like a miniature sorting office; she looked left and right for a few seconds and then said, 'Ah yes, here it is.' She passed a scruffy looking envelope to Chi Ha. He looked happily at the envelope, carefully examining the writing on it. Then he placed it in his pocket and passed her some money.

'Thank you,' she replied. 'Now what can I help you with?' Chi Ha explained that they all wanted to get out tonight. Could she arrange it and how much would it cost?

They negotiated for about half an hour and eventually an agreement was reached. It was going to cost twenty-four thousand won for all of them, including Chi Ha. Reluctantly, Miss Woo handed the money over, not in the sense that she regretted the cost, but with the realisation that this was virtually a whole year's wage for the average North Korean manual worker.

Chi Ha took Miss Woo's hand. 'Thank you for this. I have only ever come here to get letters. I would never have been able to get out. Thank you.'

They smiled at each other. Her mother just wished to get going and her brother was getting worried.

'What happens at the other side?' asked Chi Ha.

'We have people the other side who will get you into the next town,' explained the woman, 'then you will be able to stay there while the passports are arranged. You will have to pay separately for those but once you get to China, you are three-quarters of the way through your journey.'

They stood around for another five minutes while she made a call on a cell phone she pulled from her pocket. Then someone knocked on the door and the woman quickly turned the room lights off. She opened the door, and two people could be seen in the half-light that shone in from the road: a man and a woman.

'Where's the other one? The regular one?' asked the woman in the house.

'He's not well, but she is a friend of mine, we go with her.'

Miss Woo and the others thanked the lady and she wished them good luck. They walked into the street following the man and woman into the night.

They had been walking mostly on rutted back roads, sometimes through muddy fields, but here the ground was hard. Winter was setting in, and normally around this time of year they would be expecting snow, but it had held off so far. Soon they reached thick woods, and eventually, after another ten minutes, they stopped at a clearing.

'Now we wait here for a while. When your guide is on the other side he will call me.' The man produced a cell phone, its face suddenly throwing light into the sea of black that surrounded them. The sound of the Tumen River rushing past was clear but they were not close enough to see it. Miss Woo's mother said, 'It sounds deep. Will we be able to wade across?'

'Yes, don't worry. It's quite low at the moment. It's just the stones that make it sound fast. I've got torches.'

It was as he was fiddling with his phone that Miss Woo noticed the woman's face in the light from the phone screen. She looked closely, and then she began to study her, from top to bottom then back again. She walked slightly closer to Chi Ha, and rubbed his shoulders.

'You look like you need warming up.' She moved closer to him. He looked shocked.

'Woo, I'm fine . . . really.'

She continued, then stood on her toes and, leaning towards him, whispered, 'Don't look at her now, but that woman with him . . . there's something not right about her.'

Chi Ha replied loudly, 'Oh, okay, Woo. I'll let you warm me up.'

Miss Woo smiled at him, as he had given her the opportunity she wanted to continue her whispered conversation. 'I'm sure she's from the military. Look how lean she is, her gait, everything . . . believe me, I can tell.'

Chi Ha carried on loudly. 'Oh do my shoulders a bit more. They're still cold!'

Miss Woo's brother looked over, embarrassed, as if this was some overt display of affection. She leaned in again. 'If anything happens, promise you'll get my family over.'

He whispered back, 'Of course, don't worry. I'll deal with her if she tries anything.'

Miss Woo looked him straight in the eyes. Her mother looked away with embarrassment; she thought they were kissing. Woo said, 'Chi Ha, believe me, if she is who I think she is, you won't stand a chance. She'd kill you. Just promise me . . . get my family over.' She gripped his hand then moved away.

She moved closer to the man with the phone and stood perfectly still. 'Ah, I've got a message. We have to go this way.' He signalled for them to move to the right. Miss Woo tapped him on the shoulder.

'Why? I've been looking, and this is the narrowest point. It widens up there, and where is your man? Shouldn't he signal us from the other bank first?' He turned and froze. Miss Woo's piercing eyes burned into him. He started to stutter, then dropped the phone and ran off.

The other women turned and shouted after him. 'You fool!' She turned back quickly, looking at Chi Ha and the rest of the group. 'You are all under arrest. I am an officer of the People's Army. You will all come this way.' She produced a small gun and pointed it at them.

Miss Woo's mother started to cry, her brother tried to reason with the woman. Miss Woo eventually spoke: 'You are wasting your time, this piece of shit licks the dear father's arse and she probably fucks him too.'

Miss Woo's mother put her hands to her ears. Her brother was so shocked he just shouted, 'What language, stop it!'

But she continued. Miss Woo looked at the woman directly. 'You make me sick. You hold that gun to us, and two small children. You are nothing but a coward.' Then she spat in contempt.

Miss Woo's vitriol had the desired effect. She knew exactly what she was saying and it was cutting into the woman like a scalpel. The woman put her gun back in her pocket.

'Okay, I'm giving you this one chance. If the rest of you can get away before I finish her, then . . .'

Miss Woo's mother screamed. Then Miss Woo shouted, 'Go, all of you, now.' She looked down and kicked the man's phone over to Chi Ha. 'Take that with you. Just go!'

Chi Ha grabbed it and then, picking up both of the children, ran over to the river bank. Woo's mother just looked; her brother pulled her. 'Come on, Mum, come on.' She was screaming, but as he stumbled down the bank Chi Ha shouted up:

'To San, if you don't come now, your boys will be in China and you will be in prison.' To San grabbed his mother and they slid down the bank and started to cross. The water was freezing but it was shallow; they kept going.

Miss Woo just looked at the woman, knowing she was probably going to die. *'After all this,'* she thought, *'all this way I have come. . .'* Suddenly she went reeling. A kick directly into her chest sent her flying backwards. Then advancing, the woman launched another perfect kick, which threw Miss Woo to the ground.

'Well?' The woman looked down. 'I'll give you one more chance.' She stood back and let Miss Woo get to her feet. Still out of breath, she was not going to be taken by surprise again. Miss Woo circled, and after a few feints, managed to grab the woman's arm. She pulled and twisted it, then, as the woman's body twisted, she kicked her in the stomach. The woman didn't flinch. Her stomach felt like steel. Miss Woo continued to twist her arm, but suddenly she found herself on the ground again. She got to her feet, went in close and managed to get her opponent by the throat. Usually, she could disable a man with this hold, but the woman head-butted her. Dazed, she went backwards, but managed to get in a kick, just halting the woman's progress for a few precious seconds.

Miss Woo's head was spinning; she felt sick, her nose was starting to bleed, and perhaps one of her ribs was broken. They re-engaged. Miss Woo fought hard to prevent her getting a hand anywhere near her throat. If the woman did, she knew it would be over. She would snap her neck, no question. They continued to struggle, matching blow for blow. Then, as they both began to weaken, the woman went for the gun in her pocket. They crashed to the ground. The woman was trying desperately to get her gun out, but suddenly a single shot rang out. Miss Woo couldn't see. Blood was all over her face, in her mouth. Coughing and coughing, she wiped her eyes. The woman rolled to one side.

Chi Ha stood over the woman. He had got back across the river, climbed up the bank and, using Miss Woo's gun to full effect, he'd shot the woman in the back of the head, the bullet narrowly missing Miss Woo. But the blood had spurted over her face.

Chi Ha threw the gun down and looked at her. 'I am glad I killed her, I've never hurt a human being in my life. I am a pacifist.

I was a teacher. . .' He started to cry, then was sick. She got up and walked over to him.

'Come on, let's go.' Looking at him with a comforting smile, she said: 'Well, Chi Ha, I'm glad you killed her!'

They put an arm round each other and, after Miss Woo had tossed the gun away, they crossed the Tumen River.

As they climbed the bank on the opposite side she knew the worst of it was over. They were on Chinese soil.

The cell phone started ringing. Chi Ha answered and a man speaking Korean with a Chinese accent directed them towards the road. A few minutes went by, and then some headlights came into view. A car stopped and a man opened the door. He took one look at Miss Woo.

'What the hell happened to you?'

She just smiled, 'Nothing. I'm fine. I just paid the price of freedom, that's all.'

They got in. Miss Woo turned to Chi Ha. 'Thank you. You're a brave man.' She hugged him. To San shook his hand and his boys did the same. Her mother hugged him and thanked him again.

Then Chi Ha turned to her mother: 'Thank you all, but I have to tell you, your daughter is the bravest woman I have ever seen. When I came up that bank and saw you fighting with that bitch, I could not believe it. I am never going to forget this, I feel I have lived a lifetime in a day!'

Miss Woo's mother looked at her and said, 'Yes, she was always a crazy child, but thank you, my daughter, you are so brave, thank you.' She wiped her eyes and held her daughter's hand.

Finally Chi Ha said, 'Well?' looking at Miss Woo, 'well, what is your full name? We are free now, no more *Miss Woo*, so?'

She turned to him and smiled. 'Yes you are right: my name is Ti Woo, but well, being as you saved my life: just call me Woo!' They all laughed.

*   *   *

The car drove on through the night, arriving eventually at one of the Chinese safe houses. For many Chinese families in that area taking refugees in was a very lucrative trade.

They explained that they wanted to get to South Korea. Miss Woo had money and was prepared to pay, but North Korean currency did not have much value. However, once she revealed who she was, the family agreed to lend them money as it was clear that she would not only be getting the usual resettlement grant from the South Korean government but she would also be able to cut herself a good deal with the South Korean newspapers, as well as international press, who would love the story.

Their Chinese hosts would stump up money for them in return for a good profit on the loan. It was done on trust but it was rare that anybody defaulted. To do so would jeopardise others that wished to get out of North Korea; the stain on a person's reputation would be indelible. It all worked like a well-oiled machine and suited everybody concerned. Once the deal had been concluded, they were told that after a few weeks they would get false passports and eventually a flight into South Korea.

Seven weeks later, Miss Woo, Chi Ha, To San, their mother and the two boys arrived at Seoul's Incheon airport on separate flights. They confessed who they were and asked for asylum.

Miss Woo, as a high-ranking police officer, was a great coup for the South Koreans. They debriefed her for just over a week, and she was happy to tell them all about life in the North: the brutality of the place, the depravations. . . She held nothing back, after which she got her prearranged deal with a South Korean newspaper, and with the money from that, she settled her debts to the Chinese family through an agent.

Eventually, the family received resettlement money from the South Korean government to get them back on their feet and a specialist agency assisted them in finding work and places to live. The story was all over the papers.

Woo's brother was given a home and he eventually found work;

her mother got a job as a domestic cleaner. Chi Ha, after intensive and exhaustive enquiries, located his son. Ti Woo moved to her own apartment and was considering working back in the police force, having spoken to them about it, but in the meantime found work in a nearby factory.

She came home one day to find a message on her answerphone from Ca Foo of the resettlement section: 'We had a call from a man at *The Washington Post*, who heard your story. He has news for you about a man who knows you, an American. We would not give your number but he left his, asked us to pass it on. Call him if you wish. . .'

She listened to the message again and wrote Bill Orson's number down. That evening she would listen to the message two or three times. She went to bed that night wondering what this was all about; who could possibly know her? And then it struck her: could it be? Could it really be *him*?

30

Her phone was buzzing; it woke her from a deep sleep, and she grabbed it from the side of the bed. 'Hello.'

'Woo, it's Chi Ha, how are you? Hey, I have not seen you for a while, I was going to call round today; you're not working over the weekend are you?'

'No that's fine, look, let's meet for lunch.'

'Okay, look forward to it, say about one?'

She looked at the bedside clock; it was showing 8.45 on the digital display.

'That's fine, see you then.'

She turned onto her side, wanting to grab another few hours' sleep. After hearing that message she'd received yesterday she could not get it out of her mind.

Since they'd arrived in South Korea, Ti Woo and Chi Ha had become firm friends. And once they were reunited Chi Ha soon took his son over to see Ti Woo. They got on really well. The boy was shocked that someone like her would have wanted to escape, but he could see her strength of character and she was so smart.

Over the next few months they met a few times as a group. Chi Ha's son had a South Korean girlfriend now and she loved to hear Woo's stories of what it was like to be a senior police officer in the North's capital city. One day the son said to his father:

'Dad, why don't you and Ti Woo get together? Mum would not want you to be on your own, and, well, Dad, she might be a bit young for you, she might be even too fit!' He winked at his father and laughed.

'You hold your tongue, son.'

The father and son chat went on for a while and eventually the younger man left to meet with his girlfriend later that day. Chi Ha sat for a while thinking: although he had been jesting with his son and they'd both been teasing each other, the truth was he had fallen in love with Ti Woo. They had been through a life-changing experience, something that could bond people for ever; she had made it possible for him to escape. Her sense of purpose and determination: he found it totally intoxicating. He had saved her life, and they were interlinked now.

As the weeks had gone by this feeling had grown in him, but somehow he'd always been too embarrassed to say anything. Firstly, they both still had programmed in them the years of behaving formally between a man and a woman. Overt shows of intimacy or displays of affection were practically forbidden in North Korea, and in public it would be unheard of. But they were both changing, enjoying the relaxed atmosphere of the South: the bars, the busy streets, loud music, neighbours calling round for no other reason than social conversation. It was like they had landed on another planet. He'd asked her a few times in a roundabout way if she was seeing anybody, and what her plans were but he'd never actually plucked up the courage. It went on and on like this. Until today; today he would finally make his feelings known.

They met, as arranged, at a restaurant in town. He was early. He saw her walk in: she was no longer wearing those drab, ill-fitting North Korean clothes; but was instead dressed in beautiful, perfectly tailored western clothes. She looked like something out of a magazine. She wore a figure-hugging knee-length skirt with a large flashy belt and silver buckle; on top, a white blouse, partially covered by a short, black leather jacket. Red stiletto shoes and flesh-coloured tights finished the look. Her black, shiny, shoulder-length hair was flowing around her face. Her lips were full and pink. And those green almond-shaped eyes and quizzical eyebrows. As she locked on to him, that beautiful, elfin-like face broke into a captivating smile. He noticed that a few men's heads turned. She was thirty-five but could have passed for a woman ten years younger.

As she neared the table, he stood up and greeted her with a hug. That's when he knew: that he wanted to share the rest of his life with her. Yes, today was the day. . .

She had realised of course that he was very interested but she was not sure. She knew she did love him after the experience they'd shared, but she loved him like a brother, so she kept a friendly but formal appearance up. Eventually though she got tired of it. It was becoming the same as if they were back in the North, and she certainly was not going back to that. The day before, on that Friday, she had considered calling him and saying that although she was not sure perhaps they would give it a go. Then suddenly, as if preordained, the landscape had changed. The message she'd received had made her heart race. She knew the American the message referred to could only be one person. What if Greg spoke to her? How would she feel? She knew something had started all those months ago. . .

She'd tossed and turned all that morning. Then she got up and made a decision. She left her apartment around 12.15 for her rendezvous with Chi Ha.

During their meal she asked how his son was and he enquired as to her family and her two nephews. They shared a bottle of wine and as he poured the last of it, dividing it equally between their respective glasses, he found his moment. He had pre-empted her: 'No, let me speak first, Ti Woo.' He leaned forward and held her hand. 'Listen, I want to tell you something. I think, no, no, I *am* in love with you. I want us to, well, go out together. I think you're so beautiful and, well, I am both in love with and frightened of you at the same time!'

They both smiled and he laughed. She looked down and her heart sank. She knew what she was going to say, but he continued.

'Look, we have been through so much, and I know I am older than you but I think we could be happy. That's it really, Ti Woo, but I have told you how I feel.'

She looked at him and squeezed his hands.

'Chi Ha, listen, I really appreciate this and you are a good man, but I am not ready.' She decided at the last minute to change her narrative. Her usually frank manner had given way to a softer side; she was not going to hurt his feelings, and he did not deserve it. She would keep the door open; even *she* was not sure. 'Look, let's give it a few weeks, please.' She could see the disappointment etched on his rugged features. His eyes went down to the table and he slightly pursed his lips.

'Oh, okay, if that's how you feel.'

'I am sorry, Chi Ha, but please let me think about it.'

'I feel embarrassed now.'

'Don't be, it was a lovely thing to say; please, we will talk soon.'

She needed to leave now; no point prolonging the conversation; so she sipped the last drop of her wine and offered to pay the bill.

'No leave that to me, it's fine.'

They hugged each other and she left the restaurant.

As she walked round the shops later that afternoon she could not get it all out of her mind. Chi Ha was a good man and should she have said yes? Perhaps if she had not had that message? For some reason it was nagging away at her. She walked through the large downtown mall; that was it, she was going to call Bill Orson.

'Hello, is that Bill Orson?'

'Yes. Who's that?'

'Mr Orson, this is Ti Woo, I think you would know me as Miss Woo?'

'Miss Woo, thank you for calling me. I'm so pleased they passed my message on. I got back here a couple of weeks ago and saw your story in my office. I did a big article on Greg Sanderson.' She could not believe her ears for a second.

'Greg Sanderson you say?'

'Yes, I am sure you know who I mean? Well, he talked about you, off the record, and I did a bit of investigating..—'

She interrupted him; she couldn't help herself. 'Is he well?'

'Yes, he's getting his life back on track, but I know he'd love to hear that you got out. He thought they were going to send you to a labour camp or worse. He does not know about your escape, but as I say, he spoke a lot about you. I'd love to do your story.'

She remained silent; she wasn't going to commit herself to anything rashly, not after everything that had happened.

'I know you've been approached by a few people here, but I must get you and Greg together, do a big article on both of you guys. . .'

She wasn't sure about any of this. She just wanted to know about Greg. She interrupted again: 'Mr Orson, I'll consider all that later, but how do I get hold of Greg? Do you have his number?'

'Yes, but I would rather get you guys together with me; then I can do the story.'

'Mr Orson, if you don't give me Greg's number, you will have no story.'

Bill Orson had never met her, but from her uncompromising tone he knew if he did not acquiesce to her demand she would terminate the conversation.

'Mr Orson, I told you, we will speak soon. I am a woman of my word. Now, give me the number please.'

She waited until the next day. She'd checked the time difference; it would be around 8 p.m. on a Saturday evening in New York.

The phone rang two or three times.

'Hello, hello.' Greg shouted into his cell phone; the noise of the downtown bar was muffling the sound.

'Hello, Greg, how are you?'

'Hello, sorry, I can't hear, it's noisy in here, hold on please.' He put his drink down. He was with a few friends in Manhattan, guys who he'd gone to college with. They would meet up occasionally.

'Hey, guys, let me just take this call. Sorry I couldn't hear; who is this?'

'Greg, I hope you are behaving yourself?'

'Sorry, who is this?'

'It's not been that long, don't you recognise my voice?'

'Sorry, it was noisy, who is this?'

'Greg, if you are not behaving yourself we might have to lock you up, but you might have to share a cell with me; then we could discuss what freedom feels like. I mean, Greg, you can physically imprison a person, but can you imprison the mind?'

He did not answer for a moment.

'Miss Woo?'

'Hello, Greg.'

'Miss Woo, but how? I mean, where are you?'

'Yes it's me. I am no longer Miss Woo and I am no longer a prisoner and I am free, your type of freedom, Greg. Greg, I got out. . .'

'Oh my God, how, when, where? How did you find me?'

'It's a long story, this guy Bill Orson. . . Look, I don't want to tell you now, but I am living just outside Seoul. I have my mother, brother and two nephews with me. Greg, I will never go back, never.'

'Miss Woo, but, I mean how?'

'Greg, you won't believe it, sometimes I don't. . .'

'I don't know what to say. Listen, it's so good to hear your voice. Hey, I always thought about you; I thought you were in serious trouble.'

'Yes I was; look, let's not talk now, I would really like to see you.'

'Hey, come out here to New York, I have—'

'Greg, no, really, I can't financially, and my family is only getting settled. Please, will you come out to see me, yes?'

'Well, yeah, I guess I could get some time; yes of course. Hey, look, let me call you in the week. I will have to make arrangements with my firm, but yes, okay, look, we will talk soon.'

'Goodbye, Greg, I will await your call.'

31

Greg sighed as he waited to get through Incheon airport security. Finally clearing passport control, he made his way to the exit. The last time he was here he had been on a crazy search for the truth about Natasha's story, about her death, about whatever it was she had got herself mixed up in.

And all of that had led him to Miss Woo, and here he was again, travelling halfway across the world on a whim. He couldn't wait to see her.

Emerging from the airport, he looked around expectantly but to no avail, his heart sank, perhaps she had changed her mind? He knew that was a ridiculous thought. He scanned the airport concourse left and right, still no sign. He tried to call but his cell phone did not seem to work. She knew the flight he was on and had told him if there were any problems communicating just to wait outside. After taking one last walk around, he exited the arrival lounge, walked out into the warm morning air and waited. Half an hour went by. It seemed longer to him. More thoughts began racing through his head. Suddenly a taxi pulled up and the door swung open:

'Mr Sanderson, please get in. I am arresting you for loitering outside an airport in an ill-fitting jacket.'

'I am to be interrogated, I assume?'

'Yes, but first you will have to pay for the taxi and take me to lunch.'

They chatted as the cab sped along. 'Greg, let me take your bags to my apartment first; you have had a long flight and will want to get cleaned up. Get some sleep and we will go out later.'

'No, look, it's okay, I feel fine.'

'Greg, please do not argue with me. If I had my gun with me I would command you to sleep!' He laughed and noticed the cab driver glance in the rear view mirror with a questioning look.

The journey took about an hour and eventually they reached a smartish suburb. At least it was clean and all the buildings looked relatively new. They turned off the main road and then drove past a few side streets, finally turning right and stopping outside a small, low-rise apartment block.

'Come in, Greg, and welcome to my humble apartment, a better place than the first time we met.' He looked round: it had large windows, and a view at the rear onto some beautifully tended communal gardens with a small car park. The room was bright with freshly painted walls and wooden floors with a large white carpet in the centre. There was a large mirror on the wall and some abstract paintings hung here and there. A dark brown leather settee sat in the middle with two amply proportioned armchairs. It smelt fresh and clean.

'Let me take your bags, I will put them in here.' She disappeared with Greg's two bags, then, returning, she said, 'Would you like a drink?'

'Orange juice please, Miss Woo.'

'Greg, you have to stop this: my name is Ti Woo, I told you.'

'Sorry, old habits.'

She returned with two glasses of orange juice topped with ice. She placed one on a table at Greg's side and she went with her glass to the opposite chair.

'Greg, can you believe all this! Can you believe what has happened?'

'I know, I know, there's so much to talk about; what was it like getting out of there? They must have really hated losing you.'

Over the next hour or so Miss Woo went into detail about

how she'd begun to have doubts. Then when Sie Roo attacked her and she fought back, her fate had been sealed. Greg sat in silence and listened to the whole story. He admired her guts and tenacity; he was also warming to her, to the new her. Gone was the cold, hard exterior; she was warm, she was beautiful, she was an amazing woman, but still an enigma. Even now there was still something about her, something deep and hidden, but for the moment he was not going to probe further; this was a good time to listen and make friends.

Finally, having said enough, she turned to him. 'So, tell me your news. I assume you've found a good-looking woman to share your life with?'

'Hardly,' he said. And he told her everything, the whole story, the truth at last behind that crazy trip to North Korea. He began with the death of Natasha and the mother contacting his boss at Noble and Black, how he thought it was just a fantasy and the ravings of a distraught mother; then things had begun to unravel. He told her that the authorities back in the US had discovered that Natasha's death had been no accident, that she had been murdered as a result of her investigations into the North Korean counterfeiting conspiracy, but that no leads had ever been found. Whoever had got to her had done a sleek, professional job, and then disappeared again into the night, leaving no clues.

Although she'd known right back when she first interviewed him that he had stumbled across something, she knew that his whole story about coming to the North would have been quite plausible if they had not found and read the diary. He was just unlucky, she told him, that one of her staff could read shorthand. Once they saw the notes about the dollar production, his fate was sealed or would have been if it hadn't been for the World Trade Center attacks and the necessity to prevent an international incident. He'd been in enough danger as it was, what with those notes in his diary, she reminded him. How could he have been so foolish as to attack Sie Roo? It was crazy. But she went on to explain that it was when he did that, put himself at enormous risk to protect her, that she began to think about him, a man who would be prepared to do that for her. Nobody in her own country would have done that.

'You know, Greg, if it had not been for the international situation I doubt you would have ever been released, seriously.'

Greg half smiled. 'I know, I know you are right.'

After a long pause Woo spoke. 'Greg, there's something you must know about the girl's death.'

'Natasha?'

'Yes, you said that there was no trace, no evidence, no trail that led anywhere.'

'It's true, nothing, apparently.'

'And they won't find anything either, Greg,' she said.

'What do you mean?'

'The people who killed her are serious, consummate professionals; there will be no trail, nothing of any consequence anyhow.' She sipped her glass of orange juice, put it back down and looked straight at Greg. He was quiet for a few seconds, then said:

'How do you know?'

'Greg, you have been to my old country, you have seen it first hand. We lived in a dystopian state, they were obsessed with control. Control can only be attained by fear, that is the key to running a country like that. Every thought, every action can be scrutinised in great detail and if it does not fit into the normal pattern of behaviour then there are penalties to pay. But that's just low-level stuff; to try and do what I did, to try and actually break out of the place, that is treason. So to prevent people getting to that point there has to be the ultimate sanction, the knowledge that you will be killed, that's how it works.' She moved back into the chair slightly, reaching again for her glass.

'Are you saying people are sent to kill dissenters.'

'No, Greg, they can't look into people's minds, they wait till they make a move, then if they catch them they simply disappear. We all know who is responsible but nobody speaks of it.'

Greg was intrigued. 'Who are they? Are these the people who killed Natasha?'

'Yes, as a straight answer, Greg.'

'It does not explain how they got her to drive her car though. The New York authorities know she had a drug introduced into her body, but that would not get her to drive a car into the back of a truck; how would you explain that?' Greg was pressing his questions now. Gradually as his interest stirred he was transforming into the reporter, his journalistic instincts rising. He wanted an answer.

'She was hypnotised, that's how they would have done it.'

Greg laughed. 'Ti Woo, I am sorry but it sounds like something out of a movie.'

'You don't think it's possible, Greg, do you?'

'If I am honest—'

She cut straight in. 'Greg, many years ago in America, a famous man was killed by an assassin. His name was Sirhan Sirhan. If you don't believe me, Greg, read his story. I believe he is still incarcerated in the US. He will never admit the crime, and he has claimed for all these years that he was hypnotised, but if you choose not to believe it that's fine, though I am telling you the truth.'

'The woman you fought with, just before your escape, was she—'

'Yes, Greg, now I am finished with this, please. I told you I have a new life now, so please, as you would say, let's let sleeping dogs lie.'

Greg realised she would not say any more on the matter. He agreed with her that it was time to let the authorities deal with it, but deep down he knew he would probe again. For now, though, he would forget about it.

It was 6.30 p.m. He had slept since 11.30 that morning, the long flight having caught up with him. She had suggested he get some sleep and they would talk more later. He heard a faint tapping on the door. 'Greg, can you get up please, I am making a dinner for us.'

He grabbed some fresh clothes and came into the kitchen. She was preparing the vegetables by the sink. He looked at her. She was wearing white trousers and a small T-shirt. Her jet-black hair was tied back. She wore large earrings and her wrist bangles jangled as she busied herself with the food preparation.

'Something smells good.'

'Yes I am making you a traditional Korean dish.'

'North or South?' he said rather sarcastically.

'Very funny, Greg,' she laughed and continued her preparations.

Ten minutes later they sat in Ti Woo's dining-room drinking the wine she had provided. They ate and talked. Later that evening they walked around her neighbourhood. For two hours they talked, this time she revealed more about her escape from North Korea and her incredible endeavours to secure her family's freedom. She told him about Sie Roo, about Chi Ha and their desperate journey across the border into China. And then about how they had turned their lives around and begun to sow the seeds of a new future in the South, where freedom was a given thing, not just some fleeting pipedream.

They got back to her apartment around ten.

'That story of your escape, it's incredible,' said Greg. 'Are you going to let Orson have it? He's dying to get hold of your story and he says you made a deal with him.' Again Greg bristled at the thought that another journalist was going to get the story, the story that should rightfully be his, but hadn't they just said to let sleeping dogs lie? It didn't come naturally, but he would try. To be honest he didn't really have any choice.

'I know, I'm still thinking about it. A lot happened back there, a lot of things I'm not sure I want to go back over, so we shall see.'

'Yes, I understand. What I'm not sure of is what happened there at the end,' said Greg. 'Do you think they raised the alarm before you got out? I mean that woman you told me of, at the end, do you think she was searching for you?' He thought she might say a bit more now.

'I really don't know. They have teams that are forever trying to infiltrate the border-smuggling operations, but they will never fully eradicate it. From what I hear now more and more people are getting out all the time. All they do to try and counter it is to become increasingly brutal with the people they catch; that's why that woman was there.'

'Yeah, she sounded really bad news. Are there many like her?'

'I think so, I don't care now really, Greg. Look, I don't want to talk about it any more. Listen, have you had a good evening?'

'Ti Woo, really, it's been great. I am just relaxing now. Hey, have you any more of that wine?' He looked at her shaking the empty bottle.

'Greg, time for talking is now over.'

'I suppose you need me to wash up now. Surely you've got a dishwasher. I don't mind packing that for you.'

'No, Greg; not that at all.' She sat forward and turned to him. 'Now, I want you to make love to me.'

Greg raised an eyebrow and just half smiled. 'Oh I see.' He laughed. 'Can I think about it. . .' He never finished his witticism.

Afterwards, they kissed and lay together, not speaking, just enjoying the moment. He got up. His mouth was dry. He returned with two glasses. Just lying there, naked, she was the most beautiful thing he'd ever seen. He wanted her again. He pulled the bedclothes over both of them. They made love once more.

She was fit, strong and insatiable. And he, he took her to another place altogether. She had been with men before but not like this; this was special. They say to have intimate relations is halfway to love; the rest is the desire to complete the journey by having no fear of what might happen, good or bad. If you let it happen, it will. She knew what she wanted for now: the best sex she had ever had. But later a bond, an unbreakable bond; that was her wish. She would pursue it and she would have it, have it all. They eventually got to sleep in the early hours of the morning.

Greg spent two weeks there in total. She took time off work. It was only a temporary job and she was not worried if they did not take her back. Maybe she would make a deal with Bill Orson after all. It was her story to tell, and what could they do to her now? She was free, she was finally free, and with that freedom came the liberty to tell her own story as she saw fit, without fear of retribution. And make a tidy profit at the same time? Yes, why not, this was capitalism after all, and a girl had to live, didn't she?

Greg eventually returned to the US, telling her he would be back in about eight weeks.

Ti Woo did her first interview with Bill Orson. She got her deal, agreeing with Orson that she would do a minimum of five separate stories beginning with her early life. Orson told her if he got the syndication rights it could even be made into a film. It would be more money than she would have made in a lifetime in North Korea, and if the movie deal came off she would be in the financial stratosphere. Life was getting better for her every day, but something was niggling away at her. She had something to do; she was dreading it and was sad because she had to hurt someone, but she had to be truthful, that was her way. It was around two weeks before Greg was due to fly back. He planned to spend perhaps three weeks with her and was hoping that after that she would fly back to New York with him.

It was three in the afternoon when they met in a busy bar in the centre of Seoul. Chi Ha was smiling as he came in and sat down. 'Hey, stranger, how have you been? I haven't seen you; you kept saying you were busy, I mean—'

'Chi Ha, sorry to cut in. Please listen to me.' She looked at the table and was silent for a few moments; then she looked straight at him. 'Chi Ha, listen, you are like a brother to me. I

love you like that. You saved my life, what can I say? But, look
. . . I have to tell you I am in love with Greg, you know, the
American I told you of.'

Chi Ha looked devastated. 'But I love you so much, I thought
. . .'

She could tell he was on the edge of tears. 'Chi Ha, I am so
sorry but you know I would not lie to you or deceive you.'

'I want you, please, I love you with all my heart.'

She tried to console him, but it just seemed to make things
worse. His sadness soon turned to anger and bitterness.

'That fucking American, fuck him, I hate him.'

'Calm down, calm down.' She put her arm round him.

'No, fuck you, I am so upset.' He threw his glass on the floor
and it smashed.

The manager came over. 'Is there a problem here?'

Ti Woo stood up and apologised to the manager, offering to
pay for the damage.

'Look, we don't tolerate this kind of behaviour in here. I am
sorry but you will have to leave.'

Ti Woo apologised again, feeling slightly embarrassed. She and
Chi Ha walked out. They continued arguing and although he
had calmed down somewhat the emotional outburst had stirred
him into pouring his heart out. He told her that what with all
they had been through and how good their lives were here now,
she should at least give it a try. They walked round the town
centre for a while, eventually finding a bench just outside of the
main mall. He was absolutely distraught and she was crying. To
hurt Chi Ha was unthinkable, and right at this moment she hated
herself, but at least she had been honest. She wiped her eyes.

Eventually Chi Ha calmed down, composing himself.

'Listen, I will always love you, Ti Woo; don't they say that
unrequited love is the greatest of all?'

She grabbed him and hugged him tight: 'Chi Ha, I must go
now, please don't hate me, please.'

'How could I hate you? I can see that you are upset as well.

Look, you have told me the truth; I don't like it but what can I do?'

'You have to always be in my life, Chi Ha; you know that I value your friendship more than anything, but, look, forget Greg, it's still how I feel, please understand.'

He held her tight and apologised for his behaviour over the last hour or so.

'Look, let's leave it now; perhaps we can speak soon; if you want some time I understand.' She kissed him and walked off, tears flowing. Eventually she caught a cab home.

A week later Greg called her from the airport. 'Hi, beautiful, listen, I have just got in; I will go straight to the apartment.'

'Hey, sorry I could not pick you up. I found some temporary work; it's a friend of mine. I did not want to let her down, you understand?'

'Sure. No problem. Look, I will let myself in.'

Greg arrived at the apartment. It was its usual immaculate condition, smelling of fresh flowers and her distinct perfume. He got washed and changed and went for a walk. At 5.30 he heard the door open.

'Hi, darling, how was the flight?'

'Great, good to see you. Listen, I am going to stay for three weeks, how's that? Then we will go back to New York, is that okay?'

'Of course it is. Hey, come on, I am starving, let's go and eat.'

They had two fantastic weeks together. Ti Woo had to work for one of them then she finished. She did not need the money now and Greg was treating her to so many things; life was getting better each day.

It was during the last week before they were due to leave for New York that she woke up one morning and said, 'Come here please, there is something I must tell you.'

'Well what's this? Am I being interrogated by Miss Woo!'

'Greg, this is serious, darling.' She took his hand. 'Greg, darling, I am pregnant. Greg, I am having a baby, your baby!'

He grabbed her and they held each other tight.

'Miss Woo, will you marry me?'

'Yes I will, Greg Sanderson.'

That morning they drove over to her mother's apartment and broke the news. She was ecstatic. They all went to lunch. Greg got quite drunk and that afternoon Ti Woo and her mother went shopping after she had admonished him and left him to walk home.

Two days before they were to fly back to America Ti Woo left Greg at the apartment. She needed to go and see Chi Ha. She realised that once she saw New York Greg would try and persuade her to live there, and they had a baby to consider now. She wanted to tell Chi Ha the truth and hoped that in time they would rekindle their friendship. It was the only black cloud in a shining new world that she inhabited.

It was just gone 11 a.m. Greg glanced at the clock, and carried on reading the newspaper. Ti Woo had told him she was seeing Chi Ha. Greg suspected that Chi Ha was in love with her and that he probably hated him. He did genuinely feel sorry for him, but never questioned her about it. It was just an unspoken thing. Though he'd never met the man he had tremendous respect for him, and hoped in time things would be okay between them. He folded the paper and took one final look at the front page. *'Right, I am going into town; I need a walk,'* he mused as he went to get up.

There was a gentle tapping on the door. It surprised him as the apartment had an entry buzzer. Getting up, he walked to the door, thinking it was probably one of her neighbours who would pop in now and again.

'Hello, are you Mr Sanderson?' A woman was standing in front of him. She was half smiling, but he noticed she had the darkest eyes he had ever seen. She seemed to be looking right through him.

'Yes.'

'Greg Sanderson, the American; you were in North Korea once?'

'Yes that's right.' He looked at her again. It was her eyes; they just burnt right into him. It felt like his eyes would catch fire.

Ti Woo buzzed two or three times. There was no answer. She had bags of shopping and was in a good mood. Chi Ha had taken the news well and promised he would go to New York if she decided to move there, but she was getting annoyed, not wanting to look for her keys as the shopping bags were weighing her down. '*Where is he? Must have gone out. . .*' she thought, as she placed the bags on the floor and rummaged around for her apartment keys.

After letting herself in the front reception and walking along the corridor to her apartment door she placed the key in the lock. Just at that exact moment something came over her: a chill. It went right through her bones. She shrugged her shoulders and went in.

'Greg, why didn't you answer? Greg, darling are you here?' Silence. A slight breeze moved the lounge blinds a fraction as she walked into the room. It was empty. The dining-room was empty too, but there was a smell. She sniffed twice, a third time: a smell of perfume was discernible. It wasn't her mother's, or her neighbour's or Greg's aftershave, but it was there. She dropped her bags and backed out of the room. Moving slowly, she went into the kitchen. With stealth, she opened the second drawer down and quietly took hold of a large carving knife. She flicked her shoes off. The place was silent.

Slowly, she went down the hallway. Gingerly, she pushed the bedroom door open. This was Greg's room; it was where he stayed that first night. She pushed it till it was all the way against the wall. Nothing. She kneeled down and tried to see under the bed, but realised all her beds would be impossible to hide under. Next, her bedroom. She was sweating now, her heart was

214

thumping so hard she was sure it could be heard round the apartment like a small drum. Thud, thud, thud, it went. The bedroom was empty. Slowly and panther-like, she moved to the bathroom door. It was open a fraction. She could hear a dripping sound. She slammed the door back. This was the only other place a person could hide. She crept in. . .

She screamed and dropped the knife: Greg was lying in the bath, blood everywhere. His wrists were slashed and the pupils of his eyes had rolled up and were just staring, glazed over as he lay utterly motionless. The blood was dripping from one of his wrists onto the marble bathroom floor. She screamed again, and grabbed him. She pulled him up but knew, she knew the minute she saw him: Greg was dead. She held him and cried and cried. Then she got up, soaked with his blood. She looked down and the room started to spin. Faster and faster it span, then suddenly her legs gave way. She collapsed on the floor, smashing her head as she went down. She was out cold. All that could be heard was the dripping of blood from Greg's wrist hanging over the edge of the bath. The breeze went through the apartment and soon the smell of that perfume disappeared as if it had never been there. As the blood stopped dripping, there was complete silence, nothing but a macabre silence.

32

The screaming sirens broke the quiet afternoon of the suburb. Ti Woo's neighbour was waiting at the apartment entrance holding the reception doors open. 'Quick in here, apartment two, look here,' she indicated as the paramedics raced into the building. She had blood smeared all over her. Ti Woo had eventually come round and thrown up. She'd then managed to run out of the apartment and bang on her neighbour's door, so distraught and hysterical that her neighbour had called the emergency services. Then the woman had gone back in the apartment with her. She'd screamed and held her hands to her face. Ti Woo had gone back and just sat with Greg, sobbing and screaming. 'Why, you fucking bastards!' She'd held Greg and put his hand on her stomach. 'This is your baby, darling, your baby.' She was sobbing and sobbing. Her neighbour ran out and knocked on a few more doors. Soon a crowd had assembled in the downstairs lobby.

Two minutes later the police arrived. They began to cordon off the area and started taking witness statements and moving the neighbours away from the proximity of Ti Woo's apartment. The paramedics could do nothing for Greg and eventually persuaded Ti Woo to release him and go with them. They only got her to the lounge and she started to wrestle with them. 'No, let me stay with him. . .' She tried to break free but with the aid of two police officers they managed to hold her down and the paramedics had to sedate her. As she succumbed to the sedation

216

they stretchered her to the ambulance and then it sped away back to the hospital.

A detective arrived about fifteen minutes later. Nodding to the uniformed officer on the door, he went into Ti Woo's apartment. Another uniformed officer was inside, standing in the hallway. He nodded at the detective. 'It's all in there, sir,' he said, indicating the far end of the corridor. The detective looked in: it was a scene out of a horror movie. He looked down. Lying on the bathroom floor was a large knife. He went no further.

'What happened?' he said as he returned to the officer. They both went into the kitchen.

'Sir, when we got here both the paramedics were in the bathroom. They told us the man—'

'Name, officer? What's his name?'

'Greg, sir, that's all I could get from her, sorry sir. Oh, sir, her name is Ti Woo.'

'Okay, officer, carry on.'

'Right, sir, well the paramedics told us the man had slit his wrists and she came in and found him. Oh, sir, do you think that she might have done it? I mean, did you see that knife on the floor? And there is another one just by the bath.'

'Thank you for that, officer. I am going to get the crime scene team here now; look, you know the routine, nobody in or out now.'

'Yes, sir.'

With that he left the apartment. As he walked out a few more police cars arrived. He chatted with the sergeant and told him briefly what had happened. He told him to make sure his officers had the place sealed off and to get us much information as they could from neighbours and take statements. Also to check CCTV footage if available. He walked around the entire block and the small communal gardens. After studying the area intently, he left.

Back at the hospital Ti Woo began to come round after the heavy sedation. She observed that a hospital gown had replaced her clothes. Trying to lean forward but feeling weak, she looked over to the glass door. It was closed but a uniformed police officer was standing directly outside. Suddenly her brain kicked in as the mist began to clear. She began to recall the events of a few hours ago, then started to shout out. The officer turned and immediately called for a nurse. She rushed in and tried to prevent Ti Woo getting out of the bed. Eventually they had no choice: she was sedated again.

A few hours later the detective called. She was calm now but dumbstruck. A nurse was in the room now and the officer still outside.

'Ti Woo, I am Detective Lee, I am sorry but can we. . .'

She cut across him: 'It's fine, I was a police officer myself, please, let's get this over with. I know how it works . . . fresh in the mind and all that.'

'Thank you, miss; you said you were a police officer?'

'Not any more. If you look up my file you will find that I escaped from the North some . . . well about seven or eight months ago. Now, sorry, I am still in shock; you know we were having a baby.' She lost her composure again; tears welled up in her eyes. The nurse passed her a tissue.

'Thank you.' She wiped her face and rubbed her head. The sedative was beginning to wear off but she still felt drowsy.

'Look, miss, can you tell me what happened?'

'Yes, I came home . . . well I am not sure, I think it was one-thirty, maybe two. Anyhow, I kept buzzing but there was no answer.'

'You don't have keys?'

'Yes I do. I just had a load of shopping and didn't want to search for them. Well there was no answer, so I had to find them, and I let myself in. That's, that's . . . well then I found him.' She broke down again. 'Sorry, forgive me,' she continued.

'Take your time,' said Detective Lee.

'I went into the apartment, it was so quiet, but I knew they were in there.'

'Who? Who do you mean?'

Ti Woo ignored the question; she went on: 'I got a knife from the kitchen and looked for them but when I got to the bathroom I found him. You know they killed him?'

'Sorry, miss, I don't understand, who was in the apartment?'

'Look, you won't believe me, but these people, they are assassins, they killed him.'

Then a doctor arrived at the hospital room and informed Detective Lee that she was heavily sedated and really he should leave. He realised that of course she could be deluded about this assassin business, the brain simply refusing to accept that things like this can happen; but he was keeping an open mind: she seemed to be so sure.

A cloud of suspicion hung over Ti Woo for weeks. Then, eventually, with no other evidence to the contrary, they had to conclude that Greg had slit his own wrists. They were going to close the case. During the investigations, Chi Ha was questioned intensely. He initially became a suspect. He had a motive – jealousy – and no alibi that afternoon. He admitted he was in love with Ti Woo and had become jealous of her and Greg, but in the end a woman came forward to confirm that he had been seen drinking in her bar later that day around the time of Greg's death.

The forensic evidence supported by the position of the body, and the fact that there had been no sign of a struggle only led to one conclusion. Also the knife that Greg had cut his wrists with matched both his wounds and was from the apartment. There had been no sign of forced entry and the other knife had not been used. All these factors pointed towards a suicide, albeit an unexplained one.

It did puzzle the detective why Ti Woo, by her own admission, had taken a knife from the kitchen. She must have suspected someone was in there? He could not get her words out of his head: *'they are assassins, they killed him.'* He questioned Ti Woo many times about what she had said to him at the hospital, but she denied it. When he persisted she told him she had been delirious and under the influence of extreme shock and sedatives.

Detective Lee and other senior officers could find no plausible reason why Ti Woo would have killed him, and the forensic evidence supported a suicide, even if it was not fully conclusive.

Two months went by. Ti Woo worked a few days just to keep herself from going mad. But eventually she could take it no more. She knew the truth, and it would have to come out. She owed it to herself, she owed it to Chi Ha, she owed it to Greg. So she arranged a meeting. She called Detective Lee and told him that she needed to talk. At the same time she called Chi Ha on the pretext of needing his support. She would tell them both together.

Ti Woo sat forward in her chair. They were gathered in her apartment. Initially, both men had been suspicious and not a little put out. Particularly Chi Ha who had had quite enough interrogation for one lifetime. But they both knew that Ti Woo wasn't the sort of person to mess around. She had something to say, and she was going to say it. And they had better listen.

'Look, I know this is going to seem hard to believe. . .' Christ, that was an understatement if ever there was. How was she going to convince them? She knew it would sound preposterous, but she had no choice. She carried on: 'But what I have to tell you, what I have tried to tell you is true.'

The two men sat in silence.

'Chi Ha, you know what life was like in the North; even now we do not speak of some things; some things you swear never to tell. I told Detective Lee here that Greg was killed and I speak the truth.'

Chi Ha looked up at her. She was pacing the room while the two men sat side-by-side on the settee. 'I know, Ti Woo, the detective told me during my interrogation.' He gave Detective Lee a scornful look. 'But it is just a story, Ti Woo, just something you dreamed up in the shock of the moment; you admitted as much to the detective. There is no evidence; Greg committed suicide and that is the tragic truth of the matter. Why not let it lie?'

She turned to Chi Ha. 'You saw one of them that night, you saw her. . .'

'Who, what night?' he said, alarmed.

'That woman, the one you shot.'

Now it was Detective Lee's turn to look alarmed. 'Shot! Now hold on, who shot who?' He looked at Chi Ha.

Chi Ha looked up to Ti Woo again. She nodded. After a long pause and a deep sigh, he continued: 'The night we escaped from the North; it was at a spot by the Tumen River. This woman, she was posing as a guide. . .'

Again he looked to Ti Woo for some sort of affirmation.

'Go on,' she said, 'it's all in the past.'

'Well the next thing,' he continued, 'she pulled a gun and ordered us to go with her. Ti Woo fought with her and, well, I got her nephews to safety then came back. I had this gun, so I just shot her.'

'Look, Miss Woo, what is the relevance of all this?' asked the detective, impatiently.

'I will tell you, but what I say never goes outside this room. I am having a baby, my two nephews live here now, my mother and my brother, and there is you, Chi Ha. Yes I care and love you like my own brother. So do I have your silence?'

Chi Ha nodded. Detective Lee said, 'Miss Woo, if this sheds further light on the investigation I may have to ask you to make a statement.'

She just looked at him. 'No, Detective Lee. Yes, you can look into this; yes, you can check it out; but you will never hear it from these lips, never, now do you understand? Before you answer, think. If you put that gun you are carrying to my head and ask me to sign a statement I will refuse. You would have to pull the trigger. Now, do I have your word?'

He nodded.

'Okay then.' She moved to the far corner of the room. She paused for a few seconds.

'There are these women in the North who are used as assassins. You will have heard stories now and again: people who disappear; Japan, China, even from here, and are then taken back to the North. Some have mysteriously died.' She looked at Detective Lee. He nodded.

'Well some of that is known; what you don't know is who they are. They use these women. Kim Jong-il had them trained in all sorts of infiltration techniques; some are even able to hypnotise their victims. . .'

'Her eyes,' said Chi Ha, 'I remember her eyes. . .'

'Go on,' said Detective Lee. 'And these women, these assassins, where do they come from? Where does he find them?' This was all beginning to sound like something out of a comic book.

'Mostly they are taken from the highest echelons of elite military units. They are extremely intelligent, speak two languages at least. Each one will be a specialist in some particular field; they blend in easily, often with disarming personalities. Sometimes they travel with men, even children, passing themselves off as ordinary families going on holiday. Often they are very attractive and will induce men to go with them. Then they will either kidnap them or kill them; they don't care either way.'

Chi Ha spoke: 'And that is who that woman was that night?'

'Chi Ha, you saw the way she attacked me?'

He nodded, then said, 'Yes, she was frightening.' He turned to the detective beside him: 'I told you, I had to shoot her; I think she was trying to break Ti Woo's neck.'

'You really shot her?' said the detective.

'I had no choice.' Chi Ha looked at the floor.

Detective Lee looked at Ti Woo. 'Miss Woo, how do you know it was them? I mean, we looked carefully for evidence of foul play. I promise you, forensics were aware that you'd informed me that you suspected somebody had killed Greg.'

She continued: 'Very rarely will you ever find evidence. But I am telling you now the full story, and as I said, I will never admit to it and it will never be linked with me or my family.' She glared at Detective Lee. She moved around the room for a few seconds then continued.

'I don't know how she did it; it may have been two of them; but when I arrived back in that apartment there was a smell of perfume. That's when I knew; it's part of their *modus operandi* to always leave a calling card.'

'We went over the place, your apartment. There was nothing, nothing at all.'

'No, that's because I have got it.'

Detective Lee looked at her. 'Where is it? Show it to me please.'

She walked back to the corner of the room, turned, then put her hand inside her jacket pocket. She pulled something out and then passed it to Detective Lee. He stared at it for a moment then passed it to Chi Ha. He scrutinised it in turn then passed it back to the detective.

'You can keep it,' she said.

Detective Lee looked at the small photo in his hand. It was a picture of Kim Jong-il. On the front was written: *Greetings from your Dear Leader, Miss Woo.*

'It was in Greg's hand when I found him.'

'But what does it mean?' said the detective.

'It's their calling card, that along with the distinct perfume.'

Detective Lee looked puzzled.

'Who do you mean? You mean they sent somebody to kill him?'

'Yes, Detective Lee, I can assure you.'

'You have no proof. We examined the entire apartment, and this photo, you could be—'

She cut in. 'I don't care what you think, I am telling you the truth. Look, I have been cleared, you have closed the case, I don't need to tell you any of this but I am. But when I am finished, as I told you, I will never speak of it again. If you wish to look into it fine, but it never came from me. I have a baby coming, I have to protect my baby, that's all I care about now, and of course my family who are here now. We have a good life here now in the South, I am not going to risk anything, Detective Lee.'

He realised she was coming to the end of her revelations. He knew she was serious, and something in him told him she was telling the truth; her voice, her body language, her demeanour. And she was right, she did not have to say any of this. But he wanted a bit more, before she closed off.

'Okay, Miss Woo, look, tell me then, who are they?'

'They are all women and they are extremely dangerous. And these women, they all have a tattoo in the small of their back, about an inch, maybe smaller, in diameter, quite discreet, but it's there all right; they wear it with pride. It is the name of their group.'

'What is the tattoo of?' Detective Lee asked.

Ti Woo looked straight at him and said: 'The face of the Medusa.'

The room went silent. She walked over to Detective Lee. 'If you ever catch one, kill her; believe me, they are the most dangerous women in the world.' She was about two feet from him. 'Could you stand up a moment please?' He looked at her, then got up.

'Yes, Ti Woo.' A moment passed. Suddenly and without warning she grabbed at his throat and instantaneously twisted one arm. She pressed his neck, twisting his arm further. He made no sound but gradually sank to the floor, turning as his legs buckled from under him. Chi Ha gasped.

Ti Woo released her grip on the detective and he collapsed in a heap. She opened his jacket and, taking out his gun, threw it into the middle of the room and went back to sit down. He groaned, then slowly and gradually got to his feet; he was holding his arm and neck. He glanced at Ti Woo, then walked over, bent down and retrieved his gun. He stared at her, not annoyed, but shocked.

'Well, the point was?'

'Detective Lee, I am thirty-five years old and three months

pregnant; if I can do that to you can you imagine what these women are capable of?' She walked past him. 'I told you I shall never speak of this ever again. Chi Ha, I am leaving now, please come and see me. I have told the truth and I have no more to say.'

She turned and went to leave the room. Detective Lee called to her. 'Miss Woo, how do you know all this?'

She came back into the room. This was it: she had hoped she would be able to keep this part of her story to herself, but she could see that in order to make them believe what she'd told them, she would have to complete her tale.

'Detective Lee, they, well let's just say they requested me to join them. I trained with them for a while. When I found out they wanted me to kill people I refused. I was twenty-five years old. As you can imagine, I was punished severely for refusing, and no doubt they would have killed me in an instant if I hadn't been invaluable to the regime. They needed good people, strong people, disciplined and well-trained people, and I made a deal. I would keep my own counsel and would serve out my life for the Party in the People's Police. And, well, that's my story.'

The two men sat in silence. Ti Woo looked down at them. 'I hope to God you never meet them. If you do, I told you, kill them or you will be dead. You saw what I just did and I am half your size, out of condition and not a killer.'

She walked out of the apartment and just made it to the street when Detective Lee ran out and caught up with her. 'Miss Woo, before you go.'

'Yes?'

'What you did back there to me, I mean, I could say that you did that to Greg?'

'Yes, detective, you are right, you could indeed, and I tell you another thing,'

'What's that, Miss Woo?'

'If I had continued you would have been dead, make no mistake about that, but I loved that man with all my heart and soul. He changed my life and now I am having his baby, but if you really think it was me then I suggest you arrest me.' She moved closer, Detective Lee shifting slightly backwards.

'Don't worry, I won't resist. I am getting too old for that and I have to consider and protect my baby now.'

'No, Miss Woo, actually I do believe you. Part of the reason I came here was to tell you—'

'Tell me what?'

'Some new information has come to light.'

'Yes, what is it?'

'Well we never found anything on CCTV and, as you know, only a few of the apartments round here have it. But we did check the main street and made the usual house-to-house calls. At first nothing came in and our inquiries produced nothing. Then two people eventually came forward.'

'Who? Who came forward?' She couldn't believe this was happening.

'They were an older couple and did not want to get involved. They were quite frightened. They have an apartment, well let's just say it's close by.'

'And what did they see?' she said, growing impatient.

'I'm coming to that. They claim to have seen two people acting suspiciously late that morning, around the time Greg died. They did not see much but the one thing they were certain of was that they were both women.'

She looked at him, did not say a word, turned round and kept walking. He called her again:

'Ti Woo, just one thing, please, before you go.'

She stopped and turned to face him; he looked into her eyes.

'Yes, detective?'

'The tattoo?'

'What of it?'

'Do you have one?'

She just turned and walked away. Ten minutes later she caught a taxi home. As it drove along she held her stomach and whispered, 'Don't worry, son, you will be okay. I will protect you now; your daddy has gone to a better place.' She wiped a tear away and looked out the window. It had started to rain.

33

It was the early hours of 5 April 2003 when Ti Woo gave birth to a beautiful baby boy. She named him Greg, after his father, his middle name being Woo. She knew Greg would have liked that.

Greg's affairs were eventually settled in New York and, after the usual legal wrangling, most of his money went to Ti Woo. After Greg's death, she had backed out of her deal with Bill Orson; she simply couldn't go through with it. He often called and would implore her to reconsider telling her stories, but she steadfastly refused to give a reason why she would never again speak of life in the North.

Greg's case was never officially closed but she managed to get them to record an open verdict, subject to any new evidence coming to light. She did not want that suicide stain on Greg's character. Though she had pretty much convinced Detective Lee with her Medusa story, and though the evidence of the two elderly neighbours backed it up, it was still all circumstantial. And she would never testify even if he managed to track them down, the chances of which, after she described who they were and their tactics, were decidedly slim. He had no real descriptions, no positive IDs and no forensic evidence linking anybody to Greg's death, so he reluctantly had to draw a line under the case.

Ti Woo's two nephews soon adapted to life in the prosperous South. Her brother retrained and got a new job with an electronics company and was doing well. Ti Woo had bought a new apartment close to the city and a large house out of town. The rest she invested. Gerry and Tanya became good friends and she promised them she would come to New York one day when Greg Junior was a bit older. But South Korea was her home now. Her old life was well behind her.

She was looking to go back to work, but nothing serious. She and Chi Ha were as close as they ever were. He had been badly affected by Greg's death and felt it would be offensive to take advantage of her when she was vulnerable. So he never asked her again whether she wanted more than friendship. In any event, he went back to teaching and met another woman. His son is getting married next year.

Occasionally her past would surface, sometimes in the most unexpected manner. She was out shopping one day with Greg Junior when two men ran from a store apparently with stolen watches. Unfortunately for them Ti Woo was just outside. One of the men smashed into her, knocking her and Greg Junior's pram over, as he tried to get away. 'Get out the way, you stupid bitch,' he shouted. She managed to grab him; the other man got away. When the police turned up, the jeweller, happy that he had got most of his goods back, was trying to explain that he never touched the thief but that this woman had grabbed one of them. The next thing he saw the man was on the floor. The jeweller had been so busy picking up his goods he hadn't noticed her leave. Some witnesses thought she had a baby with her but were not sure.

Detective Lee happened to see a report that one of his officers was going through; the thief had suffered a broken jaw and two broken ribs. Lee laughed to himself; he knew who was responsible.

Ti Woo loved her house, just outside the suburbs, and became a keen gardener; she would often have garden parties and eventually was quite well known on the local social scene. As the months passed her persona mellowed. She was an avid reader and one day discovered a book at her local library about Ghandi and his teachings. She was fascinated by his doctrine of passive resistance and how he had rid his country, almost single-handedly, of one of the world's most powerful empires. And virtually without bloodshed. She prayed that this is what would eventually happen to her old country. Perhaps that was the answer: not a bloody revolution, just non-compliance. She would often discuss it with friends and others she met who had recently escaped.

Childbirth had changed her; she was comfortable in her own skin. Her old life was gone now. Sometimes in her private moments she would think of Chan. She guessed he had got into serious trouble over her deception; she even suspected he'd helped her escape. He was no fool. But then she would be sad; they'd probably sent him to a labour camp or he could have even been shot for dereliction of duty if they suspected his involvement.

Greg's death played heavily on her mind; she'd had to receive counselling and had tried to come to terms with it. The story she told Detective Lee that day about Greg's death and the assassins she had never repeated.

It was a few days after Greg Junior's first birthday. She'd had all her friends and family over and the house was a mess. She had been feeling tired these past few days. He was becoming difficult at times and being a mother was not easy for her, but she was adapting and loved him like any mother loves a son, with her whole being. He was her life now.

That morning she got up and reprimanded herself about the mess. Greg Junior was in the lounge asleep in his pram. She had started in the kitchen, occasionally eating bits of his first birthday cake, but feeling guilty and annoyed at the weight she had been putting on. The washing machine was on, humming away, and the dishwasher. She smiled to herself at all these gadgets she now had. How things had changed! She went back to chastising herself about her weight. She was going to have to start running again soon. . .

She stood perfectly still; then just started shaking. It was like an electric shock passing through her. Feeling her legs going, she gripped the sink, shaking even more now, like she was about to have a fit. She took a massive breath and, letting go of the sink, walked towards the lounge. It took for ever; her legs were like lead weights. She got to the lounge door; it was closed. That was the sound she'd heard; and a smell, a smell of perfume. She opened the lounge door.

They were just standing there, two of them, either side of Greg's pram. One of them had her hand on it; the other one just forward of it. Ti Woo had no fight left in her: these two were standing by the most precious thing in the world, her son. There was complete silence. A few seconds passed. Then, realising that her situation was hopeless, for the first time in her life she dropped to her knees and pleaded. 'I beg you, I beg you, please don't harm him, please.' Tears were streaming from her eyes and saliva ran from the corner of her mouth. She felt a trickle of urine run down the side of her leg. She couldn't breathe. She put her hands out.

'Please, I am begging for his life. Kill me if you want but don't touch him; for God's sake no . . . no . . .' She broke down, falling flat to the floor; she had her face in her hands. A minute or so passed, then one of them walked forward. Ti Woo heard her footsteps and looked up.

'You have a choice. You will leave with us now; we don't need your baby. He will be unharmed.'

She got back on her knees. 'What choice do I have? I can't, I can't leave my baby.' She just sobbed.

'Then both of you will be dead in the next thirty seconds; we will set fire to the house and it will just be a tragic accident.'

The room fell silent again. Ti Woo had no choice, she was no match for these two. Even ten years ago she would have been lucky to have overcome one of them, but two of them, both younger, probably armed and with a propensity for killing; she was finished.

'Okay I will come with you. What about my baby? I need someone to come here.'

The closest one walked to the phone, took it from its holder and threw it next to her.

'Call your neighbour or someone who is close by. No family, get them here in the next ten minutes.'

Ti Woo picked the phone up and, shaking, she dialled the number.

She spoke to a neighbour, a woman who had teenage children and was at home most of the day, but those two already knew this; they had done their homework. 'Yes thank you, it's, well it's just an emergency you see. No, I will close the door but it won't be locked. When? When?' She looked at the one who was nearest. She held her hand up, indicating five fingers. 'About five, yes I know, yes, really I am sorry, yes, I know, but, look, I will pay you. Sorry again, okay around five then, thank you, goodbye.'

She dropped the phone; it was picked up and replaced. Ti Woo got to her feet. 'Let me hold my baby before we go.'

The one closest to the pram and still with her hand on it said, 'No, we go now.'

Ti Woo looked at her. She picked herself up off the floor, steeled every ounce of resolve she had left in her body, and walked steadily towards the pram. Ignoring the two assassins, she bent over and lent in to the pram. She kissed her boy on his head as he slept. 'I love you, son, I love you so much. Goodbye and stay safe.'

A year passed: rumours circulated that she was alive and living back in the North. Bill Orson took up her cause and with the help of a few connections managed to get letters into the place. Some investigative journalists even crossed the border a few times. Some got caught and were never seen again. The South Korean ambassador got involved but it was categorically denied that the North had kidnapped her. The previous year, not long after Greg Junior's birth, two famous South Korean film stars, Choe Eun

Hee and Shin Sang, were kidnapped and taken to the North. It was 'suggested' that they should remarry and make films under instructions from Kim Jong-il. Around the time of their disappearance three women were seen in the area but never identified.

Another report came in about a man who had made it out from the North and was living in an old Chinese town close to the Tumen River. Before he escaped he had been a member of the large domestic household staff responsible for cleaning and maintaining the many homes Kim Jong-il had around the country. The man would tell how the Great Leader kept women at these homes for his pleasure, but he asserted that Kim was an impotent fat pig and would generally cast aspersions on him. The man met a woman in a bar one night and they became lovers. A week or so later, early one morning neighbours heard screaming. When they managed to break his door down he was lying in a pool of blood; his penis had been cut off. A few days later he committed suicide.

Detective Lee would often spend time studying these reports and making detailed inquiries. He discovered many of them had veracity. The story of the film stars and many others that came in proved to be true. In the case of the movie stars, they had managed to get letters out to their families, but again in the North it was officially denied.

Some time later Lee received a call from Bill Orson. He had been out to the border area and stayed in the Chinese town with a guide and interpreter. They made contact with someone who knew the man who had killed himself. At first he refused point blank to talk about it, but after Orson paid him about a year's wages and promised he would never reveal his identity, the man eventually agreed to tell them what he knew about his friend.

The story went that he had met a woman in a bar one evening. She was beautiful, down on her luck and wanted somewhere to stay. His friend told him they had become intimate, he could not believe what a beautiful body she had, but there was something else, something that intrigued and fascinated him. She had this tattoo in the small of her back. The next thing he heard, his friend had killed himself after she attacked him. Naturally the detective asked if he knew what the tattoo was. He told him: it was of the face of the Medusa.

Greg Junior is a beautiful baby and has a loving family around him. Ti Woo's mother and brother look after him. They use Ti Woo's money for all his needs and to run and pay for the cost of her home. Her car has never moved, still parked exactly where she left it. The garden is tended and the house always kept clean; fresh flowers are a regular feature. Nobody has heard from Ti Woo. All her family hope and pray that she is still alive. Perhaps she is, and perhaps her story is not finished. . .